The Heartwood Box
A Fairy Tale

By Lilia Ford

For my long-suffering husband and sons.

Chapter One

Of all the great magic users in our world, only one sought love above all else, Titania, Queen of the Northern Fae. Most Faeries are vain, selfish creatures, but Titania was different. The continental Fae drove themselves close to extinction with their divisions between Seely and Unseely, their obsession with pure blood, and their wasteful wars with the wizards. Titania had no time for such pettiness. Her realm lay in the British Isles, a few short leagues from the only demon gate in Europe. She understood that demons and their half-human spawn, the Reavers, were the true threat to wizard, human, and Fae alike.

Titania was no fool to ignore weapons and warriors, but she knew in her deepest heart that over time, love is the only weapon that can prevail against cruelty.

Her greatest warrior was the Black Prince, Declan. Declan was loyal to his queen, but he had little respect for what he saw as her romantic nonsense. He lived only for battle, fighting to the point of madness until Titania feared he would destroy himself. She knew that Declan's disdain for love grew from frustration and loneliness. Though a man of great honor, he was ruled by dark and fierce passions, lust and a will to dominate. Faerie women are proud and exacting creatures, demanding worship from their males. They could find no pleasure in submitting to Declan's fierce will.

Finally Titania could stand it no more: she called Declan to her and told him she was releasing him from her service. She commanded him to go out into the human world and not return until he had found the woman who could be happy with him. She knew humans to be strange, varied creatures, no two looking the same, each village showing different customs and personalities, unlike the Fae who are far more similar to each other.

To make sure that Declan was able to find a wife who could love him, she gifted him with a box made from the wood of the heartwood tree that grew in a sacred grove in her own garden. It was a box of miraculous properties because it would change color to reflect the deepest heart of the person it belonged to. She told him he must give the box to the woman he sought to marry, and if the box turned black that woman had a heart that could meet his in love and trust. And if the woman trusted him to unlock the box, inside they would discover the deepest desires that lay hidden in her heart.

So Declan left and was gone for many years. Titania missed her champion, but she trusted that he had found happiness with a human woman. Then came the day he returned: to her astonishment, he was utterly distraught and threw himself at her feet. He had found a woman who could love him, and they had lived together in great happiness and had three sons. The sons had all grown up to be warriors, devoted to honor like their father, but sharing his dark passions.

But when the two eldest had married, disaster had struck: the oldest son had tried his best to conform his heart to his wife's nature, but doing so had broken something in him. Like Declan he had thrown himself into battles to drive away his despair, and finally had been killed. His second son's story was even more tragic: he had revealed his nature to his new bride on their wedding night, and the poor girl had panicked and taken her own life, leaving his son broken and in despair. Now he had only one son left, and he prayed Titania to find some way to help him.

The queen thought and thought, but she didn't know what she could do. Even if she helped Declan's son, his children would only suffer the same fate when it came time to marry. On a whim, she decided to ask the priestess of the town that lay on the other side of the gate between Faerie and the human world.

The priestess was a wise and clever woman, and realized this might be the chance to help all of the people of the valley, not just Declan's son. She counseled Titania to gift each unmarried girl with a box made from the heartwood tree. When it came time to marry, the girl's box would change color to point to the man who would best suit her. Any girl whose box turned black would marry one of Declan's descendants. But, she warned, such girls were not common, and though she prayed there would be one for each generation, there might not be more. The sons of his family must promise not to try to win over any girl not meant for them, even if it meant that some of them must stay unmarried. In return she promised the townspeople would revere Titania and serve her as best they could according to their different gifts.

Titania was so impressed with the priestess' words, she blessed her with immortality and set her to guide the town in their new rule. The town prospered greatly. Love and trust became the rule between married people, so that even in times of tragedy, the people could take solace in the knowledge that they had made another person's happiness. And after a few generations, everyone forgot that the boxes had been originally given to help Declan's descendants. They were now seen as a blessing to everyone, and the true source of the town's unusual happiness and prosperity.

Declan's descendants remained in the hills above the town, guarding the demon gate and always showing unusual devotion to Titania. From time immemorial they had produced only male children, all sharing Declan's nature. As the priestess had warned, they could not all find brides, but in each generation there was one girl whose heart was drawn to their darkness....

The Bridal Week had finally arrived. All over town, girls who were to take part were putting on new dresses, arranging and rearranging their hair, watching the clock until it was time for the first event, the picnic. Only Genevieve Miran was in despair.

It was not her dress. Her mother hailed from a family known for its gifts with the needle—their color was yellow—and she had created a dress so beautiful, it made Genevieve's heart ache. They had no choice but to make it in white, but her mother had chosen the most delicate fabric she could find and then crafted dozens of petals that made Genevieve think of flickering butterflies. She knew her mother had carefully picked a creamy shade that would flatter Genevieve's complexion, but there was no hiding that she was pale and drawn. She looked like what she was, a recluse who for the last few years had refused to mix with their neighbors and rarely ventured outside.

It hadn't always been like that. Genevieve had been an energetic, carefree child, who made friends easily and enjoyed school and play and being with people. Her father was a carpenter by trade, his color red, but he was also a passionate musician. On evenings and weekends he could be found at the tavern playing his wooden flute before a spellbound audience. When Genevieve was barely old enough to walk, she became fascinated by their little clavichord.

Soon it was clear she had an unusual gift. Not only could she play any piece she'd heard just once, but she could effortlessly adapt and rearrange it, discovering lovely and unexpected dimensions. As soon as she was old enough to properly study music, she began writing her own compositions. Her parents happily scrimped and saved to purchase a beautiful pianoforte, which had pride of place in their small parlor. Soon Genevieve was accompanying her father to play at weddings and festivals, where she would delight neighbors with her improvisations on familiar tunes. But when she was fourteen, her life took an unexpected turn. Genevieve was playing before the whole town at a feast for the Bridal Week when suddenly her music just... changed.

The sweet, pretty tune she'd been playing was suddenly filled with harsh dissonances and jarring shifts. Instead of evoking the pure joys of childhood, it brought to mind ugly passions and disappointments, bitterness and clawing fears, sentiments that were mostly foreign to the cheerful villagers.

Genevieve was horrified at her creation, but she couldn't stop. Her music was spontaneous and had always grown out of her feelings. Looking out at the audience, she saw astonishment and fear. The people who had known her all her life looked at her like an alien. Genevieve couldn't bear it.

As soon as she got home, she went to her room and in a frenzy burned every last notebook that held her compositions. She announced to her parents that she would never play again.

Unfortunately, for Genevieve that was only the beginning. Though she'd quit music, she found she could not escape that song. Soon, she couldn't even remember the happy girl she'd been. She was tormented by horrible mood swings, fits of temper followed by crippling sadness. Genevieve hated this side of herself. When the moods gripped her, she secretly feared a demon lived inside of her who would take possession and perhaps one day drive her to harm the ones she loved. She detested the uneasiness she saw or imagined on the faces of her neighbors, and she began to refuse to go out.

Even her parents were a source of pain. At times she flew into rages that they understood nothing of what tormented her. At other times she was buckled under with guilt at the pain she was causing them. Worst of all, she was consumed by wicked doubts that they couldn't possibly love her given all the anguish she was causing them.

The worst moment came the following summer, on the anniversary of that first disaster. Her parents had left her at home while they attended a wedding feast. Jealous and bitter at being left, she attacked the beautiful pianoforte in the parlor. When her parents arrived home later that night, they found her sobbing, huddled amidst the splinters of the instrument, her badly torn hands covered in blood.

The Mirans were utterly baffled. They adored their daughter, but Genevieve was right that they had no understanding of the dark moods that consumed her. They took her to the healer, but the woman could find no illness, no cause for Genevieve's change.

After, they went to the priestess, fearing that some demon really had taken possession of her. The priestess calmed their fears. She told them there was no cure, but promised that their daughter's sadness would not color her whole life.

The Mirans were simple people, so they received comfort from the priestess' words. They never stopped loving their daughter, found patience to cope with her moods, and never lost their hope that someday she would find happiness. Later when Genevieve reached the age to marry, they again consulted the priestess, who told them firmly that Genevieve must join the Bridal Week. So they went about all the preparations, divided between hope and fear at their daughter's destiny.

Genevieve had also gone to the priestess and begged her to say she was too ill. It was the only reason any girl ever delayed. The entire idea of marriage terrified her. What would her husband think? How could she bring such misery down on some unsuspecting man? She secretly feared that alone of the girls in the town, her heartwood box would never change color, would always remain locked.

The priestess refused to excuse her. She told Genevieve that she was beloved by Titania and must never turn away from her gifts, no matter what the price. Genevieve became impassioned and warned of dire consequences if she were forced to go through with it. The priestess strongly rebuked the girl, saying her words were akin to blasphemy, and warned her that it would destroy her parents and curse her family if she ever harmed herself. And so Genevieve had no choice but to acquiesce in the preparations.

Her mother came in, showing none of the uneasiness she must have felt. "You look so lovely, Jenny, truly."

"It's the dress," Genevieve said sourly. Her mother clutched her hands in despair at her daughter's habit of decrying everything about herself. Genevieve hadn't wanted to upset her and tried to give a cheerful smile. "Thank you, Mama," she murmured.

Genevieve didn't hate her looks. Though she'd probably never be considered the rival of the Fae Queen, she had a wholesome village prettiness. Her hair was long and thick, and a striking mix of honey and gold, and she had clear, frank blue eyes. But several years of poor eating and sleeping had taken their toll: the pallor and thinness that might look attractive on a more elegant woman didn't suit her. When she was younger, she was always tanned and lightly freckled and strong enough to run and climb trees. Now she looked like an invalid.

"It's time to go, Jenny," her mother said gently.

Genevieve's face fell. "Mama, I can't face them."

Though she'd had friends when she was younger, after her music changed the boys and girls her age became wary of her—not unkind but uncomfortable, unsure what to say around her.

Her mother said, "There now, it's just a picnic. I was nervous when my year came, but you'll see. It's like everyone's had a glass of champagne—the week brings out their best nature. Please give them a chance, Jenny."

Genevieve turned from her mother and reached for her shawl, frowning when she saw it. Like all girls joining the Bridal Week, she had woven it herself of her family's colors. Most of it was red, but it was not the cheerful red her father favored, but a deep, uneasy shade mixed with brown and black. At random points were clashing strands of yellow, her mother's color. When she'd first woven it, she'd been intrigued by the unexpected patterns and strange energy of her creation, but now it just seemed as disturbing as her music. She wished she had created something beautiful like the dress Mama had crafted. Why must everything she did be so ugly and harsh?

Her mother kissed her gently. "Give them a chance, Jenny—you are as much a part of this town, as much Titania's daughter as the others, and you will be blessed as they are." Genevieve fought back her tears and nodded. Mama was right. It was time.

Chapter Two

Genevieve and her mother made the short walk to the village green where a throng of girls had gathered, each wearing a shawl with their colors. They were engaged in admiring each other's designs, shooting looks every now and then at the young men, who stood in their own group twenty feet away. Unlike the girls, the boys wore only one color, that of their craft or profession, though they had choice of the shade. Some chose showy displays with bright scarves or hats, while others were more discreet with just a band on their cuffs or cap.

Genevieve had no choice but to join the girls, shyly trying to stay on the outside. To her surprise, Sally, an old friend from school, burst out, "Jenny!"

Several other girls greeted her. She saw nothing but warm smiles when they admired her dress and shawl. Her mother was right—the excitement and hope of the Bridal Week brought out everyone's most generous side.

The topic soon turned to the boys who had joined this year. Though girls almost always joined at eighteen, families often preferred their sons wait. Sometimes they needed more training at their chosen craft or to save money to set up their own household.

It seemed this year the main gossip concerned the presence of Damian Black. It was the first Genevieve had heard his name. Everyone knew the Blacks were warriors who lived in the great fortress on the hill that overlooked their valley, but she couldn't remember ever having seen them in the village. Most likely they lived too far to attend the village school, so the children were taught at home. She had an uneasy sense that there had been times when she'd come upon her parents talking about one of the families in the town, and they had suddenly gone silent. She felt certain now that it had been the Blacks.

"His brothers attended the Bridal Week, Derek three years ago, and Donal two years ago," one girl was saying, "but they both failed to find brides."

Genevieve hadn't heard that—she'd thought everyone found a partner during the Bridal Week. She wondered if such a thing could happen to her.

"My sister married three years ago," another girl said. "She told me that Derek Black scared the daylights out of all the girls. He rarely spoke and glared at everyone. They all said he must have a fearsome temper."

"What of their sisters?" Genevieve asked.

Sally looked at her as if she were crazy. "Jenny you goose—everyone knows the Blacks have only sons." Genevieve didn't hide her amazement at this. "It is said because they are warriors, Titania's most loyal guards, but

I don't know." Sally shivered. "There must be some reason they haven't found brides—theirs is the only family this ever happens to."

Several of the girls whispered their intention of avoiding Damian Black as much as they could. If they didn't get to know him, they conjectured, there was no chance that their box would turn to his color.

"Ooh," Sally hissed, "there he is, Damian Black himself." Everyone turned at once. He smirked when he noticed their stares, and the girls squealed and quickly turned away.

Sally whispered in her ear, "Just look at those eyes of his. That is a man who knows how to get his own way, or I am much mistaken. He may be handsome, but you can bet he never forgets for a minute that he's descended from the Black Prince."

Genevieve couldn't disagree. She looked at Sally more carefully. She'd forgotten how bright her old friend was. As a child she'd been a tiny spitfire of a girl who didn't take nonsense from anyone. She had grown to be a very pretty woman, with pale blond hair and sharp hazel eyes, and so confident it was easy to forget she was barely over five feet tall.

But unlike her friend, Genevieve felt a certain kinship with Damian Black and his brothers. They knew what it was like to be part of the town and yet feel themselves outsiders. The very thing she had feared so much had really happened to them, and yet everyone seemed to agree that they were ever among the most devoted to Titania and made great sacrifices defending the demon gate. She couldn't blame them for remembering their illustrious heritage. Declan was a great hero, and they seemed to be living up to his legacy. She resolved that she would not be one of the girls who avoided Damian Black.

The topic soon changed, and Genevieve was able to sneak a better look at the mysterious son of the Black family. There was no difficulty picking him out. He was taller and more powerfully built than the others and appeared older—she guessed he was at least twenty-five. He stood off to the side, away from the central group of boys who were joking and play fighting each other. Genevieve agreed with Sally that he was handsome—very handsome. His inky black hair and almost black eyes made him seem fierce, but Genevieve saw plenty of good humor in his expression. There was no missing the confident way he held himself, but he wore an ordinary brown suit and showed his color with a plain black scarf, hardly the dress of a man trying to make everyone aware of his superiority.

Another boy approached him and asked after Damian's family. Genevieve felt a moment of trepidation at the boy's boldness but relaxed when she saw Damian smile and answer easily. She saw no contempt or impatience in his expression—nothing like cruelty in his face. But she didn't deceive herself: he was nothing like the boys she'd grown up with. He looked like what he was, a fighter trained from his youth for war, the descendant of Declan. She must have looked too long because she realized with a start that he was looking back at her. He made a shallow bow, which made her face flame up.

Genevieve bit her lip uneasily, wondering if she could look a greater fool. Fortunately, the awkward moment was interrupted by the approach of the elderly priestess and her votary, along with various neighbors bringing picnic baskets.

Sally was beaming, having exchanged a glance with Peter Crane. Genevieve couldn't help laughing. She remembered Peter well: he had mercilessly tormented them when they were nine, loving nothing more than to pull a girl's hair or put a spider down her back when the teacher wasn't looking. The obnoxious skinny boy had grown into a very handsome man, with blond curly hair and dreamy blue eyes. He was an artist, a painter, and displayed his color with an outlandish blue satin scarf. He still had an infectious smile that even Genevieve couldn't resist.

Genevieve winked at Sally, who clapped her hands joyfully. Both of Sally's parents were healers, their color green. Sally had trained as a midwife, and her shawl was pale green with a vine pattern in darker green twining through it. Green and blue were harmonious shades, and she knew it would be considered a good pairing.

Something in Genevieve relaxed, and all of a sudden the Bridal Week didn't seem so terrifying. These were her people, her traditions. For the first time since her music changed, she could almost believe that she was one of Titania's beloved children just like all the others.

The priestess called to the boys to each pick up a basket and attach it with their color. They all started together towards Titania's Altar, which was in a grove of rowan trees about a half-mile from town. Away from the village green, the two groups dispersed, and boys and girls gradually fell to walking together. Sally grabbed Genevieve's arm and pulled her along to speak to one boy after another—except for Peter Crane.

To Genevieve's surprise, she found it easy to make small talk and ask about their crafts and families. No one raised the kind of excitement that Sally seemed to feel for Peter, but the walk passed pleasantly. She couldn't help but notice that though the boys began to warm up to Damian Black, the girls all kept their distance.

At the grove, the girls and boys separated again until the priestess called them all to order. "Welcome all of you to the Bridal Week. As you know, our events are designed to give the girls the chance to spend time with the boys in our group. Today is simple: each girl will choose a color from my bag to know whom she will share lunch with. After lunch, you can mingle again and if you choose walk in the forest. Enjoy this time together. Do not forget that we serve Titania in all that we do here. Be true to yourselves and respectful of each other, and Titania will smile on you and bless the unions you form this week."

There was a moment of pious silence at her words, and then the girls approached to choose their ribbon from her bag. Soon they were laughing and squealing, but Genevieve had lost the easiness she'd felt just a few minutes before. Everyone had been warm and friendly so far, which pleased her—it had felt like a gathering from her school days before all her troubles. But this wasn't school—it was the Bridal Week—and by the end of it, these laughing girls and boys would be married couples.

She held back as long as she could, but finally she could delay no longer. To her surprise, before she could reach into the bag, the priestess took her face in her hands and kissed her forehead. "Titania bless you, Genevieve," she said. She placed something in her hand and whispered, "Don't look until you've sat down."

Chapter Three

Genevieve was too preoccupied with trying to get away from the others and their oppressive gaiety to notice the ribbon in her hand. She threw her shawl down beneath a tree at the far end of the meadow and plopped down, fighting to get her temper back in order before she shocked the poor boy cursed to share lunch with her.

Unfortunately her valiant efforts were all for naught. She noticed Damian Black approaching her spot and quickly opened her hand: in it was a black ribbon. She now cursed the nerves that made her choose a spot so far from the others. She wasn't afraid of Damian Black precisely, but she would have preferred if they'd at least been within earshot of the other couples.

Damian came to the edge of her shawl and just stood there. Genevieve stared up at him, blushing like a schoolgirl, with no idea why he was standing there. Finally he said, "May I join you?"

"Of course!" she burst out, appalled that she would forget her manners. As he placed the basket and took a seat, she fumbled for something to say and then remembered that they'd never been formally introduced.

"I actually know your name," she stammered. "Damian of the house of Black. People call me Jenny."

She groaned inwardly—her parents and school friends called her Jenny, but she hated that nickname. Jenny was the girl who'd existed before her music changed. "Don't call me that," she added hastily. "Genevieve, I'm Genevieve Miran."

"Genevieve," he said as if testing it out. "Much better. I am indeed Damian Black, and I am delighted to meet you, Genevieve."

She looked at him sharply—something in the way he spoke made the words sound like more than just an empty civility. He met her eye almost like he was challenging her, which made her flush violently and look away. She hated how easily discomposed she was and was suddenly terrified she might burst into tears—how foolish!

To her surprise, she felt his fingers gently grip her chin, pulling her face up to meet his gaze. "Genevieve, darling, what's wrong?" He watched her face carefully.

"I'm sorry, please, I didn't..." she fumbled. "I don't mix much with strangers—I'm sorry. I get nervous—it's so foolish. Please don't be offended." It all just sounded worse and worse.

"Never, Genevieve. Don't apologize again. You have nothing to be sorry for."

Again, the words sounded like they meant something more—like he felt deeply, which only alarmed her more.

She realized he was still holding her face. She instinctively tried to turn her head, but he held her face more firmly.

"Don't look away from me, Genevieve." He was watching her, studying her face, as if looking for something. She tried to pull away again, but his grip tightened. "What did just I say?" His tone was laced with iron, and she suddenly swayed dizzily.

"What is happening?" she gasped.

"Get up and walk into the trees," he ordered.

"But the lunch... the Bridal..." Nothing made sense.

"They don't matter. Listen to my voice. Walk into the trees. Do it now, Genevieve."

She stumbled to her feet and did her best to walk purposefully, as if she had a perfectly good reason to leave the picnic. As soon as she was out of sight of the rest, she wondered why on earth she'd done this, just like that, because he'd told her to? Would he follow her?

Suddenly it was all too much. She hiked up her skirts and started running blindly. She hadn't gone far before she slammed into something, which some part of her knew was Damian, but her mind wasn't working properly. She struggled and flailed, tears running down her face.

"Stop struggling, Genevieve."

"What's happening?" she cried again.

Damian pulled her into his arms and clasped her tightly. She struggled for a moment before realizing her arms were pinned. She started to come out of her panic and allowed herself to relax, somehow trusting that he wasn't disgusted by her lunatic behavior. He was even taller than she'd realized—almost a foot taller than she was, not that she could call herself tall. She was exactly her mother's height of five foot three.

He loosened his hold slightly and gripped her chin to make her raise her eyes to his. She was surprised at how warm his gaze was, which calmed her further.

"Are you better?" he asked gently.

"Yes, thank you. You must think me a lunatic. I'm so sorry," she said lamely.

He tapped her cheek firmly. "Kneel down, Genevieve, and don't apologize again."

His words brought on the dizziness again. She slipped down to her knees, not even trying to understand what was happening. After her panic, it was soothing to just be off her feet, out of the sun, away from all the others. So for a long time, she just stayed there, enjoying the cool grass under the trees and the quiet forest sounds.

Finally she became curious about Damian and why he'd insisted on coming out here, so she looked up. He was standing against a tree, watching her. He'd said nothing for all those minutes—attempted no apology or explanation for the oddness of his demand that they leave the picnic.

There was something intimate about that—that way of ignoring the usual rules of interaction, the expected topics of polite conversation between two people who'd never met before. Those rules were a boundary between people, and somehow it had just been shunted aside. It was freeing: she felt no more pressure to pretend she could chat about tea parties and sewing. She suddenly wanted him to understand. "I'm not like them—the other girls."

"I know."

"I have moods. My thoughts aren't... right—they're not nice... Something's wrong with me. I used to think it was a demon. The priestess said no, that Titania gives her children many different gifts, and mine was harder to bear. I don't know what to think. I'm babbling." She cut herself off before she apologized again. "I just didn't want you to get the wrong idea."

"Wrong idea?"

"You asked me to come out here with you...." She paused to see if he would help, but he remained silent. Suddenly she felt annoyed. "You obviously have your reasons, Damian Black, whether you say them or not. I'm telling you now, I'm not totally right, so don't ever say I didn't tell you."

"I never would, Genevieve. Are you trying to warn me off?"

"The other girls are afraid of you."

"Answer my question, Genevieve."

"I don't know.... No. I just wanted you to know, in case...."

"In case of what?"

"In case there was some reason you asked me out here. Don't treat me like a fool." Her voice was rising again.

"Hush, Genevieve, you know I'm not. Perhaps I just wanted to watch you kneeling."

"I don't understand you—can I get up now?"

"No. I'll tell you when you can get up. Be silent now, Genevieve." She slumped down, tired from dealing with such a confusing male. "Close your eyes, darling."

"Damian..." she protested, her anxiety rising again.

"Do as I ask," he responded in a soothing voice.

"This doesn't make sense!" she cried, letting her eyes fall shut. But it was too difficult to hold them closed knowing he was there, wondering what he was doing. She blinked and then realized he was no longer in front of her. Suddenly a soft cloth covered her eyes and then was tightened. She stiffened in panic and reached to pull it down, but he gripped her wrists and pulled her firmly against him.

"Easy, darling. You're safe. Stop struggling." He rested his cheek against hers—it scratched—and then she felt his soft lips touching her face. "Are you calm?" he asked.

"Yes," she said, though her voice was shrill.

"Keep your hands here," he said, placing them on her thighs. When she started to protest, he covered her mouth and said, "Hush, Genevieve, you mustn't speak." He gave her a little kiss on top of her head, and then he moved away.

So she knelt there, like he said, blindfolded. She was beyond fear, beyond misery: her emotions were in chaos. Her body began shaking, so she fisted her hands, gritted her teeth, and held herself rigid, as if she might suddenly shatter into pieces. She could feel the tears dampening the blindfold, and finally she let out a sob, which turned into a scream.

A second later he was in front of her, pulling off the blindfold. He kissed her on the lips and sat back against a tree, pulling her into his arms.

Genevieve huddled there, sobbing, feeling like she'd turned into a small child. "What is happening? What do you want?"

"Shhh, love," Damian soothed. "Easy now, it's over."

"Who are you?"

"You need to trust me—I would die before I let you come to harm; quiet now."

So she lay there enclosed in his arms. She just caught a trace of his scent, oakmoss she thought sleepily, and leather. It was extraordinarily pleasant. And so masculine.

The tension drained out of her, leaving her utterly exhausted.

She was startled when Damian nuzzled her face. He looked elated. "You fell asleep, love, but we should return now."

Genevieve moved to get to her feet, but Damian suddenly stood while holding her, which she vaguely recognized must be very strenuous.

"Can you walk, darling?"

She nodded, and he gently put her on her feet. She was dizzy and clutched at his arm. He shook his head and swung her up again, kissing her forehead. Genevieve didn't argue but lay there passively, resting her head on his shoulder as he moved swiftly back to the picnic area.

The other couples had finished their lunch, and some part of Genevieve realized that every person there was staring dumfounded at the two of them. Her hair had come out of its combs, and her beautiful dress was stained with grass and twigs.

So apparently this was to be the start and finish of her Bridal Week—creating a scandal with Damian Black. She had no idea why it had happened or what she might have done differently, and finally she just closed her eyes.

"Damian, what have you done?" the priestess demanded.

"Do you impeach my honor?"

"Have care, Damian!"

"She is unharmed, I swear it, but I am taking her home. I must send for the rest of my family."

"I gave her your ribbon and this is the return you make me! You could not wait?" the priestess said angrily.

"No I couldn't! This is everything to my family, Holy One."

"Your family! What are they to her? This is her Bridal Week—a week of pleasures she has waited for her whole life. She deserves to be courted and feted. Are her feelings so little to you? I will have words with Declan over this—he has allowed his zeal for you to blind him."

Damian dropped to his knees, gently placing Genevieve on the ground next to him. "Forgive me, Holy One," he said, bowing his head. "Do not blame Declan. I let my fears rule me. Her well-being is my first priority at all times, on my honor I swear it. Declan would repudiate me if he thought it otherwise."

Genevieve felt herself swaying dizzily—nothing made sense. Declan? Titania's champion? "Damian?" she squeaked out. "What is happening?"

"Silence, Genevieve." He looked carefully at her, tapping her lips, and then turned back to the priestess. "Please, Holy One, I need your help. It will be many hours before Declan can get here. I need you to ease matters with her family. She is mine now, and I will allow no interference, even from her parents, but I have no wish to trample their feelings."

The priestess gave him an annoyed rap with her staff. "Get up, Damian, enough of this."

Genevieve felt herself flying up as Damian got to his feet in a smooth motion, hoisting her up at the same time.

"I see you've arranged matters so that I have little choice. I will speak to them, but you will not forget what is given to you, nor treat lightly the challenges she faces becoming your bride. She must have a proper wedding, surrounded by her friends and family, before you sweep her off to that castle of yours."

"I know," he said, sounding deeply moved. "You cannot guess.... Just trust that every member of my family knows what we are being given, but please, come as soon as you can."

Chapter Four

Damian had no intention of putting Genevieve down as he made his way back to the town and her parents' home. She was so slender, she weighed practically nothing and while she was in his arms, he felt there was no chance of her escaping.

He was astonished and touched by how peacefully she lay there—trusting her future to him—though she understood nothing of what it would mean to marry into his family, or what would be demanded of her.

He wanted to howl with triumph—she was his! He'd actually found her. He wondered what his brothers would say. No doubt Donal would ask if she were pretty. How strange that he'd barely even taken note of her looks beyond the basics: blond hair, blue eyes, small. Except for her mouth: he'd noticed immediately how innocently carnal it was, as if made for taking a man between her lips. Donal would be driven mad by her.

He supposed by conventional standards she would not be considered a great beauty. Her figure was feminine, with small, gently rounded breasts, but not particularly well endowed. Her thinness and pallor hinted strongly of ill health. His bride clearly needed someone to take proper care of her!

But it was those clear blue eyes of hers that continued to stagger him. They hid nothing. Right now they wore a glazed expression, as they had every time he'd shown her even a hint of dominance. He was forced to shift his hold slightly. Just the thought of her responses made him shoot impossibly hard for what seemed like the fortieth time that afternoon.

There had probably been girls at the picnic whose beauty stood out more, but Damian hadn't noticed anyone after he'd caught sight of Genevieve. The awkward way she'd stood outside the group of girls, as if she knew she could never truly belong, had called to him. The frothy, feminine dress she wore only underscored for him how tense she was. Then he'd caught her staring at him and noted the nervous, guilty way she'd looked away, as if she'd been indulging some very unmaidenly thoughts about him.

At that moment he'd known—she was his. Declan had told him to trust his instincts, but nothing could have prepared him for that overwhelming sense of certainty. From then on he'd not stopped watching her. Her movements and expressions were remarkably easy to read even from a distance. But still, his observations had been nothing to the reality of meeting her, hearing her voice, seeing her adorable confusion.

It was as if a force had taken over, impelling him to push until he could feel that she was his irrevocably. He would stake his life that her heartwood box had changed to his color.

Unfortunately that was not the end of his problems. Declan had also given him strict instructions on dealing with the girl's family. They must be treated with courtesy and their attachment to their daughter honored, but Damian must also assert control of everything to do with her immediately. He could allow no one, not even her mother, to speak to her without a member of his family present.

Now was the time that posed the greatest risks to both of their happiness. There were very few outside his family who could understand or accept their ways, and there was a great chance that the girl's family or some well-meaning friend would poison her mind and lead her to fear marriage to one of the Black family.

He only had himself to blame that he must now appear to trample over her parents' natural rights and keep them from their daughter. Declan was the proper person to explain matters to them and ease their fears for Genevieve. The Black Prince's authority was such that they would find it impossible to deny anything he asked for, and they would trust his reassurances more than they could Damian's. Declan planned to come, but he had many duties and no reason to think he would be needed today—the very first day of the Bridal Week.

The moment Damian arrived at the village, he found the servant who had accompanied him and ordered him to ride with all haste to the fortress, informing his brothers that they were needed. They would understand the urgency and would not delay, but it might be many hours before a message could be gotten to Declan in Faerie, and as many more before he could make his way to the village.

But first he must deal with Genevieve's parents. The moment he knocked, her mother threw open the door. Her expression told him she already knew Genevieve's box had changed color and did not regard the news with joy. Her uneasiness only grew when she saw her daughter's confused state. "Jenny! Is she hurt?"

"She's not hurt, just a little dazed," he said. "May I enter?"

Mrs. Miran reverted instinctively to proper village courtesy and showed him into the parlor, calling out to her husband. Genevieve's box had been placed in the center in honor of her joining the Bridal Week. He could imagine the Mirans' surprise when the pale wooden box had darkened to the same lightless black as his hair.

Damian ignored the seat Mrs. Miran pointed to and sat himself and Genevieve on a small sofa that enabled him to keep himself between her and her parents. She slumped against the back, so he pulled her to lean against him, keeping his grip on her arm. Genevieve's parents both took seats across from him.

He didn't waste time with the usual civilities but said his family's traditional betrothal words. "I am Damian of the house of Black. I beg the honor of being allowed to guard the key to your daughter's heartwood box."

Damian wasn't surprised that her father did not immediately hand over the key but said gruffly, "This is full hasty, sir—I don't half like this."

Damian could see the man's suspicions growing as he took in the details of his daughter's appearance—her shawl lost, her skirt stained with grass, her hair disheveled. He knew what it looked like, but still it took some effort to master his rage that they might suspect him. To take a girl's innocence as a way to force a change of her heartwood box would be the gravest dishonor and an unthinkable offense to Titania. But the father and mother in front of him knew little of his family but the rumors.

"Let me take her upstairs," the mother said, thinking to let her husband confront Damian.

"No!" Damian said more harshly than he intended. "The priestess promised she would come. I cannot let her out of my sight—I will not."

"Well now, sir, this is my house!" the father protested.

Thank Titania the priestess arrived. She seemed amused at the sight of him clutching Genevieve. "Let him take her upstairs, poor creature," she said with a wry smile.

"Priestess, what is going on? What has he done to her?" her father demanded.

"Tsk, tsk, she is fine, Cyrus. He is Declan's brood—you mustn't cross him. They are madmen when it comes to their brides. Genevieve's so shy. I'm sure he turned the poor girl head over heels with his wooing, that's all."

The priestess' words helped mollify the father. "I didn't know what to make of it—she isn't herself. I feared...."

"No descendant of Declan's would ever dishonor himself or his bride that way, you may trust me on this, Cyrus. But they are an overwhelming bunch the lot of them. He knew they were matched, and he just couldn't help rushing to the point with her. Take her upstairs, Damian."

"I must have the key to her room."

"What?" the mother cried.

The priestess rolled her eyes and said lightly, "That's Declan speaking, I'm sure. Humor him. You'll see: he'll want to guard her as if she were Titania herself now that he's found her. There's no reasoning with this clan, I'm afraid."

Damian wanted to kiss the priestess. Her light tone was exactly right. The father shifted from wordless terror at the thought that his daughter might have been molested, to grumbling about hot-headed boys. The mother looked unsure but led him upstairs to Genevieve's room and showed him where the key was kept.

The priestess called from downstairs, "I'm sorry to trouble you, Lilia, but I'm a bit overset from rushing to get here—if you could spare a cup of water or perhaps a spot of tea?"

The mother was horrified at the idea of failing in hospitality to the priestess. She hurried downstairs, leaving Damian to gently place Genevieve on her bed.

"Damian," she said dreamily, still too dazed to question why he was in her bedroom.

"I'm here, Genevieve—you're safe. Can you take off your dress yourself, darling?" Genevieve just blinked at him. He kissed her forehead. "Here, love, I'll help you."

He quickly undid the back of the dress and pulled it off, leaving her in her shift. He removed her shoes, undid her garters, and took off her stockings. Through the whole process, she sat passively. He knew that tending to her needs like this each night would prove to be one of the most gratifying aspects of their life together, but after the scene in the wood, his desires were roaring.

Making a superhuman effort, he mastered his will and forced himself to behave exactly as if her mother hadn't left the room—the most difficult thing he'd ever done. He would have given anything to be able to tie her to the bed and teach her some of the pleasures that awaited her. Such intimacy would go a long way to counteract any officious counsel she might receive.

But he had already pressed his limits too far. Declan would be seriously displeased if Damian acted as if he had no regard for the sensibilities of Genevieve's family. Moreover, he knew that if the Mirans had deep reservations about the marriage, there was no way he could keep Genevieve from knowing. It would cast a shadow on what should be a happy day for her, one that might extend to their married life as well.

He helped her settle under the covers and said softly, "Genevieve, you are tired. You must rest."

"What is happening?"

"Your heartwood box changed, love."

"Yes," she said vaguely.

"Genevieve, this is very important. You may not leave your room until I come for you."

Once again her eyes glazed—she seemed incapable of resisting him when he asserted authority over her. He needed to leave before he lost control.

"You are mine now, darling, and must obey my will. Do you understand?"

"No, not really," she said, curling up sleepily against him, "but I won't leave."

He felt a rush of affection for her and kissed her forehead. Suddenly, more than anything he just wanted to crawl under the covers and hold her while she slept. Soon, he reminded himself, very soon.

He locked the door to her room, pocketed the key, and crept downstairs quietly. Though he doubted Declan would approve, he couldn't stop himself from listening at the door to the parlor. Genevieve's happiness was at stake, he reasoned. She would be miserable if her parents were, and he owed it to her even to stoop to listen at a door if that would help him ease things for her.

The parents were far from reconciled to this unexpected turn of events. "Priestess, this can't be right," her mother pleaded. "The Blacks... we hear such stories."

"Fie on you for listening to gossip, Lilia," the priestess said firmly. "Their ways are not for everyone, to be sure, but they are men of honor. And let us not forget: this is Genevieve we speak of. How happy would she be married to one of our village swains? Her torments are painful enough, but the guilt she'd feel would crush her—it's crushing her now."

"Guilt?" Cyrus said fiercely. "She's our daughter—how can she feel guilt? We would do anything for her. We've always only wanted her happiness."

"Would that it were that simple," said the priestess. "Genevieve has long tormented herself for many imaginary sins. Lilia, Cyrus, you must listen to me. You carry no guilt for Genevieve's troubles. Now, she needs your love and to know you accept her."

"He did something.... If he hadn't..." Lilia pleaded.

"There is no forcing or fooling the heartwood box. This is her path. I swear by everything holy: every member of the Black family considers her the greatest blessing Titania could give them. No action of hers, no dark mood will change that for them. You have raised and loved her, but she is a woman now, and she belongs with them. The only question for the two of you is can you let her go? Damian acts as he does because he fears you will poison Genevieve's mind and make her fear him. Is he so unreasonable?"

The Mirans must have acknowledged the point.

"Let it go. Let the Blacks do things their way—it will be very hard to stop them anyway. So don't fight it. Show Damian the hospitality that is his due and make

Genevieve feel her wedding is a day of joy for you. It is the greatest wedding gift you can give her."

Damian bowed his head in silent thanks and then retreated up the stairs and came down again with loud steps. He received a rather forced invitation to stay with them from Mrs. Miran, but nothing suggested they were readying themselves to refuse his suit outright.

"Damian, I would have your arm back to the temple. I am old, and all this walking is hard on me," the priestess said.

Damian was on his feet in an instant offering his arm and promising to return as soon as he had seen the priestess home and made arrangements for his horse.

As soon as they were out the door, the priestess released his arm and said angrily, "I will see Declan as soon as he arrives."

"Holy One...."

"I did what you asked, but I'm not pleased about it. You swept her off her feet and used me to pacify her parents, but Genevieve has rights. Tell Declan I would speak to him."

She held up her hand to stop him from following her and bustled off.

Chapter Five

Damian felt some contrition that he'd upset the priestess, but not enough to overcome his joy. He could hardly believe how well things were going. His satisfaction was greatly increased when he saw his youngest brother standing near the green—the servant must have found him. That he'd arrived so quickly told him that Donal had been lingering on the road close to the village. He must have suspected something would happen today. How well his brother knew him!

They embraced, both feeling an emotion too strong for words. For a moment, Damian felt almost staggered by the momentousness of what had happened.

It was a great event for Donal as well. By the traditions of their family, the unmarried males of his generation were charged with his bride's well-being, in this case Donal and their middle brother, Derek.

The hope was that his brothers would share their house, so that when Damian's duties required him to be absent, one of them would be present at all times to see to Genevieve. Neither brother had found a bride during their Bridal Week, so they had a great stake in Damian's success.

"Where is she?" Donal asked.

"Asleep in her room."

"You left her!" Donal bristled.

"She is safe—she's locked in her room." He showed Donal the key.

Donal's eyes widened. "How did you manage it?"

"Thank Titania the priestess arrived and smoothed things with Genevieve's parents."

"Genevieve," Donal said, savoring the name. "Is she pretty?"

"Beyond anything I'd dared to hope for," he said with utter sincerity.

A sharp voice accosted them from across the green. "You left her unguarded?" Donal gave him a sympathetic glance as Damian steeled himself to face their brother Derek, who in his mellowest mood could be described as abrasive.

"She is asleep, locked in her room," Damian repeated.

"Which is her house?" Derek demanded.

"Derek," Donal said, "Damian doesn't need you terrifying the girl's parents. It would delay the wedding if one of them died of an apoplexy after meeting their new in-laws."

Derek's expression did not relax by so much as a hair. "Which is her house?" he demanded again.

Donal and Damian exchanged a glance, but there was no arguing with their middle brother. Damian pointed to the small white cottage with bright yellow shutters and window boxes overflowing with red geraniums. It would be hard to imagine a building more antithetical to their austere, temperamental brother.

"Her name is Genevieve Miran—in case you're interested," Damian added dryly.

Derek nodded and walked towards the house. Damian wondered if he should begin praying to Titania for mercy, when Derek called over his shoulder, "Declan is just behind me."

"Say the word, brother, and I'll skewer him," Donal said. Damian shook his head. In truth neither of them could take Derek in a fight when his blood was up. "Go after him. I'll bring Declan as soon as he arrives."

Damian jogged after Derek, who spared him only a cool glance. Damian knocked on the door, conjuring up his warmest smile for Mrs. Miran, who paled as soon as she saw Derek. Though all three brothers closely resembled each other, there was something in Derek's expression that women especially found forbidding.

"As you see, I have returned," he said in his most soothing tone. "Mrs. Miran, may I present my brother, Derek, of the house of Black."

Though Derek's manners within the family were abrupt to say the least, he had been raised by a knight of

Titania's royal court, who demanded they all follow proper forms of courtesy.

To Damian's relief, Mrs. Miran seemed more awestruck than terrified when Derek bowed over her hand and said with grave formality, "It is an honor to make the acquaintance of the parents of my brother's bride."

"Please, make yourself at home," Mrs. Miran said nervously, ushering them into the parlor. "May I offer you something? My husband will be here in just a moment."

Derek made only a grim nod, and Damian said, "That would be extremely welcome."

The poor woman practically bolted from the room. He wished Donal were here: their youngest brother could charm a dragon into donating its gold to charity and was far better than Damian at smoothing over Derek's rough edges.

Damian had been too distracted earlier to get much of an impression of the Mirans' home, but sitting in their parlor he felt some sympathy for his bride's parents. Mrs. Miran appeared to have a taste for all that was sweet and feminine. There were crocheted lace doilies on all the furniture and framed satin hearts on the walls. Various surfaces held small vases filled with silk flowers along with a collection of ceramic terriers at play.

It had its charm and wasn't at all ugly, but the decor provided a poignant contrast to Genevieve's heartwood box, standing black and stark on a delicate painted table. It would be next to impossible to imagine anything belonging to the Blacks inside this room.

It occurred to him that Genevieve's bedroom was nothing like this parlor either. He did not think there was a single picture on the walls, and it was completely free of the expected feminine bric-a-brac: little pillows, favorite dolls, a lacy beauty table. In fact, he might have said it was almost aggressively spare, with only the bed, a wardrobe, and a small bookshelf. The only item of color he could recall was a pretty green spread on her bed.

Mrs. Miran entered a few minutes later carrying a tray with tea things followed by a small kitchen boy, who staggered under an enormous platter piled with enough cakes, sandwiches, and scones to provision an entire troop.

Barely a moment later there was another knock on the door. It seemed the queen of light decided to smile upon him today. Mr. Miran entered the room with a stunned expression on his face: immediately behind him was Donal—accompanied by the Black Prince.

If he'd been less nervous, Damian might have been amused at the sight of the enormous Fae prince, whose very name made the Demon King tremble, sipping tea from a dainty pink cup, nibbling on a bit of jam tart.

But as he'd hoped, Declan smoothed all problems. His authority and stature were such that no one, least of all the good-hearted Mirans, would dream of opposing anything he suggested. Within minutes, they'd agreed it would be "best" if the marriage took place in a mere two days. Then as if it were completely expected that he would make such arrangements, Declan added, "Derek and Donal, you will split the watch for the next two nights so that Damian may sleep. I do not anticipate any dangers, of course, but it is not the way of the Blacks to leave a bride of our family unprotected under any circumstances."

Mrs. Miran stumbled out an apology: unsurprisingly, the tiny cottage contained only a single spare bedroom.

Declan turned his most forbidding expression on Derek and Donal as if both had loudly complained about the accommodations. "No son of mine would dream of inconveniencing you. Such would be a poor return to those who are entrusting our family with their greatest treasure. You will not give it another thought. They are trained soldiers, accustomed to life on campaign. A chair in the hall outside Miss Miran's bedroom would be more than generous. The other may sleep on the floor of Damian's room. You may rest easy that your daughter will be protected. I assure you Derek and Donal are prepared to meet any danger. I trained them myself."

And with that, the Fae prince swept away any lingering reservations about Damian's admittedly outrageous request to be given the key to Genevieve's room. Both parents were in awe that the great Declan was concerning himself with their daughter's protection.

Derek excused himself then to take up his duties, and Mr. Miran abruptly decided that it was still early enough to call upon several neighbors and begin issuing the invitations. Damian suspected he also wished to stop off at the tavern to spread the news that the Black Prince had taken tea in their parlor.

Damian saw his moment to say, "Sire, the priestess asked to speak with you as soon as you have a free moment."

"I've no doubt she did," Declan said with the barest hint of a smile. "We'd best pay our call then." They gave their thanks and dispersed, he and Declan to the priestess', and Donal to send a rider to the fortress for their clothes and to let their servants know to begin arrangements for the wedding.

So twenty minutes later, the two were again taking tea, this time around the large wooden table in the priestess' kitchen.

"This is lovely, Maura," Declan said.

"Thank you again, Holy One," Damian said, taking a generous sip.

The priestess snorted. "Very pretty. We could have had more of these nice manners at the picnic. Declan, you've let these boys run wild. I've walked my legs off putting out their fires. Next time you do it yourself."

The priestess was the only human who would dare speak that way to the Faerie prince.

"There, there, Maura, I'm sure you haven't had such an exciting day in decades," he said good-naturedly.

"I apologize deeply that my rashness caused you such trouble," Damian added. "I am greatly in your debt for what you said to Genevieve's parents."

"Were the Mirans uneasy?" Declan asked. "They seemed quite satisfied to me."

"The priestess eased their concerns," Damian said carefully.

"Concerns was it? What would you call it when Damian shows up at their door, their daughter practically unconscious in his arms, and then demands the key to her bedroom so he can lock her in?"

"He only did what is necessary, Maura," Declan said, revealing a little of the ferocity that made him the most feared knight in Faerie.

The priestess was not cowed in the slightest. "Damian forced things today with her, Declan, rather than let her affections grow naturally over the week."

"Damian?" Declan asked.

Damian bowed his head. "Genevieve hides nothing, sire. I did what you suggested, and I don't know how to explain it—she submitted to me instinctively, as if she has no ability resist. I couldn't help myself."

"And because she couldn't resist, her rights were ignored. This is her Bridal Week!" the priestess said angrily. "I'll tell you bluntly, Declan, I don't think this promises well for how he'll treat her once they're married, and she's completely in his power!"

"I agree, he should have waited—it was selfish. But you mustn't be too hard on Damian. There isn't a male in our family who would have acted differently—the instinct to claim is too strong. And Maura, just because Damian was selfish doesn't mean he was also wrong. You and I go through this every time one of mine claims a bride. What you, her parents, or even the girl herself believes is 'right' or 'best' for her is irrelevant. Ultimately, it comes down to whether you trust the heartwood. The girl belongs with us, and the sooner Damian can claim her, the better—for her."

No one had an immediate response to this, and they all sipped their tea in silence for a minute, when Damian

48

found the courage to mention something that had bothered him. "Holy One, Genevieve said something at the picnic—she spoke of troubles and said she feared a demon lived inside her."

"Suddenly worried she might not be the docile lamb you thought? Maybe you shouldn't have forced things with her then," she said crossly.

"Maura," Declan warned.

She sighed and then went and fetched a basket that sat near the kitchen door. "Declan, I would have you see this." She pulled out the shawl that Genevieve had left behind at the picnic. "All the girls weave one for the Bridal Week—this is Genevieve's."

Declan examined it carefully, taking in the strange, chaotic design. Finally he said, "Thank you for showing me this, Maura."

"Genevieve is troubled. She suffers terribly from dark thoughts, fits of temper followed by uncontrollable despair. She has spent the last few years hiding from the world."

Declan took the tiny woman's hand and said feelingly, "We owe you much for setting aside your own doubts and doing your best to help Damian's cause. You may put those fears to rest, however, Maura."

Damian knelt and said, "I know what you did for us, and I am truly grateful."

"Take care of her, Damian. She has had a hard journey. She deserves some happiness."

"From the moment her box changed, my son's first duty became his bride's happiness. You may trust him." Declan kissed her cheek. "I will keep this," he added, picking up Genevieve's shawl.

When the two of them were outside, Declan gripped Damian in a strong hug.

"You're not angry, sire?"

"No," Declan said. "I spoke the truth—not one of us could have held back."

Damian wanted to faint with relief. Somehow he had gotten through the most dangerous part; he'd won his lady, reconciled her parents, soothed the priestess, and even managed to introduce Derek to his in-laws. All that was left was to introduce Genevieve to her new family. Declan and Donal would be simple enough. Derek... was a problem for another day.

"Make time to visit Titania's Altar. Her priestess did you great service today."

"I know she did. I promise I will tomorrow."

"It is traditional to unlock the bride's heartwood box immediately after the ceremony. I will be present."

Damian was unprepared for the explosion of primal possessiveness set off by Declan's words. "My bride's box is given to *my* keeping! No man but I will look within it!"

50

"You are no boy to reject aid when it is offered!" Declan said fiercely. "You with your vast experience in these matters! You are a Black. You would risk your bride's happiness over a childish jealousy?"

"My apologies, sire," he said, lowering his gaze. An unbearable idea arose. "Do you have some reservation about Genevieve?"

Declan turned on him in surprise. "Of course not, but you are not ready for every challenge. You need not face them alone—you will not, for both your sakes. Never doubt that you have been blessed in her, Damian."

Chapter Six

Genevieve awoke with the heaviness that accompanies an unusually long sleep. She had no memory of coming to bed and couldn't fathom why she was wearing only her shift instead of her nightdress. An instinct warned her that it had something to do with Damian Black and their strange scene in the wood.

Suddenly she needed to know what had happened. She threw a robe over her shift and went to the door, only to discover that she was locked in. She shook the handle loudly until the door was opened by a young man who looked so much like Damian, he could only be another member of the Black family. One of the chairs from the parlor had been placed outside the door. He stood in the door, blocking her from leaving, a warm smile on his face. "Genevieve, you're awake. I'll tell Damian."

"Who are you?" she asked.

"I am Donal, his brother. Wait in your room, sweetheart. Damian will come for you in a few minutes."

And with that, he shut the door again and locked it.

Genevieve plumped down on the edge of her bed, so astonished she couldn't even feel angry. As promised, a few minutes later, she heard the key in the lock, and

Damian entered without knocking. He shut the door behind him. "Did you sleep well, love?"

"Damian, what's happening? Why is your brother sitting outside my door?"

"My brothers arrived after you fell asleep, and your parents kindly invited all of us to stay here."

Genevieve wondered that her mother would agree to host three young men—where on earth would they put them? Then she looked up at Damian suspiciously. "Why was the door locked?"

Damian gripped her shoulders gently. "Your box changed color, Genevieve, which means you're mine, my responsibility. It makes no difference that we're not married yet. It is very important that I know at all times where you are."

"So I must be locked in?"

"Yes, you must, and you must not argue with me about it, darling."

He took her chin and tilted her head up so she met his eye. He waited until she made a small nod and then lifted her off her feet and kissed her warmly on the lips. "Good girl. Now get dressed. There's much to do today."

He looked almost giddy with joy, and Genevieve couldn't help but share it. She reached up and touched his face, this man who would be her husband.

His gaze softened and on an unexpected impulse, she leaned in and touched her lips to his. "This is real," she murmured half to herself. "It's really happening."

"Yes it is," he rasped, holding her at arm's length. "I'd best go. Don't be long, darling."

It was still her Bridal Week, even if her box had changed. All of her old clothes had been packed away in traveling trunks, and inside her wardrobe were only newly made items, every one in white. At the far end, carefully wrapped, was the wedding dress that she and her mother had worked on over the past year.

Genevieve chose a simple linen dress with a boat neck, three-quarter sleeves, and wide inverted pleats down the front. It was the one they'd intended for a day of outdoor games and was the plainest of the bunch. She dressed quickly and went to open the door, only to realize it was still locked. She tapped hesitantly, though it seemed foolish that she must ask to leave her own room. Donal was still outside.

He stood still for a moment staring at her and then said in a rapt tone, "I've never seen anything so lovely."

She patted her skirts shyly, not sure how to respond.

Then he winked and said, "I'm sure you need to use the convenience." It took Genevieve a moment to take in what he'd just said, at which point her jaw dropped.

Donal led her to the small room that held a water closet. She was too stunned to protest, so she went in and took care of her needs. He was still outside when she came out again. "The family is at breakfast. May I have the honor?" he said, holding out his arm.

Genevieve just stared at him. Were all men like this? When she didn't answer, he gave her an innocent smile and grabbed her arm and led her downstairs to the small dining room.

Damian and another young man were already at the table along with her mother. Both men stood the moment she entered. Damian put his hand on her back and guided her in. "Darling, may I present my brother, Derek."

Genevieve wrestled her brain back to lucidity in order to greet this third brother, who bowed formally over her hand as if she were Queen Titania herself, which made her giggle nervously. But when his head lifted, the laugh caught in her throat.

No one had ever looked at her like that, as if he were daring her to bolt. She instinctively tried to pull her hand back, but he didn't release it, as if to make clear that he had her trapped. Genevieve knew she should make some light remark, but she could only stand there blinking like an animal cornered by a hunter.

It was Donal who broke the spell with an apologetic cough. "I hope my new sister can forgive me if I dig in, but

I think I'll expire if I don't taste your mother's sausage pie."

There was a general movement then. Derek released her hand and took his seat as Damian held the chair for her. Luckily, there was no pressure for her to play hostess, which gave Genevieve time to recover her equilibrium. Mama spent the next five minutes making sure their guests had enough food, offering to send to the bakery if they didn't find something to their liking.

Genevieve felt some pity for her, even as she wanted to laugh. The Blacks were unfailingly polite over a spread that must be lavish by most standards. Mama was an excellent cook and had old-fashioned notions of hospitality that prompted her to awaken hours before dawn so that her table would be worthy of the Black Prince's family members. On offer this morning were baked eggs, three different types of pie—sausage, apple and quince—an entire ham, and a platter of her special sweet-cheese rolls.

While her mother concerned herself with the guests, Genevieve examined her new family. The three brothers presented an odd triptych: Damian in the middle, confident, friendly, reassuring to her mother, and somehow in command of himself and the room, then on either side his brothers, who each looked like Damian, only in some utterly foreign mood. Donal's eyes were bright with barely suppressed hilarity, his look that of a child who has just stolen the tarts off the tea tray beneath his mother's nose. Derek, for his part, sported a ferocious scowl that would have been better suited to a duel with the Demon King himself than breakfast at Mama's table.

As she looked she noticed other, subtler differences. Donal's hair had a slight curl, unlike his brothers', which was poker straight. Derek wore his hair longer than the other two, with bangs that fell over his forehead obscuring his eyes, which only made him seem more off-putting. Despite his scowl, she noticed that his lips were fuller than his brothers'—almost sensual, though she quickly put aside such an improper thought.

Without question, they were all extraordinarily handsome—and so large they seemed in danger of splintering the small dining chairs. There was a dissonance to their very presence in this room with its pale yellow walls and pink chintz curtains.

Genevieve's observations were interrupted by her mother's concerned cry. "Jenny! You've barely taken a bite! And you missed supper, too! You're going to waste away!"

"Mama," she hissed, blushing fiercely to have the old argument aired in front of her new family, especially when she realized that all three Black brothers had turned their attention fully on her.

"I'm afraid you missed lunch as well—thanks to me," Damian said apologetically.

"What!" Derek burst out to everyone's surprise.

"Oh Jenny! You missed lunch!" her mother cried, now completely alarmed.

"I'm not... I wasn't... I don't eat that much."

"Is she difficult in her eating, Mrs. Miran?" Donal asked in a sympathetic tone that to Genevieve's ear also contained a hint of irony that would be lost on Mama.

It seemed her new brother understood his mark. It was a favorite topic, and her mother immediately launched into a lengthy, detailed litany of her daughter's poor appetite, the many times they'd sent for the healer on the theory that Jenny suffered from indigestion (which she emphatically did not!), the long periods she'd been forbidden her favorite drink of water brightened with sliced lemons, the bland dishes she'd been forced to eat (as if she were an infant!), finishing up with Mama's favorite lament about its effect on "Jenny's beautiful figure," until Genevieve thought she'd die of embarrassment.

Donal's face was the picture of concern, but again Genevieve easily detected the mirth lurking beneath. She was right, the scoundrel had known! And he'd probably been mocking her about using the water closet as well!

She felt a sudden urge to empty her *water glass* on his head.

Her ire cooled rapidly, however, when she caught a glimpse of Derek's face. For some inexplicable reason he was furious and looked ready to throttle her.

Fortunately Damian made a clucking sound and caught her chin to turn her face to his. "Genevieve, this won't do! You must eat properly. Mrs. Miran, I give my word. My brothers and I will see to it that your daughter no longer skips meals. If we must tie her to her chair, she will eat her food!"

"Oh Mr. Black," Mama cried joyfully, "I'm sure she'll do it for you."

"I know she will," Damian said with a knowing smile that made Genevieve's eyes glaze for a second.

She turned to her food for distraction, realizing that she was indeed ravenous. They had company so seldom, Genevieve forgot herself and started gulping down her eggs.

"Manners, Jenny," her mother tsked. "Eat like a lady! What will Mr. Black think?"

Genevieve looked up mortified, but Damian and Donal were laughing, though Derek's look was accusatory.

"I'm afraid, Mrs. Miran, she comes to a home that has long been without a lady's influence—not since our mother died," Damian said.

"No one would notice if she gobbles down her food and then lifts the plate to lick it clean," Donal said flatly.

"Oh dear!" her mother said, patting her lips with her napkin. "Though if you can get Jenny to eat..." she said considering. "I begin to see it is an excellent thing indeed that you will marry tomorrow."

"Tomorrow?" Genevieve burst out over a bite of sweet-cheese roll. Swallowing her food, she added, "Is it always so fast?"

Since the disastrous night with her music, she'd avoided wedding feasts. She couldn't remember how soon they usually took place after the Bridal Week couples had formed.

"Not always," Damian answered with a little glint in his eye. "But Declan wishes to attend ours, and tomorrow is the best day for him."

"Declan? The Black Prince? From Faerie—he's coming to the wedding?" Genevieve was dumfounded. He might as well have said Titania herself was coming. And yet Damian spoke of Declan as he might an uncle or grandparent.

"He wouldn't miss it for anything," he said, giving her a look so warm and affectionate, her heart leapt. He truly looked happy. That seemed even more extraordinary than that a Fae Prince was planning to attend her wedding.

Which would take place tomorrow. Tomorrow!

It was difficult after that to sit and eat breakfast, but she noticed Derek glaring at her. He nodded at her plate, warning her she'd better finish. Genevieve bristled, but she did clean her plate. She reminded herself that she was hungry, and it appeared she would need her strength to cope with her betrothed and his brothers.

Chapter Seven

As soon as breakfast was over, Damian suggested that they all walk to the green to see the spot for the feast and then continue to the bakery. Wedding celebrations were communal affairs, with each family contributing a special dish. Traditionally, the bride's family provided the bridal cake and iced puddings to ensure the couple's sweet married life, while the groom's family provided the ale needed to ensure a joyous celebration for the guests.

Denied time to plan and fuss, her mother was forced to devote her worry to a long discussion with the baker about the puddings, which Genevieve didn't even pretend to follow. Damian never left her side and showed admirable patience, good-naturedly answering the questions Genevieve should have.

At midday, her mother gave her a harried kiss and turned to go home without asking any of them to come along, which made Genevieve suspect that Damian had already made some arrangement. They stopped off at the tavern and picked up packed baskets and a chilled stone pitcher. When she asked, Damian smiled and said that he was making up for ruining the picnic the day before.

So she and the three Black brothers left the village and for the second time in two days, she made the walk to

Titania's Altar. When they reached the meadow, Damian gave her a kiss and said, "I need to visit the altar, darling. Stay here with Donal."

Donal spread a blanket so she could sit against a tree and then gave her a smile that was pure roguish charm. "Now that I've got you alone, is my new sister hungry?"

Genevieve was woefully ignorant of men, even more so than most girls her age, but she instinctively recognized Donal's tone—he was being suggestive. She rolled her eyes and responded, "As it happens, I am. What do you have?"

"Tongue," he answered, licking his lips slightly.

"Excuse me!" she cried, shocked.

"Excuse *me*!" he cried back. "Is it possible my new sister is entertaining improper thoughts? I was referring, *of course*, to the excellent sandwiches prepared by our local tavern-keep, Mr. Richards, who I believe is a dear friend of your father's."

Genevieve turned scarlet at this. She was stammering out an apology when she realized that Donal was barely managing to restrain his mirth—at her expense! She shook her head and then said more tartly than she should have, "As it happens, I do not care for tongue. Is there anything else?"

"You truly don't care for *tongue*? What are we to do?" Donal said in an alarmed tone.

He really was too bad!

"Do you have anything else or not?"

"I'm afraid that there is nothing else except...." He unwrapped a second basket. Genevieve moved closer so she could peer in.

"Cherries!" she exclaimed, all annoyance at Donal's nonsense forgotten. "But they're not due to ripen for another week. Mama asked specially for me." The basket was filled to overflowing with cherries so dark they were almost black. She closed her eyes: the fragrance was mouthwatering.

"Honestly, I should have been oracle to Our Lady Titania," Donal intoned mournfully. "So I have told Declan many a time, though he chooses to ignore my advice. Before I'd ever heard the lovely name of Genevieve, I had a vision, yes a vision, that Damian's bride would be partial to cherries, so before I left, I asked to speak to Roderick, our cook. 'Roderick,' I said, 'we must have cherries for Damian's bride. No matter how reluctant she may be to marry my lazy lout of a brother, she won't be able to resist him if she tries the cherries from the Black orchard.' And what do you know, a basket of cherries was delivered before breakfast. Ours always arrive a few weeks before the valley's."

Genevieve couldn't help bursting out laughing at this brother who looked so like Damian but was capable of such good-humored absurdity. He held out one of the cherries, swinging it by the stem like a string before a kitten.

She nibbled her lip. Genevieve absolutely adored cherries, and it *had* been almost an entire year since she'd had a fresh one. She couldn't help glancing about for Damian, though, whom she suspected would echo her mother in insisting that she eat a "proper" lunch before she had dessert.

Donal was looking decidedly mischievous. "Just a few couldn't hurt. I promise I won't tattle." He held the cherry to her mouth. "Open please."

The lure of cherries was too much to resist. Genevieve obeyed and couldn't help a soft moan: compared to these, the valley cherries tasted like bland, long-storage apples. She gave Donal a guilty look as she tried unobtrusively to spit out the pit.

"No, no, my dear. To do justice to the Black cherries, you must properly dispose of the pit." He ate a cherry himself and then shot the pit from his mouth. He held another to her lips. "Try again."

Within minutes, Donal had hand-fed her half the basket, and the two were deep in a contest of who could spit their pit the farthest. In the meantime, her white dress had become liberally sprinkled with juice and had acquired a multitude of twigs and even a caterpillar.

She finally managed to hit the tree that was their target and clapped, holding out her mouth for another cherry, when they were interrupted by an angry voice demanding, "Have you visited the altar yet?" She looked up to see Derek, his face dark as thunder.

"As you can see, I have been keeping our lovely new sister company," Donal said mildly.

"You must make your devotions," Derek said coldly.

"And you think I should do that now?" Donal replied with that veiled irony he seemed master of.

The look that Derek returned was hard as granite. "I will stay with our brother's bride."

"I will leave you two to become acquainted then."

Donal smiled humorously, but underneath Genevieve could have sworn she caught a glimpse of something... canny. It would be a mistake to underestimate this comical new brother of hers.

As soon as Donal was gone, Derek wordlessly unwrapped one of the sandwiches, cut it into small pieces, and sat directly in front of her. Did he intend to feed her the sandwich as Donal had the cherries?

"No, thank you..." she protested, trying to sound polite. "Please, I don't care for tongue.... I had a large breakfast."

"Cherries are not lunch," he said accusingly, holding a piece to her lips. "My brother gave his word that you would not skip any meals."

Genevieve flushed violently. He was treating her like a child, but she wasn't sure how to refuse without being unforgivably rude. "Fine, just give it to me," she said through her teeth, wondering at how angry she sounded, but by Titania, this Black brother was difficult.

To her consternation Derek said, "No," and brought the piece closer to her mouth. Everything in his expression was daring her to defy him. Suddenly she wanted nothing more than to slap his face, but she managed to control herself and opened her mouth and ate the bite of sandwich.

The meat tasted well enough, of course—Mr. Richards took justified pride in his curing—but she'd always disliked the greasy richness of tongue, which even the sharpness of the mustard did nothing to cut through. She chewed slowly and swallowed. "Is that enough?" she asked, unable to keep the sullenness from her tone.

"No," Derek said. "You will finish your sandwich. Next time you will think twice about having dessert before your lunch."

Genevieve looked him in the face, astounded at his gall, but all thought froze under his gaze. It was no longer angry but something else, something predatory. Like this morning, she felt like a cornered animal too scared to run away. Her mouth reflexively opened for another bite, which she chewed without tasting, repeating until the sandwich was finished.

The spell was broken by a cough. She looked up to see Donal watching them a bit too closely. Suddenly hands grabbed for her, causing Genevieve to let out a loud shriek. She grimaced when she realized it was Damian. She tried to slap at his hands, but he ignored her struggles to pull her onto his lap, gripping her wrists and holding them against her waist. He nuzzled her neck and then kissed the bare skin where her neck met her shoulder, just touching her with his tongue. Genevieve gasped at the pulse of desire that shivered through her body, and for a second her eyes closed.

But then she recalled that they were not alone. She flinched and tried to elbow Damian and shake herself free. "Damian, let me go!" she cried, but he just kissed her again and forced her to settle.

In the meantime, Derek had risen and was standing off to the side, while Donal took a seat in front of her again. "Did my cruel brother make you eat your sandwich," he said mockingly.

"I'll get you for this, Donal Black," she snapped. She was sure he'd known Derek would make her eat that sandwich.

"You'll get me? You'll get me? What are you nine?" Donal scoffed.

Genevieve was so annoyed she threw her napkin at him but then worried that maybe she'd been too forward. But when she glanced over her shoulder, her disloyal, good-for-nothing betrothed was laughing at her too! She glared at both of them, which unfortunately only caused Donal to explode in loud guffaws. When he finally caught his breath, Donal cried, "Oh Genevieve, sweetheart, if you could see your face. Didn't your mother ever tell you not to scowl in case your face stuck like that?"

"You... you..." she tried to come up with some truly devastating insult or threat, but she'd not grown up with brothers and couldn't think of anything worse than the all-purpose *"I'll get you,"* which she recognized now was pretty weak.

"Peace, sister," Donal cried. "After your sufferings at Derek's hand, you deserve some reward." He held up the basket of cherries. "We must show Damian and Derek the progress you've made spitting cherry pits."

Genevieve was mollified and could even laugh at their ridiculous argument. To Damian's wry amusement, Donal insisted on holding up the cherries for her to eat, and the three of them spent several hilarious minutes comparing shots. Only Derek remained stone-faced. Neither of his brothers seemed surprised, and Genevieve was too annoyed with him to mind that he wasn't enjoying himself. He finally joined them when the basket was empty, and the three brothers set to eating their sandwiches, Damian refusing to let her move from his lap.

"I notice that Damian and Donal are allowed to eat their dessert before lunch," Genevieve said tartly.

Derek just glared at her, but Damian kissed her temple and said, "I'm sorry, love. When I made that promise to your mother this morning I meant only to reassure her, forgetting that my younger brother would consider himself honor bound for the rest of his life to ensure you never again miss a meal."

"Derek's younger?" she asked, distracted from her annoyance. "But I thought...." She stopped herself before she repeated the gossip she'd heard before the picnic.

"You thought what, darling?" Damian said, nestling her neck again.

She wondered that she was becoming so accustomed to his freely touching her, but his affection was so easy and natural, she would feel ludicrously missish for stopping him.

When Genevieve still hesitated he said in that iron tone he sometimes used, "Say what you were going to say, Genevieve."

"I'm sorry," she answered, flustered.

"Genevieve, you're apologizing again; now answer," Damian whispered, giving her a little bite on her ear as a warning.

"It's just that I heard that Derek attended the Bridal Week—that both of you did. I assumed you were older." Though now that she thought of it, they didn't seem older.

There was an uncomfortably long pause before Damian said, "I'm the eldest, but I command the garrison that guards the demon gate. We were experiencing some problems with the Reavers the first year we discussed my attending, and Declan asked me to postpone and let my brothers go first."

"Honestly Damian," Donal said. "Declan knew you had the best chance. He made no secret of it to Derek and me. He wanted us to have our try, of course, but we never questioned that you should go last."

"I don't understand," she said. "The best chance?"

"Well obviously, since Damian's so much prettier than Derek and me, we knew you village maidens would be falling all over him," Donal said, winking at her.

Genevieve grunted. Except for her foolish self, the "maidens" had kept their distance, and anyway the three brothers were so similar looking, it would be hard for those who didn't know them to tell them apart.

She turned to Damian. He gently pushed a strand of her hair behind her ear. "From the time Titania first gifted our people with the heartwood boxes, only one son in each generation of the Black family has found a bride."

"Declan always knows which brother it will be," Donal added in an eerie tone. "It's maaaaagic!"

Genevieve frowned as the information sank in. Both Derek and Donal had gone to the Bridal Week knowing they would not find a bride—how painful that must have been. And to sit now with their brother who had found a bride, knowing that they would likely never marry. Wouldn't they feel resentful? Jealous of their brother's good fortune?

Her expression must have given her away. Donal gave her a puzzled smile. "You look so worried, little one. It's not like that."

"No Black would ever dishonor himself with petty jealousy," Derek said angrily, and to her dismay he walked off. Donal gave her a rueful smile and jumped up to follow him.

"I didn't mean..." she stumbled.

"A bride is a blessing to us from Titania herself—the greatest she can give us," Damian said carefully. "To envy our brother is to turn away from her, to say that such a gift is not enough. It would be a great dishonor."

"Damian, I meant no offense!" She squeezed her eyes closed, afraid she might cry.

"Hush, darling, I know you didn't. To cope with Derek, the first thing everyone must learn is that he is absolutely impossible," he said, kissing her nose.

"Brothers can be jealous, even when they know it to be wrong and unfair. We can't always control our feelings," she whispered, thinking of her own dark moods.

"What do you know of brothers, little one? What you say is true of other families. You must trust me on this. Derek's honor is everything to him." Damian hesitated and for the first time since she'd met him appeared uncertain. "I haven't spoken to you about what our life will be after we're married."

"No, you haven't." She turned on him in surprise. She hadn't had a moment's leisure to even think about such topics, and yet they would marry tomorrow.

"The castle is really a military fortress, designed to hold the entire garrison, especially during the winter. So in the time of Declan's grandsons, a separate house was built within the grounds, specially warded, where the bride may live. You need to understand, Genevieve. From the moment your box changed, your protection became the first priority of all the males of my family. I will have to be away at times as part of my command. During those times, Derek and Donal will take care of you. Either of my brothers would give his life to protect you, just as I would."

"Damian!" she protested.

"That is the male's right, darling, and not for you to question," he said, firmly tapping her chin.

His tone brooked no argument, and she shivered at how serious he sounded.

He kissed her nose again and then continued. "One reason we work hard to root out even the hint of jealousy is that the tradition within our family is for the unmarried brothers to share the household with their married brother."

"Your brothers will live with *us*? All the time?"

"That is our tradition," he said, looking at her carefully, "so long as the bride agrees."

"You mean if I said no, you would respect my wishes?"

Damian looked deeply pained but said, "Yes. It's the bride's right to say who will share her household. You may refuse one or both of my brothers. I would not hold it against you—no one would."

"They'd really wish to?" she asked. It made no sense to her that Derek and Donal would wish to be saddled with any responsibility for their brother's wife, let alone live with her.

"You must trust my judgment on this, Genevieve. They wish it more than anything. *Both* of them."

His tone was urgent and looking into his eyes, she could not doubt his sincerity. She knew at that moment that her answer was supremely important to her new family, though she still couldn't understand it. There was no hesitation in her response. "I will trust your judgment then, Damian. If you're *sure* they don't mind, I certainly don't. I appreciate your giving me the choice."

To her surprise, he clutched her tightly, and she felt how great his fear had been. It was a measure of his love for his brothers. She squeezed him back, feeling the rightness of her decision. Indeed she felt deeply grateful that she had found a man who felt such devotion for his younger brothers. It told her much about his priorities.

When he finally released her, she felt the need to lighten things after his solemn request. Her eyes brightened mischievously. "So your brothers are to live with us."

"I believe that is what we just decided," he said with an answering smile.

She pretended to ponder and then said, "Damian, I do not like tongue—neither in a sandwich nor in any other preparation. I also do not like headcheese, mushrooms, or blood-rare meat. I detest liver and will not eat it under any circumstances, including starvation." She raised her eyebrows in challenge.

Damian laughed loudly. "Understood. Fortunately, it is the wife's right to decide the meals. But I must warn you, darling. Unless I am greatly mistaken, Derek has decided that you do not take proper care of yourself. And now that I have made a promise to your mother, you will have the chance to discover why Declan calls him the most stubborn male in the history of the Black family."

"Damian, no!"

"I'm sorry, darling, but it is the male's right to intervene if he feels the bride is not taking proper care of herself."

"You keep speaking of rights—what does that mean?"

"It means that in our home there are areas where you decide and none of us may challenge your decision. And then, my love, there are areas where I decide, and you may not challenge me."

He gave her a devilish smile, which left her licking her lips, wondering that his look could promise wicked things, though she didn't yet know about any wicked things. Damian read something in her look because he pulled her up and pressed his lips to hers. He'd been giving her little kisses since they met, but none like this. This kiss was intimate, sensuous, and left her body humming with desire.

She reached up to grasp his shoulders, suddenly desperate to get closer to him. He responded, clutching her neck and tilting her head so he could take her lips more thoroughly. Gentle but insistent, he explored her mouth, guiding her until her lips parted just enough. And then suddenly the kiss shifted. He drove his tongue into her mouth ruthlessly, as if he were demanding her surrender. As new desires cascaded through her, Genevieve felt helpless, desperate for things she didn't understand, but which some part of her recognized she could only get from Damian.

"Children, children, the wedding night isn't until tomorrow."

Blessed Titania, it was Donal! Genevieve had never felt so mortified. She shoved away from Damian, who pulled her in so that she could hide her face against him. "Donal, did you require something?" Damian asked impatiently.

"Nothing but my dear brother and sister's company," the rogue answered.

Damian shook his head in helpless resignation. "Where is Derek?"

"About," Donal answered blithely.

"I give you leave to take back your consent, love," Damian whispered in her ear. "My brothers can live in Devil's Swamp for all I care."

"Will you at least ban them our bedroom?" she whispered back, and then gulped, appalled at how wicked that sounded.

Damian's eyes blazed, and he leaned her over and gave her a deep kiss, which left her breathless. "I don't know how I will survive the next twenty-four hours," he whispered, before turning to his brother, who was making the world's poorest attempt not to laugh. "Donal, what shall I do with you? Here I have been using all of my powers of seduction, every bit of flattery and bribery I could think of, so that my poor bride will consent to take in my two good-for-nothing younger brothers, and instead of helping me make my case, you give the final proof of why you are utterly unfit for polite company."

"Not so polite," Genevieve muttered and then covered her face. "I can't believe I just said that." Mama would faint if she heard her. Donal burst out laughing. She looked up nervously at Damian, suddenly worried that he would disapprove.

He was smiling merrily and gave her a reassuring tap on the nose. "You are adorable," he said kissing the top of her head. "And altogether too sweet for such rotten brothers I am cursing you with. I should get you home, love."

Genevieve noticed now that the afternoon was almost spent. Damian and Donal firmly ordered her to sit still, while they packed up the remains of the picnic. Derek still hadn't returned when they were finished, so Donal roared out, "Derek, you worthless oaf! Come and help us with these baskets, or will you make Damian's bride play the pack mule for your lazy self."

Everyone was startled to hear Derek's voice a few feet away. "Cease your noise, Donal, I'm here." He'd crept up so silently!

"I hate when he does that," Donal grunted.

Derek picked up a basket and started off without waiting for the rest of them. Genevieve made a sudden decision and without saying anything to Damian, she jogged after Derek. When she caught up to him, he only gave her one of his scowls. It should have been intimidating, but Genevieve was becoming accustomed to his ways and decided to imitate his brothers and not be put off by Derek's hostility. She took his arm. Luckily, he was too well-bred to shake it off, though his good manners did not extend to making conversation.

"I understand you and Donal are to live with us," she said finally.

She could have sworn a wave of surprise flashed over his features before they resolved into an expression of stony indifference. Was he deliberately trying to offend her? It seemed incongruous behavior if Damian was accurate about his brothers' wishing so much to share their house.

She couldn't help wondering if despite Derek's best efforts, he felt some lingering resentment. Far from being offended, however, Genevieve was becoming curious about this prickly new brother of hers, who unlike the other two seemed at the mercy of a difficult temper—much as she was. Either way, she had no intention of living with a man who thought he could quell her with a look—or force her to eat foods she disliked!

In a tone that perhaps approached the border of saucy, she said, "Damian assured me that you and Donal both wish it. Of course he also told me that I'm to have charge of the meals. Please be aware, if you care greatly for tongue, you'd best get it at the village tavern for it won't be served at our table."

She gave him an excessively sweet smile and let go his arm to return to Damian. But before she could go back, he caught her wrist and said in a low voice, "Don't forget, sister, that Damian also swore you'd be tied down if you refused to eat your meals."

There was nothing in his expression to indicate he was joking. Genevieve gulped a moment and then steeled herself. In a tone that definitely crossed the border over to insolent, she retorted, "You can try," and ripped her hand away.

She jogged back to Damian and Donal, relieved that they could not have heard the little exchange. With a bright smile, she told them, "I was just informing my new brother that I would have charge of our meals now, and if he must eat tongue, he should get it at the tavern."

The two brothers stared at her with such shock, she suddenly feared she'd displeased Damian with her forwardness. But before she could apologize, he dropped his basket and swung her up in his arms, kissing her on the mouth. "Damian!" she protested.

"Must I do all the work?" Donal groaned, picking up Damian's basket.

"You whine about carrying a basket!" Damian roared. "When my bride has braved that dyspeptic troll we call a brother."

Genevieve giggled and gave him a little kiss back. Damian looked at her with such affection, she felt her heart filling. It had been such a strange outing, spitting cherry pits with Donal, being fed bites of tongue sandwich by Derek, kissing Damian. She didn't think she'd ever passed such an enjoyable day in her life, and yet there had been nothing out of the ordinary in it—no fireworks display or acrobats or dancing, just a simple picnic with her betrothed and his brothers.

Unfortunately, they arrived home to find her mother in her most querulous state, full of troubles over the flowers and something about icing that Genevieve couldn't even pretend to follow. The many emotional tumults of the past few days were catching up with her, and Genevieve realized she was exhausted. It was not a good state for coping with Mama's propensity to worry endlessly over things Genevieve considered trivial.

Thankfully, Damian and Donal came to her rescue. While Damian listened to her mother with admirable patience, making all the proper remarks, Donal jumped up, proclaiming that Mrs. Miran looked pale and was in dire need of a restorative tea. Though Genevieve would have been bristling, her mother was greatly soothed by this evidence of worry.

Genevieve was far less pleased when Derek rejoined them for dinner and got his revenge for her earlier taunts by again taking charge of her meal. After seeing that she'd just taken a small piece of chicken and a spoonful of peas, he picked up her plate and with her mother's delighted support, piled it with potatoes, another piece of chicken, and a slice of cold ham.

She tried to refuse but found she was no match for her new brother, who pulled his chair closer and forced her to eat as he fed her until she grabbed the fork away and ate for herself. To Genevieve's infinite irritation, even her traitorous father gave his hearty approval. Damian would only wink at her, while Donal repeatedly patted his face with a napkin to hide his laughter.

Damian seemed to sense that her nerves were dangerously strained by the end and announced that she must go to bed. Her parents seemed to have resigned themselves to their new son's ways because neither objected when he swept her into his arms and carried her upstairs.

Genevieve, though exhausted, was no longer willing to be sweetly passive at Damian's autocratic ways. She gritted her teeth in sullen silence as he brought her to the room with the water closet. When she was done, he was waiting in her bedroom, holding out a nightdress for her. She ripped it from his hands and asked snappishly, "Are you locking the door?"

"Yes, darling."

"I'm not a child, Damian."

He gripped her chin firmly and forced her to meet his eye. "I never think of you as a child, Genevieve. We spoke earlier of areas where I make the decisions. This is one, and I expect you to obey me."

Her breath caught and her body shuddered in a way that was becoming familiar to her. This time, however, she noticed that Damian wore a small look of triumph. He knew exactly how he affected her! The very thought produced another jolt of desire, but this time it was countered by an unbearable idea.

"You know! You know what you've been doing to me," she cried. "It's deliberate, but I'm not always like I was today—I'm not like Mama. I'm not mild and sweet. I tried to tell you at the picnic. I've had... troubles in the past."

"Genevieve...."

"You're a grown man. You're responsible for your actions. You ask me to live with your brothers, as if I might object, but did you warn them about me! I tried to tell you before—if you accuse me of pretending, of acting different before we were married, I won't be able to bear it."

"You are overwrought, darling."

"Yes I am," she cried passionately. "Say it! Say that I tried to warn you—before you leave and lock me in my room!"

She broke out into hot tears, not even sure why she was crying, but fixated on the notion that Damian might think her easy and docile because of the way she'd been acting with him. Damian moved quickly, pulling her onto the bed with him, where he just held her.

When she'd calmed a bit, he said softly, "I swear on my honor that I will never accuse you of any pretense, any deception. To do so would be the height of absurdity, since you must be the least deceptive person I have ever

84

known. I fear that you will accuse me, with far more reason."

That was enough to stop her sobs. "Why would you say that?" she asked.

He paused for so long she thought he wouldn't answer. "I was afraid," he said finally, "almost for the first time in my life."

"I don't understand—what could you be afraid of?"

"Before the picnic, I could hear what the other girls were saying—about my brothers, my family. Our ways are different, Genevieve." She tried to interrupt, but he stopped her. "I feared you would be afraid to marry me. Yesterday in the wood, I forced things. I knew you were mine, so I pushed you until I was sure your box had changed and then used Declan to convince your parents to agree to a speedy marriage—so you wouldn't have a chance to back out."

Genevieve was stunned, though she realized she shouldn't be. It was obvious enough now, but she'd been so confused, so overwhelmed, she hadn't grasped what he was doing. She turned so she could look him in the face. She could see fear and also intense desire there—it was dizzying.

It was on the tip of her tongue to ask how they were different, but Damian touched her chin with his hand.

"Don't ask that, Genevieve," he said huskily. "Trust to the heartwood. It has never failed our family."

"Yet you fear," she whispered.

He smiled ruefully. "Not the heartwood, but if your mother or friends came to you full of dire stories about the Black family, if your father refused to give you to me at Titania's Altar...."

"So that's why you've posted a guard outside my room," she said, shaking her head at the strange ways of males. She gave him a light kiss. "We will both have to trust."

Chapter Eight

Morning dawned on the first wedding of the season. In houses all over the village, the family cook was up with the sun to make sure their special casserole, stew, or pie did credit to the household. Though the weather promised to be clear, tents had already been set up on the green next to the tavern where they would remain until after the final couple was married. No lunch would be served by Mr. Richards that day. As soon as the morning meal was over, the grooms and serving-men would begin hauling out the long tables and benches for the feast.

At the Mirans, Cyrus was already out of the house, preferring the tavern and the relaxing company of his friend, Mr. Richards, leaving his wife and daughter to cope with his new in-laws. Unlike the previous morning, the conversation around the breakfast table was subdued. Genevieve couldn't help feeling all the usual nerves of a bride on her wedding day—and perhaps some that were less usual, considering she was marrying a man she'd known for less than two days.

Her stomach was in turmoil, and she was gearing up for her usual battle with Derek, when rescue appeared from an unexpected quarter. There was a loud rap on the front door, and before her mother could even rise, Sally and two other girls pushed their way into the small dining room. "We're your bridesmaids," Sally announced with a mischievous smile. "I knew you'd be too big a goose to ask anyone, so Emily, Jane, and I decided to volunteer."

Poor Mrs. Miran was put in a terrible quandary. She'd rather have died than turn away a guest without offering refreshments, but though she'd again made enough food for twenty, the small dining table couldn't possibly fit three more people, especially with three giant Black brothers already seated. She wrung her hands, begging the girls to be patient so that she could set something up in the parlor—or perhaps squeeze in some chairs....

Sally's shrewd gaze took in the situation in an instant—Mrs. Miran's dilemma as well as the conspicuous silence of the Black brothers, who in her opinion should have been jumping up to offer their seats.

Her eyes twinkled knowingly as she looked at each brother in turn and then said, "We'd love some breakfast, Mrs. Miran, especially some of those famous sweet-cheese rolls of yours. I'm sure these boys have eaten enough. It's time for you three to be on your way, anyhow. Today is for the girls. You'll see Genevieve at the altar—don't you worry."

It was enough to startle Genevieve out of her uneasy musings. She wanted to laugh at the long silence that followed Sally's pronouncement. She easily read Damian's annoyance, Donal's smirking defiance, and Derek's indignation. Good manners or not, none of the Black males would like taking orders from this girl.

Poor mama was fluttering on the verge of panic, and Genevieve realized it was her responsibility to settle this. She took Damian's hand and kissed it. "Trust," she whispered in his ear.

She watched him closely. He was clearly reluctant to leave her, which she found a little disappointing. Did he think her that fickle?

But Damian had been watching her as well: he gave her a rueful smile that seemed to ask for forgiveness and then rose. "Of course, we're almost finished. Please, ladies, take our places." He gave an authoritative nod at his brothers that silenced all protests.

"Oh," Mama said anxiously, "if you're sure you've had enough—I could pack something up...."

"Don't worry, Mrs. Miran," he said in the soothing tone that worked wonders with her mother. "We must meet our men at the tavern in a short while anyway."

"You've plenty to do without worrying about *them*, Mrs. Miran. They're grown men, they'll take care of themselves," Sally added with a triumphant smirk.

Damian shot her a wary glance, while Sally raised her eyebrows in friendly challenge. Genevieve couldn't help chuckling at the little battle of wills taking place between them, but her laugh caught in her throat when Damian turned on her with a dangerous smile.

Before she could protest, he bent and gave her a kiss—a lingering, open-mouthed kiss that left her breathless. His message was clear: while he might have yielded to Sally's bold demand, Genevieve should not expect the same. "Until later then," he said and took his leave with his brothers.

There was a moment of shocked silence, which Mama quickly covered by fussing over her new guests, rushing about to collect the used plates and fetch new ones from the kitchen. Emily and Jane began tittering and whispering to each other, while Genevieve slumped in her seat, trying to recover herself.

Sally took Damian's place and said in a low voice, "I had to make sure you were all right after that business at the picnic. Damian Black. That man is a piece of work."

"I'm fine, Sally, honestly."

"I can tell. This is the best I've seen you in years, and good thing too. He must be treating you decently."

"He is."

"He should—you deserve it. I see you've had to take on the brothers as well."

Sally's gaze was so penetrating, Genevieve didn't even try to deny anything. "They are to live with us," she admitted.

"Of course they are. I hope he at least asked you," she said shrewdly.

"He did. If I'd said no, he would have accepted my decision," Genevieve insisted.

"No risk of that with *you*, though," Sally sniffed. "You're too sweet by half, and he knows it. It's going to be uphill work managing men like those, but I suppose you'll figure something out."

Genevieve could only marvel that Sally grasped so much, infinitely more than Mama, who seemed completely awestruck by her new in-laws. She grasped Sally's hand and said feelingly, "Thank you for coming— I'm really glad you did."

"You've a friend when you need one. Don't forget that, Genevieve. And anyway, we all owe you for taking on Damian Black."

Sally wasted no time living up to her words. She took charge of the wedding preparations, ordering up a bath, selecting perfumes, and forcing Genevieve to submit to various beauty treatments for her hands and feet. All the girls were full of gossip about the Bridal Week. Apparently, two girls' boxes had changed color the previous day.

"How is Peter?" Genevieve asked Sally.

"Week's not over," she answered. From the way Sally's eyes sparkled, Genevieve was sure it was just a matter of time.

"Sally's playing hard to get," Emily said.

"No man will rush me," Sally said firmly. "My box will change when it's good and ready."

"Not like Genevieve here," Jane teased. "I own we were all stunned. The shyest girl in town was the one whose box changed first, and for a man like Damian Black."

"Careful with those flowers, Jane. There's no getting pollen out of silk," Sally said, taking charge of both the flowers and the conversation. "Shyest girl in town?" she said in a low voice to Genevieve. "You're something, Genevieve Miran, though I don't know if it's shy."

Genevieve laughed, grateful for Sally's supportive presence. She genuinely liked the woman Sally had grown into. The day passed faster than she could have imagined, and before she knew it, it was time to get dressed.

There was a moment of respectful silence as Genevieve's wedding dress was taken out and unwrapped. All three girls looked stunned, Emily covered her mouth, and Jane sighed. Genevieve felt a rush of pleasure at the girls' reaction: Mama deserved it. Her mother was an artist with a needle, and she'd expended every bit of her skill on her beloved daughter's gown.

Rather than the expected tight bodice with a full skirt, they'd decided on an A-line: a plain white silk sheath, with lightly-puffed cap sleeves and a square neck that was overlaid with a silk gauze overdress embroidered with tiny sprigs of flowers. It was deceptively simple, but the other women easily appreciated the consummate design skill and exquisite workmanship necessary to make it.

The girls handled the dress with reverent care as they helped Genevieve put it on. Looking at herself in the glass, even Genevieve could feel how beautiful it was—and how perfectly it suited her.

Jane handed her a bouquet of baby's breath, which matched the little sprigs on the dress. The final touch was a coronet of the same flowers, which Sally placed on top of her head.

"Oh Jenny!" Mama gushed. "You were right about skipping the veil—this is better." Genevieve had insisted on leaving her hair to hang down naturally in preference to some elaborate hair-do.

"It's the prettiest dress I've every seen, and that's no exaggeration. You've outdone yourself, Mrs. Miran," Sally said with her usual bluntness. "It's perfect, Genevieve. Damian Black is one lucky man."

"Oh, my beautiful little girl," Mama cried. "I can't believe you're getting married."

"No tears, any of you!" Sally ordered firmly. "Not you either, Genevieve. We didn't spend all day getting you so pretty for you to blubber it all away at the last minute."

It was well-timed. At that moment, her father called up the stairs to say it was time to go. All four girls looked at each other and then let out a loud squeal. Sally squeezed her hand, and Genevieve smiled back at her.

It was her wedding day, and she'd never been happier.

Chapter Nine

For the third time in as many days, Genevieve began the short walk to Titania's Altar, this time accompanied by her parents and bridesmaids. It was a fitting culmination to the three most momentous days of her life so far. As they walked through the main street of the village, their small party was joined by neighbors. By the time they passed the tents on the green, almost the whole town was walking in the joyous procession.

Genevieve felt the rightness of it. A wedding wasn't just for the couple involved. It was a chance for everyone to pay tribute to Titania and thank her again for the blessing of the heartwood she'd bestowed on their people so many generations ago.

Genevieve couldn't help a slight hesitation when she saw Damian standing with his brothers next to the plain stone altar. All three of them were dressed in their uniforms, which were surprisingly sober, consisting of a long, straight-cut black jacket and matching trousers, unadorned except for the trim, which was dark green braid. The most striking feature of their attire was the silver sword each of them wore. Something in the way the swords glowed convinced Genevieve that they must be Fae-made.

Damian did not take his eyes off her once. She was a little awed by how attractive she found him. She'd been told her whole life that it was improper to stare at a man or dwell on how handsome he was. She'd thought Damian good-looking in an obvious way, but now that handsomeness felt more dangerous, as if he were luring her in, enticing her to come closer so he could pounce on her. She feared she was blushing like a fool, but his gaze was so intense and possessive she felt a sudden alarm at what it would mean to be his.

Sally's light touch on her shoulder made her realize she'd stopped walking. Damian gave her an encouraging nod, which made her wonder if she'd just imagined his earlier expression. She clutched her father's arm a bit tightly, but she did manage to walk the rest of the way to the altar.

As soon as she was in place, everyone's attention turned to the small grove of rowan trees directly behind the altar. The priestess emerged, walking with a tall man who could only be Declan. From a distance, Declan looked hardly older than the Black brothers, who resembled him very closely.

But as he came closer, Genevieve saw that his skin had a flawless smoothness and subtle glow that could not be human. Only the ancient expression in his eyes betrayed the fact that he was centuries old. To her surprise, he smiled warmly at her, his face full of good-humor and even joy. Somehow she'd imagined such a great warrior would be fierce and stern even at a wedding.

Her nervousness eased a bit under his reassuring expression. Perhaps a miracle would occur and she would be able to get through her own wedding without humiliating herself by fainting, bursting into tears, or fleeing like a cowardly rabbit. Her courage did not come a moment too soon, as the ceremony began right when the two reached the altar.

The priestess said something about Titania and blessings and sacred unions which Genevieve couldn't pretend to follow, and then her father was leading her forward to stand before Damian.

"Sir...Damian," her father said gruffly. "In accordance with Titania's will I hereby entrust you with the key to my daughter's heartwood box, and with it I entrust you with her happiness and well-being."

Damian answered, "I vow upon my honor always to cherish and protect her and pray Titania's help that I may be worthy of this trust."

The traditional words said, her father handed Damian a small gold key, which hung from a simple chain. Damian kissed the key and hung it around his neck. Her father kissed her cheek and took her hand and put it in Damian's.

They both knelt and exchanged the age-old vows, Genevieve "to love, honor, and obey," and Damian "to love, honor, and protect." The priestess gave the blessing and then nodded to her to rise.

To her surprise, Damian remained kneeling and was joined by his brothers.

Declan stepped forward. "Damian has spoken his marriage vows before this company, but in taking a bride, my descendants have ever made greater vows than are even demanded by the priestess of Titania, vows to me. Derek and Donal, you have both indicated that you wish to follow in the tradition of our family and pledge yourselves to protect and care for Damian's bride."

"We do, sire," both said.

"This vow can only be given with an open heart and clear conscience, free of any envy or malice. Can you both swear upon your honor that you so give the vow?"

"We can."

"Damian, such pledges likewise must be accepted with an open heart, free of any jealous suspicions, unselfishly, for the good of your bride and the Black Family. Can you with honor accept your brothers' pledges?"

"I can, sire."

"Queen Titania has ever understood what it means to my family when a Black marries. By her order, you three are released from the vows you made when you first took up arms for her sake. I would have your vow that from this moment forward, your first priority at all times will be the safety and well-being of the Black bride. Do you so swear?"

Donal, then Derek, and finally Damian said, "I swear." Afterwards Donal and Derek stood and took a step back.

"Damian, I restate now the values that rule our family and comprise its honor, so that Genevieve and all assembled may hear them. It has ever been my belief that there can be no true happiness in marriage without trust between husband and wife. I am proud but not surprised that no descendant of mine has ever been guilty of infidelity. As you value your honor and your family, so long as Genevieve lives you will not touch another female. You will never lie to her or deceive her for any reason. You will never mock or belittle her or give her cause to fear revealing her true nature or feelings to you. At all times you will conduct yourself so that she may feel secure in your devotion and affection, no matter what conflicts arise between you. You will never forget that the fates have vouchsafed to you a great blessing—the greatest that can be given to our family."

"It will be the study of my life to live by these precepts, sire. On my honor I swear it." Declan nodded, and Damian stood again.

Genevieve almost fainted when Declan turned next to her.

"Have no fear, daughter," he said in a gentler tone. "You have given your vows, and I know they were spoken in all sincerity. I see already that you and Damian have the makings of a strong bond that will lead to your happiness. Still, all marriages have trials and conflicts. When they should arise, I *ask* only that you recall the vows Damian has made today and the precepts he has sworn to live by."

He paused, and she nodded, unable to find her voice. He nodded back at her and then to her surprise addressed Donal. "Donal in particular, I charge you with helping your sister understand the import of these precepts. I ask that you be a friend to her and actively take it upon yourself to rectify any misunderstandings and reconcile any differences that may arise between your brother and Genevieve."

Donal looked surprised by this and said with a seriousness that was unlike him, "I promise to, sire."

Declan nodded, and suddenly Damian was before her with a smile that made her shiver. "You are truly mine now, my love," he said so only she could hear and then leaned her over one arm so he could give her a passionate kiss. Genevieve batted his arms, mortified to be kissed like that before Declan, the priestess, her parents.... But Damian deepened the kiss, until she could only cling to him lest she collapse.

The crowd erupted in loud cheers and whistles. When he finally pulled her up, she was breathless and red-faced. She covered her face with her hands and then slapped at his arm, which led to loud guffaws from Donal and the other men.

Damian pulled out the key and gave it another kiss. The last task before the party on the green was the unlocking of her heartwood box, which still sat in the little parlor at the cottage. He took her hand in his, and they started back to the town.

The trip home went much more slowly as innumerable neighbors stopped to wish them joy. Everyone's tone was warm and friendly. Genevieve knew part of it was due to the staggering amount of ale the Blacks had provided, which Emily and Jane had spoken of as a great marvel, but she felt an unexpected burst of satisfaction that everyone seemed happy for her. Somehow in finding Damian, she had ended her long isolation.

They were close to home when Declan and the priestess overtook them. The priestess took her arm and said, "Genevieve, child, truly I have never seen you so happy. I knew from the beginning that you were bringing great joy to the Blacks, but I find now that they are bringing you the same happiness. I rejoice for it—you deserve it." The priestess glanced at Declan. "Genevieve, for most couples, I am present to bless the unlocking of the heartwood box, but Declan prefers to perform this for his own family. I hope you don't mind."

Genevieve's eyes widened. Unlike the other parts of the marriage ceremony, that part was never spoken of, so she'd had no expectations of who would be present. The priestess gave her a wry look, silently acknowledging that no matter what either of them felt, it would be unthinkable to refuse a request from the Black Prince.

"Of course," she said shyly.

She looked to Damian, but his expression was suddenly closed and careful. They'd reached her home. The priestess gave her hand a gentle squeeze and left them.

The door was unlocked, and the three of them stepped into the parlor where all of her trunks were waiting. As soon as they were done, servants from the fortress were going to load everything into a cart to bring to her new home.

The heartwood box would go as well, but for now it stood in its spot in the middle of the parlor. She wondered if she would ever become used to the sight of it. No paint or stain could produce such a deep, unreflecting black—the shade of Declan's hair.

Damian made a low cough, and Genevieve recalled tardily that she was hostess. "Forgive me…. Please, welcome…. Make yourselves at home…" she stammered.

She pressed her lips together lest she make a greater fool of herself—and before Declan of all people. Damian held her by the chin and kissed her forehead.

"Please don't distress yourself, daughter," Declan said kindly. "There is nothing for you to fear in this—it will take only a moment. I would ask you to kneel down."

She couldn't help looking to Damian for reassurance as she obeyed. In her wildest imaginings, she never would have dreamt that she'd be kneeling on the floor of her parents' parlor before a Fae Prince.

Declan nodded to Damian, who without further ado took the key from his neck, turned the lock, and opened the box. The box was turned so she could see nothing of its contents. Damian and Declan looked for only a few seconds, and then Damian closed the box, relocked it, and replaced the key around his neck.

Declan then said, "As your husband, Damian has become guardian of your box and its contents. I have always believed that a bride of our family must learn to rely upon her husband absolutely—trust that he knows best what she needs to ensure her happiness. For that reason, she is almost never allowed to look within her heartwood box. I have recommended that Damian follow this, and he has agreed. As head of this family, your family now, I forbid you to look within the box; likewise I forbid you to question Damian about it, or try by any direct or indirect means to find out what is within. Most brides chafe at this restriction at first, but you will find as they did, that you may trust your husband to understand what you need to be happy in this marriage."

Genevieve tried to hold them back, but tears started streaming down her face. As Declan spoke an image had arisen in her mind: Declan staring down at her with cold fury because of some unforgivable action of hers, Damian looking at her with a mixture of disgust and dismay that he should be cursed with her for a bride. The real Declan and Damian suddenly seemed far less real than those she imagined, and it seemed a foregone conclusion that she would soon commit some act that would utterly alienate her new family.

"Damian, leave us."

"Sire..." Damian protested.

"You will obey me in this!" he commanded in such an iron tone, she understood where Damian had learned his. Declan moved closer and bent to one knee. "You wished so much to see what is in your box, little one?"

Genevieve looked up surprised. "No, I wouldn't want to!" She'd never even thought of it before now, but she couldn't imagine why anyone would want to—what horrors would they find there?

Declan took her by the chin and turned her to meet his gaze. She tried to pull away, but he wouldn't allow it, something else Damian must have learned from him. After a moment he said, "You fear my anger then—or Damian's—should you disobey me."

"I'm not good," she cried. "I told Damian.... I tried to explain, but I don't think he believed me. This all happened so fast, but he doesn't know me."

"Rise daughter," he said, pulling her up and bringing her to the sofa. She quickly wiped her eyes while he took a seat opposite. To her surprise his smile was humorous. "You must forgive an old man who sounds dire alarms that the wolves have raided the chicken coop, when really two puppies have stolen his wife's drawers from the clothes line."

The image was so comical, so unexpected, it stopped Genevieve's tears instantly.

"Really, I have no excuse at all. I've long known the uselessness of making such pronouncements having raised Donal. To forbid him anything was virtually to guarantee that he would spare no effort to do the thing forbidden. I became convinced that if he would apply even a tenth of that effort to his studies, he'd rival the most learned university scholars."

Genevieve couldn't help giggling. She would never have imagined that the fierce Declan could have a sense of humor.

"I don't expect you to fully believe me yet, my dear, but you need never fear my anger." She tried to interrupt, but he said, "I spoke to the priestess. Maura told me of your troubles."

Genevieve was silenced.

"We will address those at another time, should it be necessary. I forbade you the box not because there is any ugliness within that I would protect you from, so stop fearing that." He spoke so firmly she shivered. "Had I known better, I would have phrased my request differently: I would ask as a favor to Damian that you put your trust in him. For a man such as he, it is a gift beyond measure."

He stood, and Genevieve had no choice but to nod her acquiescence, though she found his remarks needlessly cryptic. "Thank you, sir," she said because the moment seemed to demand it.

He smiled knowingly. "There are privileges to being my daughter, and one is that I would have you call me Declan."

"Sir!" she cried. He raised his eyebrows until she couldn't help biting her lip. "Declan," she said tentatively.

"See, lightning did not strike you down." He pulled her in and kissed her on the top of her head. "Welcome to our family, Genevieve. You will do well." He called out loudly, "Damian, you lazy rogue, come fetch your bride before she misses the whole celebration." Genevieve was still giggling when Damian returned. "You'd better hurry before your brothers come looking for you. I would have the third dance, daughter."

"Thank you, *Declan*, I look forward to it." She looked up nervously at Damian to see what he thought of her calling the Black Prince by his first name.

"I see she has worked her witchcraft on you as well, sire," he said laughingly. "She even charmed Derek, who has never spoken civilly to a woman in his life. But now, we are late to the feast!"

Damian gave her a quick kiss and then pulled her out the door and started running full bore towards the tents. "Damian," she protested. "I can't run in this dress, please it will tear...."

"Vanity, thy name is woman," he lamented dramatically and swung her up into his arms, jogging quickly until they reached the tents on the green.

Chapter Ten

As soon as they went under the tent, there was a thunderous cheer. The crowd had grown from the ceremony at Titania's Altar. A number of men wearing black uniforms had arrived—fellow officers from the garrison. Genevieve also realized that while they'd been occupied, the ale casks had been breached, and the guests were already well along in the revelry.

Moments after they made their entrance, Donal was on hand with a great stein, apparently some family heirloom, insisting that they drink to their marriage. Damian put her on the ground so she could drink first. Genevieve couldn't abide ale and took the tiniest sip possible, which led to mock cries of outrage. Apparently it was bad luck if they didn't finish it.

The cup was given to Damian who had to drink it down as the men counted. Thankfully, Derek was also there, holding a cup to her mouth that turned out to be filled with iced lemon-water. She was parched and for once didn't mind his bossiness.

There was an explosion of cheers as Damian drained the stein and turned it upside down. Donal immediately began yelling for the musicians to begin. Genevieve just had time to return her cup to Derek, when Damian spun her into a fast reel.

The next half hour passed in a blur of motion as she danced with her father, Declan, Donal, and several officers. She was relieved when she saw Donal leading Sally to the floor—at least one of the Black brothers had decided to make peace with her friend. She was even happier when she saw Sally joyfully spinning around the floor with Peter Crane.

She was less relieved when Donal dragged her over to a shadowed corner where Derek was standing (hiding really), enjoying himself about as much as the average prisoner of war. Derek had not danced once and gave his brother a deadly look when Donal shoved her hand in his. Genevieve tried to back away, not wanting to make Derek uncomfortable, but he made an impatient sigh and pulled her out on the floor.

To her surprise, he was an excellent dancer. For all his stiffness with people, he moved with the same uncommon grace of all the men of his family. His refusal to dance was just his usual temper.

Genevieve felt some pity for him. She knew too well what it was like to be surrounded by people enjoying themselves while she felt like a miserable blotch on their happiness. Her good will was short-lived, however. They'd circled the floor one time, when Derek demanded in an accusatory tone, "Have you eaten anything since breakfast?"

Genevieve's back was immediately up. In fact, she'd been too nervous to eat, but she had no intention of bowing to Derek's tyranny at her own wedding. "Congratulations on your marriage, Genevieve, I wish you every joy. What a lovely dress," she said, with insincere pleasantness. "Why thank you, Derek, how kind of you to say that."

His expression became livid, and he gave her a very sharp shake. "I asked you a question!"

Genevieve wasn't sure what possessed her, but she said in an insolent tone, "Not a single bite!"

She'd never spoken to anyone like that in her life, but something in Derek made her desperate to provoke him. Derek immediately stopped dancing and grabbed her by the upper arm. Genevieve turned crimson but forced herself to smile in spite of her rage as Derek marched her over to the banquet tables that had been laid out with all their neighbors' contributions.

He gave her a warning look, before letting go of her arm so he could fill a plate. Genevieve sensed that if she tried to escape, Derek would simply drag her back. She searched the crowd for Damian or Donal who might rescue her from Derek's tyrannical form of care. But

Damian was dancing with the priestess, and Donal with her mother.

When he'd piled her plate, Derek pulled her along to one of the long tables, which were mostly filled with old men who preferred ale to dancing. He found them an unoccupied end, pushed her onto the bench, and took a seat next to her. She took the fork he offered and looked at the plate. In the middle was a large slice of tongue, surrounded by applesauce, peas and carrots, and plain boiled potatoes—bland dishes for those with indigestion.

He was punishing her! His expression said unmistakably that he would feed her himself if she didn't cooperate.

Genevieve was seething. If they'd been at home she'd have dumped the plate in his lap! But unlike Derek, she wasn't totally indifferent to the opinions of everyone around her. She couldn't face making a huge scene at her own wedding, distressing her parents who were so happy for her, and causing even more talk than she'd already done. She gritted her teeth and started eating.

When she'd finished everything but the meat, she pushed the plate back and hissed, "I'm done!"

Derek flashed her a look of dark warning. Genevieve swayed dizzily, instinctively sensing that beneath his cold stubbornness lurked something dangerous. Once again, she felt that overpowering urge to run from him.

She was saved for the second time that day by Sally, who walked up practically dragging Donal behind her.

"You or me, Donal Black," Sally said, giving Donal an elbow in the ribs.

"Ouch! You undersized termagant!"

"Oh for Pete's sake!" Sally said impatiently. With an overly sweet smile, she said, "You all right, Jenny?"

"Perfectly fine," Genevieve answered, drawing courage from their arrival. "I was just reminding my dear brother, Derek, that I do not eat tongue. He seems to be suffering from memory loss."

Derek gave her a thunderous look, and Genevieve, possessed by some alien mischievous spirit, stuck her tongue out at him.

Donal roared with laughter and then elbowed Sally back. "Told you she could handle him. I've seen blood-soaked Reavers quail before that scowl of his." Sally and Donal joined them at the table.

Derek visibly made an effort to master his temper and finally said coldly, "You've not eaten enough." He moved the piece of tongue onto another plate and stood up to refill hers.

Insufferable despot!

"Fine!" she snapped. "Please be sure to take plenty of the Crane's stew then. I'm quite partial to lamb."

He leaned over and whispered in her ear, "I warned you what would happen if you refused to eat your meals," and went to get more food.

Luckily Genevieve's reaction to this threat was covered over by Damian's arrival. "There you are!" he said, kissing her lavishly on the mouth to Sally's smirking disapproval. "Look darling!" He pointed to the other side of the tent.

Her father was mounting the little stage holding his wooden flute! "This is for my little girl. I love you, kitten," he said awkwardly. He was ever a man of music, not words.

He began one of her favorite ballads. Genevieve kept a smile pasted on her face, but her emotions were rising dangerously. Her father played the rustic instrument so beautifully, it was impossible not to feel her own loss. If she'd not had all her problems, she would be up there playing with him. Her parents had always shown her so much love and patience, so much more than she deserved....

Thank Titania Damian had his eyes on the stage and couldn't see her distress, but Sally and Donal were watching her closely. She felt Sally take her hand. Grateful as Genevieve was for rediscovering her old friend, Sally's kindness was in danger of pushing her towards one of her attacks—at her wedding, the happiest day of her life. What would it do to Damian?

At that moment, however, Derek returned with the second helping of food. "Finish it!" he said in that iron tone so beloved of her new family. Her irritation succeeded where her willpower had failed to wrestle her unruly emotions. This time Derek had filled her plate with all of her favorite dishes. The wretch had been deliberately baiting her!

She made a silent vow of revenge as she dug in, genuinely hungry. She could listen now like everyone else, appreciating her father's rare talent, without feeling overwhelmed by regrets. There was wild applause when he finished, and Genevieve felt nothing but joy when she jumped up to embrace him.

Her mother had her moment of triumph soon afterwards as a splendid cake was unveiled and the puddings simultaneously set alight to enormous cheers. As was tradition, she and Damian held the knife together and cut the first piece. Damian seemed almost giddy as he fed her the first bite. His happiness was contagious. She could almost believe in the old superstition that the sweetness of the cake foretold the sweetness of their married life.

As the cake and puddings were served, Donal leapt up to give a toast, followed by Mr. Richards, the tavern-keep and her father's closest friend, and then by two officers from the garrison, who said something, bawdy probably, that caused all the men to roar.

She noticed Donal whisper something to Sally, who gave him a wry nod. Sally stood and totally unabashed pretended to solemnly thank Genevieve for snapping up the fearsome Damian Black so quickly, so the other girls might relax and enjoy the Bridal Week.

Only Sally could carry off such impudence without giving offense. Damian chuckled, and Donal practically howled. Then with a mischievous wink, Sally announced that it was time for the bride to retire.

Her bridesmaids came and collected her. Rather than return to her parents' house, they'd borrowed a room in the tavern for her to change from her wedding gown into a green travel dress.

Donal met her at the door and ordered the bridesmaids back to the tent and then led Genevieve over to where her parents were standing with the priestess. "Time to say goodbye," he said.

Genevieve hugged both of them. Her mother of course burst into tears and tried to cling, but the priestess chided her to let Genevieve go and then insisted her parents return home.

Donal wished them good cheer and then grabbed Genevieve by the hand and led her back to the tent. The tent had cleared of all but the younger men and women, who'd grown decidedly boisterous. Damian was nowhere to be seen.

Donal left her with Derek and went to shepherd the girls into a group for the bouquet-toss. "It's time, little sister," Donal said.

Genevieve couldn't help swallowing nervously. Donal's eyes were dangerously bright, and even Derek seemed more intense than usual—they were plotting something. Donal made an impatient gesture, so she turned her back on the group and tossed the bouquet over her shoulder. There was a chorus of squeals, and she turned to see Sally holding the bouquet aloft.

But a moment later, the officers from the garrison moved in front of the girls, forming a wide circle around her. Something was happening. She looked to Donal, who was holding out a narrow length of black material. There was something in his expression that made her instinctively back away. The men were making catcalls and eying her like so many wolves around a doe. The instinct to flee was overpowering. She tried to run, but she was quickly caught and pushed back. She spotted a gap in the circle and bolted towards it, but again she was caught and pushed back.

Donal called out, "Men, Damian has caught himself a bride. It's time for us to deliver her to him."

The men let out a roar.

Completely panicked now, Genevieve screamed and frantically tried to fight her way out. Somehow, she ended up in Derek's arms, but his dark eyes were implacable. Suddenly her wrists were being pulled behind her and tied together with soft fabric.

Derek bent down and hoisted her onto his shoulder to the cheers and thundering stomps of the men. She caught a glimpse of Donal as he deftly caught Sally and prevented her from coming to Genevieve's rescue.

"I'll kill you for this, Donal!" Genevieve shouted, which produced another roar of laughter and loud shouts that Damian had caught himself a "hellcat" and similar nonsense.

Genevieve was furious to be manhandled so by her infernal brothers. She tried to struggle and kick Derek, but he adjusted his grip so she couldn't move. "Let me go, you oaf. I'll kill you, Derek, I swear it!"

"Quiet," he ordered, giving her a sharp slap on her rear, which led to another gleeful roar from the men.

At the edge of the tents, he stopped and someone reached for her, pulling her up. It was Damian on a massive, jet-black stallion. By now, Genevieve was in a thorough temper and struggled and kicked, but Damian wrapped an arm around her, settled her securely, and without a word kicked the horse into a canter.

Chapter Eleven

As soon as they were away from the town on the road to the hills, Damian slowed the horse to a walk. He leaned Genevieve over on one arm, causing her anger to evaporate. His smile was pure triumph. She struggled against the bonds but was helpless.

Damian laughed and lowered his head to kiss her. His tongue plunged into her mouth, ruthlessly taking possession. When he finally let her go, he pulled her back to lean into him, kissing her neck and rubbing her breasts with his hand.

Genevieve was left speechless. This was a side of Damian she'd sensed but hadn't understood enough to recognize. She was his now. Tonight he would possess her body, and there didn't seem to be any limits to what he would demand from her.

When she could finally speak, she squeaked out, "Aren't you going to release my hands?"

"Not tonight."

"Damian!" she gasped.

He turned her around on the saddle until she faced him, yanking up her skirts so she could straddle the horse as he did. He gripped her rear to pull her tightly against him. With his other hand he grasped her hair, wrapping it several times around his wrist, and then forced her head back.

She stared up at him, utterly stunned, before he pressed their lips together. She wanted to touch his shoulders, his chest, and twisted trying to free herself, but the bonds held. Being restrained only made the need that much more intense, and she let out a strange moan.

Damian released her hair and brought his hand around to fondle her breasts, which sent bursts of sensation through her. She instinctively shifted her hips, rubbing against the leather of the saddle, feeling a desperate need for something—anything—that would give relief. "My wanton little bride," Damian murmured as he made open kisses against her neck.

"Damian, don't say that!" she cried out, appalled that he would think such a thing of her.

"I do say it, little one. I consider it only fair that my bride be tormented by desire, since I am about to die of it. Soon you will be tied to my bed, Genevieve, and when I am finished with you, you will scream shamelessly for me to give you your release."

Genevieve's eyes glazed, and she couldn't help squirming again.

"Oh no you don't," he said and lifted her up by the waist. "Put your leg over again."

Genevieve mewed unhappily but obeyed. He turned her so that she faced away again, her legs in the proper ladylike position, though there was no sidesaddle. "Soon, darling, but for now you will have to wait."

Damian held her securely around the waist with one arm, while the other gently massaged her arms and wrists. In the meantime, he nudged the horse into a full gallop though the road was utterly dark. Genevieve instinctively protested, lest Damian get them both killed before he could satisfy this desperate hunger, but he whispered, "Hush, little one. This is Nightshade, Declan's horse, bred in Faerie. He needs no bridle, and day or night, he is incapable of making a misstep."

The rest of the ride passed quickly as the horse effortlessly climbed the steep road to the Blacks' mountain fortress. The smooth motion should have put her to sleep, but the light brush of Damian's hands over her breasts, stomach, thighs kept her desires stoked too high to even contemplate sleep.

Finally, the horse clattered into a dark stable yard. Damian was off in a second, hoisting her over his shoulder just as Derek had, only somehow Damian's hand found its way under her skirt to grip the bare skin above her garters.

He let out a sharp whistle, presumably for a stable hand, since he made no move to tend to Nightshade.

Instead, he walked swiftly towards a dark building, which was much larger than her parents' cottage, but wasn't nearly as imposing as the fortress she'd seen from the valley. "Welcome, my love, to our new home," he said with pretend pomp as he unlocked the door.

Genevieve couldn't refrain from an audible snort that she would enter her married home slung over the shoulder of the provoking male who called himself her husband.

Damian snorted in turn. "Perhaps if my bride is *extremely* well-behaved and obedient, she may be permitted to see beyond our bedroom within the next four days."

"Damian! You don't mean that."

"Don't I? We have been granted a mere four days for a honeymoon, darling. I warned you there were areas where I claim the right to make all decisions and won't tolerate challenges to my authority, and tonight you will learn what some of them are."

He carried her through a dark room, unlocked a second door, through more rooms, then up a flight of stairs, and down a long corridor. True to his word, she could see nothing of the house, though she sensed the coolness of the stone walls. Finally, he went through a doorway. Unlike the rest of the house, this room had at least the flickering light of a low fire. Damian slung her off his shoulder, landing her face down on the edge of a bed, her legs hanging down to the floor. "Do not move," he ordered.

Her skirt was caught about her waist, so she wriggled trying to get it to fall down, which led to a sharp slap on her buttocks.

"What did I say, Genevieve?" She stilled instantly. "Good girl," he said, rubbing the spot he'd slapped, and then moved away.

Lights came up as Damian lit several candles, though she could see little except that she was lying on a large bed with elaborately carved posts, thick as tree-trunks, that spired towards the high ceiling.

She was quickly distracted as Damian pulled off her shoes, and then reached up and untied her garters, so deftly she hadn't time to protest before her stockings were also off. He rolled her over and pulled her to sit on the edge of the bed. Before she could even look at the room, he was before her. He gently cradled her cheeks and kissed her. "I'd thought to draw us a bath first, but it will have to wait."

She pulled urgently at the bonds that held her wrists, wanting to touch him. Damian's eyes blazed until his gaze positively smoldered. "Damian," she begged breathlessly, "let me go."

He shook his head. "Not tonight, darling—don't ask again." He grasped her chin firmly to reinforce his point.

His words caused another burst of intense pleasure to shiver through her. He turned her to the side and began unbuttoning the back of her dress. She remained passive as he pulled her to stand so he could reach beneath her skirt and unbutton her petticoat. He pulled it to her feet, followed by her drawers. Finally he moved behind her and untied her wrists. Keeping hold of them, he brought her arms to the front, examining her wrists carefully.

Seeming satisfied, he kneaded them gently and then in the flash of an eye, ripped down her dress, leaving her in her shift and nothing else. She instinctively tried to cover herself with her arms, but he caught her wrists again and loosely tied them together in front of her. He led her to a small door. "Two minutes to take care of your needs, Genevieve. Don't make me come get you."

He gave her buttocks a knowing rub as a warning and pushed her through the door into an enormous bathing chamber. In addition to a massive marble bathtub, the room had a fully plumbed water closet enclosed in a wooden cabinet. She had just enough time to use the necessary and wash her hands and face at the sink when Damian opened the door and led her out again.

He stood her before the bedpost and lifted her bound hands well above her head. When he let go, they were attached to a ring high on the post. Before she could protest, he pressed his body against her back, kissing the side of her neck, his hands everywhere, caressing her breasts through the shift, up and down her bare arms, and then slipping under the bottom of the shift to glide up her sides. At the same time he pushed his leg between hers, nudging until she moved her legs apart. Something hard pressed against her hips, which she realized was his member.

Genevieve was desperate by now and groaned loudly as she writhed against him. He kissed the top of her head. "There's my wanton girl. My turn. I won't be long."

She let out a scream of outrage as he ducked into the bathing chamber himself. She tore furiously at the bonds, wishing at that moment she could get her hands on his throat!

Her anger faded when he came out: he'd taken off his shirt, and there was nothing to hide the signs of his arousal pressing against his trousers. Genevieve drew in a shaky breath. Damian stood for a long moment watching her. Her already broiling desires burned even hotter; strange mewing sounds came from her.

Damian walked closer until he was right in front. He stroked her cheek gently with the back of his hand and then reached beneath the shift and brought his hands up her sides until he could rub her breasts with his thumbs.

He pinched and fingered one breast, while he pulled her closer with his other hand. This time, his hardness was in front and rested against the vee of her legs.

She strained against the bonds, insane lust making her desperate to fondle him. Wanton indeed—she couldn't recognize herself. Damian kissed her deeply and then slowly lowered to the floor, giving her soft kisses all down her front. Once he was on his knees, he nuzzled her... private place, which woke her from her daze. "Damian! What are you doing?" she cried.

He gave her an unmistakable look. "Grip the post and do not move, Genevieve, or I will take you over my knee."

To her surprise, Genevieve felt an overpowering instinct to obey him. She gripped the post as tightly as she could while Damian lifted her left leg and pulled it over his shoulder. His head disappeared beneath the shift, and then Genevieve screamed as loud as she ever had in her life.

He gave her no time to prepare: Damian put his mouth to her sex, his tongue sweeping through her folds, over and over, before plunging inside her. Finally, after he'd tasted what seemed like every part of her, he latched onto her bud, sucking and laving with his tongue. With her hands bound, her legs pinned, she could offer no resistance, find no escape from the overpowering sensations blasting through her.

Seconds, minutes, she had no sense of what was happening except that she was hurtling towards some unknown point. Her desire was at such a pitch that she felt like she'd die if he stopped, even though she was terrified that her body had flown utterly out of her control. Damian was relentless, his tongue pushing her until finally she reached a point where she knew retreat was no longer possible. He gripped her hips tightly as her body shuddered violently again and again while she screamed his name.

Afterwards she wasn't sure how she ended up on the bed, sobbing against Damian's chest while he stroked her hair and whispered gentle reassurances. After a few minutes, she calmed somewhat and looked at him, tentatively stroking his face with her bound hands.

He helped her sit up and held a glass to her lips. She drank deeply realizing how thirsty she was. Damian's expression was hard to read in the flickering candlelight. "Darling, I'm afraid this part will be more difficult for you—do you know what I'm speaking of?" he said gently.

She nodded, gnawing her lip nervously. "The priestess explained what would happen." Though she'd apparently left much out of her brief, decidedly unsensual description of the sex act.

"If you wish, you may wear your shift just for tonight, but I'm going to bind your hands to the bed. Do you wish to keep the shift?"

She nodded slowly. Damian kissed her forehead and then untied the sash that had bound her hands together, again rubbing her wrists thoroughly. He gently lowered her down onto the pillows. Her hands suddenly free, she touched his face. He smiled but said firmly, "Raise your arms above your head, darling."

She closed her eyes and forced herself to lift her arms, though suddenly they felt impossibly heavy. They finally landed by her ears. "Further Genevieve. Spread them apart as wide as you can—no more dawdling."

She shuddered at that iron tone but did as he ordered. She couldn't stop tears from welling as he attached leather bands to her wrists and pulled her arms taut above her head. One of his legs was draped over hers, and she found even more than before that she couldn't move at all.

He kissed the tears tenderly and stood to unbutton his trousers. She closed her eyes knowing she shouldn't look, but a second later unladylike curiosity won out, and she raised her head to see. But it was too late. Damian was on top of her, pinning her with his weight. He roughly caressed her breasts as he took deep kisses from her mouth. He tasted different, which she realized with a jolt of lust was from her. Damian moved down, and suddenly he had one of her breasts in his mouth. He licked and sucked on one and then moved to the other.

"Spread your legs, darling. It's time. I can't wait any longer."

She shuddered and moved them apart a tiny bit. It was all he needed. Damian shifted until he was positioned between her thighs. He reached down, and she felt something moving along her swollen, drenched folds.

She closed her eyes tightly as he fitted himself right at her entrance. "Now, love," he said, and he thrust in fully. She cried out, shaking from the sharp, tearing pain. "The worst is over," he said gently, kissing her. "I'll hold as long as I can so you can become accustomed to me, but it won't be long, I'm afraid."

He lay still, his face taut with the strain. After a few minutes, the burning pain faded, and she became aware of the unfamiliar, hot fullness. But his stillness felt wrong somehow. To her embarrassment, her muscles squeezed involuntarily around him.

"Darling," he groaned out, "if you do that I won't...."

She made an apologetic squeak, her face burning with mortification, but she couldn't seem to stop her hips from pushing up against his weight.

"Darling, I can't..." he said huskily and started to pulse. He managed to keep the movements slow at first, but they were too careful. Genevieve couldn't bear it and struggled madly against the bonds, trying to move her hips. Damian moved then for real, rising up on his arms and thrusting powerfully inside her. To her astonishment, pleasure began to build again until she was moaning loudly. "I think my bride is ready for another orgasm."

"No, Damian!" she cried, not knowing what she was saying. "Please."

His smile was almost cruel as he shifted his movements, twisting his hips just a tiny bit. The effect was instantaneous: she shattered into pieces, her entire body wrenching helplessly. His thrusts became urgent as he drove into her with all his force and finally let out a brutal yell. She could feel the spreading warmth as he released inside her.

His body relaxed, though he used his forearms to keep from putting his full weight on her. He stayed like that, softening within her, until he slipped out. He reached over her head then and clicked something. Suddenly she could move her arms freely, though she quickly realized that the cuffs on her wrists were still fastened to light chains attached to the headboard. Damian lay on his side next to her and rubbed her arms, soothing away the tingling. Then he pulled her into the crook of his arm and just held her. Within moments she was asleep.

Chapter Twelve

Damian waited until Genevieve was in a deep sleep before he rose from the bed. There was little he could do before she woke and could bathe, but he could at least wet a cloth and do his best to clean the effects of their lovemaking so that she might sleep more comfortably. She hardly stirred as he gently washed her thighs, down her calves, and finally along her sex. He was sorely tempted to toss away the cloth and continue with his mouth, but he knew she must be utterly exhausted.

Meanwhile, the grey glow from the windows warned him it was almost dawn. He quickly slipped on a pair of linen trousers, but didn't bother with anything else as the night was mild. Though he would be away from the room for only a few minutes, he took a lingering look at Genevieve. The sight of her sleeping sweetly while bound to his bed filled him with unutterable contentment—as well as gifting him with yet another painful erection, which he tried fruitlessly to tame. Until she'd had time to rest and recover, he would find no relief. But he needed to attend to his errand.

He made his way through the hallway, down the stairs to the dining room, where he unlocked a hidden door that led to the kitchen and finally outside. The stable yard was empty, but Damian spotted Declan seated on a bench at the edge of the cherry orchard. His sire had said he would retrieve Nightshade at dawn and guessed correctly that Damian would want to speak to him— Declan was the only person other than Genevieve that Damian could even stomach speaking to today.

Thankfully, the servants had been sent away, and Derek and Donal were covering for him at the demon gate for the next few days. Food would be delivered from the castle kitchens to their door, but otherwise they would have the house to themselves.

"I can tell just by looking that your first night together went well," Declan said when Damian walked up to him.

Damian thought that a criminal understatement. "It was beyond my wildest dreams."

"I rejoice for you. Titania's gift of the heartwood has once again proved its worth to our family."

"Sire..." Damian said tentatively.

"You understand now why I wished to be present when you opened the box."

Damian sighed and sat down next to Declan. "How did you know?"

"The shawl: the girl who wove it possesses great power to torment herself."

"I would be grateful for your advice," Damian said, his face burning. It humiliated him to admit it, but tonight had been perfect, Genevieve's passion so ardent, her trust so instinctive. He couldn't bear that any misstep of his should spoil things.

Declan nodded but did not show any triumph at having been proved right. "This evening we both discovered the risks of showing her any marked displeasure. I'd just looked within her box, yet even I was caught off guard at how rapidly her mind leapt from the mere threat of *my* anger to the complete loss of your affections."

Damian nodded, hating that they'd unknowingly caused Genevieve to fear for his love. "But the box..." Damian said finally. He was still a bit staggered by what they'd found. Thank Titania Declan had insisted Genevieve not be allowed to look inside. In many ways she was so innocent, and yet the contents of her box were not. What would it have done to her if Damian had thrown it open before her with no preparation?

"I'm glad you do not underestimate the challenges you face. She will require careful handling. I advise you to focus on play, so that she may discover the sensual pleasures that accompany this part of her nature. Give her small reminders of your mastery—always with a playful, affectionate tone. You need her to feel secure enough to disobey or tease you."

"You think I should avoid any discipline?" Damian asked.

"Does that disappoint you?"

Declan's look was so penetrating, Damian realized his sire already knew the answer before he himself did. "No," he said, understanding the truth as he spoke. He needed Genevieve to submit to him, and his desire to bind her amounted almost to an obsession, but he felt no satisfaction at the idea of giving her pain. He recalled now that Declan had once admitted that he felt a strong need to punish. "I would not deny her needs, but I get no pleasure from that. But the box..." he said again. Its contents indicated that this was no small part of her nature. "You really think bedroom play will be enough for her?"

Declan gave him a rueful look. "No," he said after a moment.

"I don't understand."

"It won't be, but I fear that she could not bear anything more from *you*." Damian looked at Declan and suddenly understood what he was suggesting. "It will be unconsciously done on her part, but she will push him until he responds. That side of Derek is strong. He will not be able to resist her need. I must know if you cannot accept this."

Damian had now to discover the difference between an ideal, even a cherished one, and a lacerating, inescapable emotion. Those times he'd contemplated this as a possibility, he'd imagined his bride succumbing to Donal's charm. He'd never dreamt she would be drawn to his impossible brother, let alone have a need that only Derek could satisfy. After all their lessons on the dishonor of jealousy between brothers, he was surprised that Declan wasn't furious with him.

Damian remembered Genevieve's words all too clearly: "Brothers can be jealous, even when they know it to be wrong and unfair. We can't always control our feelings." How wise she was—how glib he'd been.

"Damian?" Declan prompted.

Damian laughed humorlessly. "Even if I did mind, could I really stop it?"

"To interfere would do violence to both of their natures," Declan said sharply. It was no joking matter. There was no greater sin in their family. "Look into your heart, Damian. If you truly cannot, I will reassign him to the demon gate."

Even if Damian could be guilty of such a dishonorable selfishness, separating Derek and Genevieve was not an option. When it came to military matters, Declan possessed an unmatched ability to discern each soldier's talents. By the time Damian and his brothers turned six,

Declan had already decided where they would best serve and had designed their training accordingly. From the beginning, Damian had been slated for command. Though he'd trained for combat, it had taken second place to studies in strategy and the logistics of managing troops in the field.

Donal was up to mischief from the time he could walk and had a talent rivaling a Fae's for anything that required stealth. His training had focused on activities such as sneaking across enemy lines, creating confusion in their camps, sabotaging their supplies, even quietly assassinating their commanders.

Derek's straightforward nature made him despise all forms of subterfuge, and he had no gift for managing men. But the stubbornness that was so troublesome in other contexts made him dauntless and utterly ruthless when fighting for what he cared about. He had trained his whole life for one thing: to protect their bride and her children. There was no one Damian trusted more to keep Genevieve safe, not even Declan.

Damian forced himself to ask the question he'd avoided since the start of the Bridal Week. "What of the Reavers?" Donal and Derek had been completely silent on the topic of their enemy—too silent.

Declan shook his head. "Their spies slipped past us. They have heard of your marriage."

It seemed he must conquer this. Damian closed his eyes, wondering at yet another unfamiliar sensation brought on by his marriage: dread. Genevieve would now be the prime target of those monsters, worse in their way than demons since they were capable of organized attacks rather than just mindless carnage. He'd known this before, all too well, since the Reavers had killed both of his parents shortly after Donal was born.

He chuckled darkly. The night before the Bridal Picnic, he'd prayed on his knees that he find someone so that he could perpetuate the Black line and thus assure the defense of the demon gate. What an idiot he was. If something happened to Genevieve would he actually care that he'd never have children? What would that be compared to the devastation of losing *her*? What a change three days could make in everything he thought he knew.

"Do *you* think I can do this?" he asked Declan.

"The bond between you and your brothers is strong. There will be some rough patches, but you will be able to cope with this. However, there is one final thing. If a scourge should appear in the heartwood box, you will summon me immediately. Neither you nor Derek will attempt to deal with that."

"No! I won't allow it!" Damian cried, again caught off guard by his fury at Declan. If he'd had his sword he'd have drawn it.

"Think carefully what you say, Damian," Declan warned.

Damian blanched, stunned that he'd reacted that way. "You really think it possible she might...." He couldn't finish. Derek disciplining her was nothing to this. The mere thought of Genevieve being subjected to such a punishment filled him with a chilling despair. He bitterly resented Declan for suggesting it—how could he even contemplate such a thing? And that Genevieve might secretly crave anything that brutal filled him with something approaching disgust.

"You will master these thoughts immediately! They are unworthy of a Black!" came Declan's furious warning. "I would sacrifice your brother to your selfishness, but this is your bride! You accepted custody of her heartwood box, vowed at the altar to cherish her, whatever the contents are. Bad enough that you might be forsworn, but have you already forgotten that your bride's greatest terror is that you will reject her when you discover the darker passions that lurk within her?"

Damian shuddered at the rebuke—he'd never in his life received one so well deserved from Declan. He instantly felt a deep shame, all the more inexcusable after Genevieve's willingness to surrender completely to him, which had led to pleasures infinitely greater than he'd dared hope for. And for him to repay her sweet trust....

To his surprise, his train of thought was interrupted by Declan's wry laugh. "Enough! None of us can survive if there are two such natures in our family."

"Sire?"

"Damian, you were guilty of an unworthy sentiment. Forgivable so long as you recognize and repudiate it. Genevieve's tendency to excessive self-blame is enough to deal with without you indulging in it as well. Examine your heart: is she truly capable of alienating your affections, especially for something she cannot control?"

Damian nodded slowly. Declan was right—it was impossible. "Thank you, sire, for everything."

"The matter with your brother can wait. We will pray our enemy has their usual problems mobilizing. If all stays quiet, I will send your brothers in four days. You will have to resume the command then. In the meantime, enjoy this time. You are truly blessed in her, Damian."

They embraced and then Declan, with the silent grace of the Fae, practically vanished into the mist. A moment later Damian heard the clatter of Nightshade's hooves leaving the stable yard.

Declan was right: he owed it to Genevieve to make this time as happy as he could. He grinned thinking of her. He couldn't wait to see her face when she awoke and realized she was still chained to the bed. She would be hungry. Standing in the orchard made him recall their picnic: Genevieve in her innocence opening her lips so that his rogue of a brother, who'd not an innocent bone in his body, could feed her cherries, knowing the sight must drive Damian insane with lust.

He relished the chance to teach Genevieve that such pleasures were not always innocent.

Chapter Thirteen

It was late morning when Genevieve finally opened her eyes. It seemed like every part of her body was stiff and tender in unfamiliar and tantalizing ways. There was no sign of Damian. When she tried to sit up, however, she realized her arms were still bound to the headboard.

Part of her was indignant, of course, but she could not lie to herself: the mere thought of it sent intense waves of desire through her. Everything about it stirred her: that Damian had done it, that she must wait here meekly for him to return and release her, that he might refuse and take advantage of her helpless state to do... wicked things.

Recalling some of those things, she felt a surge of wet warmth between her legs. She was still tender, but apparently her body didn't care. She thrashed and tried to rub her thighs together, but could find no satisfaction. Perhaps if she sat up....

Shifting herself around to turn sideways and lie across the head of the bed, she was able to raise herself to sit, though she was forced to keep her arms in an awkward position. The sheets and bedding were twisted about and damp from their activities, and her shift must be a disgrace. But of course, she could do nothing until

Damian returned. In the meantime, she had the chance to examine the room—his room and now hers as well.

It was much larger than she'd realized, practically as large as the whole first floor of her parents' cottage. The walls were dark grey stone broken up by tapestries on three walls and on the south wall, high mullioned windows. The windows were made of heavy lead glass, but the room was pleasantly sunny—in June at least. In February, she imagined, it would be a battle to keep the room warm, despite the presence of a large hearth on the wall adjacent to the main door.

Most of the furniture was massive and ancient looking, the wood black from age. Arranged in front of the hearth were a long divan and two deep armchairs, upholstered in a heavy brocade. Beneath the central window was a small iron table with a marble top and two chairs. Throughout the room, the colors were all dark and masculine: burgundy, dark blue, forest green, crimson.

She shivered a bit and tried to curl her knees beneath her arms. Everything in the room shouted of Damian and the Black family, this family of men where she was now the sole female. It could not be more different from her parents' cottage, with its diminutive rooms painted in light colors, and filled to bursting with cheerful bric-a-brac.

The main door opened, and Damian entered carrying a tray with a pitcher of her favorite iced lemon water and a tall glass. He was dressed in a pair of loose linen trousers and an undyed, open-neck shirt. Genevieve swallowed nervously, wondering that the sight of him in such relaxed attire would make her desires flare even more.

"Ah, my bride is awake finally."

She suddenly felt shy, thinking of the things they'd done the previous night. Damian placed the tray on the table next to the bed and picked up the glass. She struggled against the bonds, annoyed that she couldn't reach it.

"Do you wish something, Genevieve?" Damian asked mildly.

Her eyes flashed, but she said with forced politeness, "Something to drink, if you don't mind."

He sat on the side of the bed and held the glass to her lips so she could take several deep sips and then patted her lips dry with a napkin.

"I've prepared breakfast, but perhaps my bride would prefer to bathe first."

"Bath... and also...." The drink made her realize she needed to use the necessary.

"Of course. I will draw us a bath then."

"Us?" she squeaked.

He just smiled in answer and then took her hands and unclipped the thin chains that had held them, leaving the cuffs themselves in place. Genevieve immediately pulled at them, but he caught her hands.

"No you don't. You will now have your first rule for this room, darling. I decide when you are to be released. You are not permitted to remove your bonds—indeed, you should not even touch them."

"Damian, that's absurd."

He gave her affectionate kisses on her forehead and nose. "You are free to try me, darling, and then I can give you your first lesson in how the Blacks deal with disobedient brides."

He pulled her abruptly over his lap, grabbed her wrists behind her back, and rubbed her buttocks, letting his fingers skim across places they should never go. To her humiliation, Genevieve groaned loudly, writhing from the desires his outrageous words awakened.

He bent and gave a little nip to her ear. "We'll save that for later, then," he said and released her.

He pulled her by the hand through the door to the bathing chamber. The enormous tub was already half filled with water. Damian turned a faucet in the wall, and steaming water gushed out, mixing with the lukewarm water in the tub.

The necessary was enclosed, but still Genevieve never imagined using one while a man stood in the same room. It seemed she had no choice, so she went in and out as quickly as possible.

When she came out, Damian had removed his shirt, making clear he'd not been jesting about their bathing together. Despite the intimacies of the night before, Genevieve was not at all sure she was ready to bare herself in the full morning light before her new husband.

As was becoming the rule, however, Damian did not leave her to mull over what she wished for. He removed the cuffs from her wrists and before she could stop him, briskly whisked the shift from her body and helped her into the tub.

Luckily for her, there were bubbles on the surface, so she didn't feel quite so exposed. She averted her eyes while he slipped off his trousers and got into the tub after her, causing a generous gush of water to pour over the sides. Instinct made her try to move away, but he pulled her in to lean against his chest.

He kept his arms around her, and they lay that way for some time without speaking. This is marriage, Genevieve thought with surprise. More than the passion of the previous night, resting here in Damian's arms without any anxious need to speak was the most intimate moment they'd shared.

After a while, he began leisurely rubbing her back with a rough cloth, pushing her hair over her shoulder. He next pulled up each of her arms and washed them, carefully examining the skin on her wrists where she'd been bound. To her embarrassment, he then pulled her body up to rest her back on his knee, so her breasts stuck out of the water. He slowly circled the textured cloth over one breast and then the other.

Up until then, the washing had been soothing without seeming overly sexual. But the rubbing, mixed with the lapping of the water and the contrasting coolness of the air, created a riot of sensations that caused her desires to abruptly fire.

Damian bore an expression of relaxed concentration and seemed in no hurry. Having finished washing her breasts, he moved the cloth over her stomach, her sides, and then her thighs, keeping well clear of her most intimate parts. The thought of the rough cloth rubbing along her cleft made her squirm and rub her legs together uncontrollably.

"Damian..." she moaned.

"My poor wanton bride, so desperate for her pleasure, but for now she must wait."

Genevieve froze. "Damian, you don't mean that!" Last night they'd both been mad with lust, but today....

Wanton was almost the worst thing her mother would say of another woman.

He shifted her so he could look at her face. "You fear I mean some criticism of you, darling?" he asked, genuinely puzzled.

"No... I mean...." She nibbled her lip, unsure what to think.

He turned her so she was fully facing him and then to her shock adjusted her legs so she was straddling his hips. "You mean you were taught it is a wicked crime to be wanton, for a woman especially," he said matter-of-factly.

She shrugged—of course she was taught that. It was the truth.

"My dear girl, as far as I'm concerned, it is not possible for you to be *too* wanton—do you believe I would lie to you about that?"

She touched his chest tentatively, watching his expression. "I know you wouldn't lie," she said finally.

His look was gentle. "But I might deceive you unintentionally?"

Genevieve shrugged again. People said what they wished they felt, or they offered reassurances they thought they believed—that didn't make such things true. Damian gave her a look that was a bit too knowing. Then he made a bland smile that she didn't trust a bit. "Damian..." she said nervously.

"My adorable new bride has implied that I did not tell the truth when I stated she could not be too wanton. That feels awfully like a dare to me."

"No, Damian, that's...."

"Don't worry, darling. I am your husband, and it is my duty to teach you that I am a man of my word. In fact, I think it best that we begin our lessons immediately. I already know my bride enjoys being bound." He pulled her wrists behind her back and held them with one hand. "I wonder," he mused, running his tongue over her right nipple, "what other wicked things my wanton little Genevieve enjoys."

He moved to the other breast, opening his mouth wide enough to take most of it in his mouth and sucked hard. Genevieve let out a loud groan. His arousal brushed against her, driving her almost mad with lust. She couldn't stop herself from writhing, trying to rub against him. To her dismay, he released her and moved her off of him completely.

"Have no fear, love. I will continue the lesson after our bath. But first, it's time to wash your hair."

Ignoring her protests, he reached for a pitcher on the shelf next to the tub, dipped it, and poured water over her hair. He then gently rubbed rosewater scented liquid soap through the lengths, combing it out as he went. He gave her the cloth to hold over her eyes as he dipped the pitcher over and over again to rinse out the soap.

"My turn," he said and dunked his entire head in the water, ran the soap through it, and rinsed it—the whole process took less than a minute. How easy for a man to take care of his hair!

He stood up, which gave her a quick glimpse of his naked body before she looked away, shocked at its strangeness. He wrapped a towel around his waist and took her hand to help her out of the tub.

He used another towel to dry her efficiently—too efficiently, she thought with irritation, trying to squeeze her legs again. But then, instead of giving her the towel to wrap around her, he tossed it aside and pulled her by the forearm towards the door—entirely unclothed! She pulled back, trying to cover herself.

"No, no, darling," he said with his wickedest smile. "It's time for your lesson. I believe we will play a little game." Damian dragged her to stand by the edge of the bed. "Do not move!" he ordered.

Genevieve had had enough of his tyrannizing and stomped back towards the bathing chamber to fetch the towel. She should have known he wouldn't allow it. Damian's eyes blazed as he lifted her by the waist and carried her back to the spot where he'd placed her. Once there, he shoved her facedown over the end of the bed.

"Darling, I see we will have our lesson on how the Blacks deal with disobedient brides. Have no fear. It will make our game far more enjoyable. But for now, I must make sure my little wanton knows she must obey me."

He grabbed her wrists, and she felt something wrap around them—once again her hands were bound behind her back. "This time you will stay put!" he said, lacing his tone with iron.

Genevieve was heaving. He disappeared and returned a minute later, wearing the same loose pants and shirt.

"Now for our game. It is an old one, highly educational, and perfect for this morning: it's called the 'the barbarian's slave.'"

He pulled her up again by the upper arm and led her over to the divan before the hearth. "In this game, I play the barbarian king, while you play my lovely captive, bound to obey my every command no matter how lascivious. Since my captive is shy, we will preserve her modesty thus."

Damian pulled her hair over her shoulders, arranging it so it covered her breasts—barely. He pushed her shoulders until she was kneeling before the divan and then lay down on it himself, stroking her cheek in a lordly fashion.

Chapter Fourteen

"**M**y captive may speak only when given permission," Damian drawled.

Genevieve's eyes widened in a delicious-looking panic. As in the past, she seemed helpless to resist him. Her lips were pursed, her breathing short, a lovely blush spread over her body. In the three days since he'd met her, she'd already lost some of the unhealthy pallor she'd sported at the Bridal Week picnic.

Damian reached over his head and picked up a basket. He glanced inside and then popped a cherry in his mouth, giving her a lazy smile. He pulled out the pit and tossed it in the hearth. He ate several more in the same leisurely fashion as her eyes narrowed furiously.

Finally, he held a cherry just above her lips. She breathed in, as if trying to master her rage. He dangled it above her until she lost the battle with temptation and stretched for it. He pulled it out of the way a few times teasingly and then finally allowed her to put her plump lips over it. After she'd eaten it, he held out his hand for her to spit out the pit.

He continued to eat cherries, every minute or so allowing her to have one. Every time she stretched for the cherry, her breasts would peak through the covering of honey-colored hair. Finally, when he'd had a dozen and she'd had only five, he put the basket down against her knees—so close and yet entirely out of reach. If she'd been kneeling properly, with her knees as far apart as they could stretch, he could have placed the basket in an even more tantalizing spot. All in good time.

The sultry minx truly adored her cherries. She looked at the basket so longingly, he almost didn't have the heart to tease her—almost. He reached for a plate filled with jam tarts. Again he ate one, while she watched hungrily. Every few minutes he would feed her a bite.

It was the first meal they'd eaten just the two of them, and he was seeing a new side of her. At her parents' home, meals had obviously degenerated into a battleground, with Genevieve being picky or simply refusing to eat and poor Mrs. Miran, who was a superb cook, constantly fussing over her. He probably shouldn't be surprised that she'd instantly slipped into that mode with Derek as well. Beneath her skittish exterior, Genevieve was a stubborn, willful creature with her own quiet forms of warfare that were every bit as dogged as Derek's.

But when Genevieve wasn't fighting anyone, she relished food, savoring the texture, the flavor, taking inordinate amounts of pleasure from it. It was beyond erotic to watch. Damian made a resolution then that he would not engage in Genevieve's battles over food, but focus purely on enjoying their meals together.

He picked up a tall glass of iced lemon-water, took a deep sip, and then gave one to her. A small dribble of water ran down her chin. She shook her head rather like a wet dog, but couldn't wipe it. He smiled and traced the trail of water lazily with his finger.

When he thought she'd had enough of the tarts, he picked up the cherry basket again. This time he held the cherry so she was forced to rise up on her knees and move closer to the divan to reach it. He took another and rubbed it over her lips, darting away from her tongue, down her neck, until he got to the rosy peak of her nipple. He circled her nipple with the cherry a few times as Genevieve's eyes glazed with lust. He pulled the stem off, and placed the cherry on his chest.

She eyed it, but made no move to snatch it, so he took another and used it to circle her other breast, back up her neck, over her lips. Again he left the cherry on his chest.

Finally, her love of the fruit became too much for her and she pounced, eating the cherry with a greedy gaze of challenge. He half-suspected that if he tried to move the other one she would bite his finger off. He smiled arrogantly, making it clear he was generously allowing her to eat the other cherry from his chest.

He took another cherry and again created a little trail from her lips, down to her breast, circled a few times, and then continued to her navel. He twisted it there a few times and then raised his eyes in challenge. Her eyes widened—she knew he was up to something. He continued on through the little forest of hair, all the way to her folds. She tried to flinch away, but he hissed a sharp reprimand.

Very slowly, he brought the little piece of fruit to her bud. She was very wet. He swirled the cherry until it glistened with her honey. Then giving her a savage smile, he removed it and put it in his mouth. Genevieve let out an adorable scream of protest, but he tapped her lips to make sure she kept silent.

Though he kept his eyes half-lidded, Damian was watching her carefully for the slightest sign of distress, but her expression was the perfect mix of pique and desire, with just enough fear to keep her attentive and aroused. But it was time for him to push her boundaries and see how far she could follow him. He gave her a smile that he knew would make her shudder nervously.

"Now that my lovely captive has satisfied one hunger, she obviously yearns to satisfy another. Sadly, she still has to learn the price of disobeying her master. But I am not a hard-hearted master: if my little slave learns her lesson properly, she will be generously rewarded."

Genevieve's eyes narrowed dangerously, and she was about to protest, when he put his fingers to her lips. "My beautiful captive does not have permission to speak."

He sat up very quickly and hauled her over his knee. Genevieve shrieked and squirmed frantically. With her hands bound behind her back, it was nothing to control her. Ignoring her protests, he gripped her arms and waist firmly with his left hand, while his right roamed over the graceful curve of her arse, tickling the bend where it met her thigh and teasingly approaching those sweetest parts that he could tell were aching with need. Now would be the first test if he could initiate her into the erotic pleasures of a deeper, more difficult submission. "For your disobedience, little slave, you will receive four swats."

"Damian, don't you dare!"

"Five! You are not to speak."

He rested his hand for a moment on her arse and then brought it down on her left cheek with enough intensity to cause a slight burn, but not enough for real pain—this was the discipline of play, not true punishment.

Genevieve still let out an outraged shriek. "I will murder you for this, Damian Black," she raged, sounding not the slightest bit frightened.

Before his bride went totally mad, he slapped the other cheek and then switched off for the final three. Once he'd finished, he massaged her buttocks, allowing his fingers to stray a bit too close to the little hole that someday she might discover also had its pleasures. But for now he was just teasing, so he went just close enough to cause her to squeak and then moved towards her sex, which to his relief was drenched.

He explored her with his fingers, purring, "My poor slave endured her first punishment—I think she has earned her reward."

He continued to circle her bud, just missing the spot she wanted. Her whole body tensed as she strained for relief. He threaded his index finger fully inside her, pumping in and out, before adding a second finger.

When his fingers were soaked with her juices, he held them in front of her face. "You know what that wetness means, don't you, Genevieve? It means what I am doing is driving you mad with desire."

"I know that, you oaf," she snapped.

He gave her a harder slap, causing her to yelp. "Keep your answers polite, pet. There is almost nothing I like more than disciplining insolent little slaves."

She seethed but pursed her lips together to keep from speaking. He rewarded her by lightly massaging the spot she so desperately wanted him to reach. The reaction was instantaneous.

Her entire body tensed sharply and she gasped, "Please Damian...."

"Much better."

He gradually increased the pressure until she was groaning loudly, but kept it just short of what she needed. "Is my darling slave close?" he murmured.

"Damian please," she begged.

"Very nice. You will wait for my command." He gave her another half-minute before he ordered, "Come for me, now!" and flicked her bud.

Genevieve sobbed out her release.

When her shudders died down, he undid her wrists and clutched her in his arms. She clung to him desperately, while he soothed her. He was viciously hard, but he didn't want to push for intercourse so soon after her first time, especially since he wasn't sure how comfortable she would feel refusing him if she truly didn't want to make love.

But it seemed he'd underestimated her desires. She must have felt his erection poking against her thigh. She froze and looked at him, her face full of uncertainty. She reached down to touch him but then winced and pulled her hand away. He nodded at her in encouragement, so she moved her hand down again, tentatively tracing the outline of his cock through his trousers.

Damian was surprised and felt unexpectedly humbled. What Genevieve was doing took genuine courage. After all, it was literally the morning after her wedding—to a man she'd known for three days.

He'd indulged in countless fantasies of his bride throwing herself into their lovemaking—fantasies that turned out to be absurdly tame compared to reality. But his sober self had reminded him that it was unlikely that his bride would immediately overcome the rubbish strictures all girls were raised on. But Genevieve was incendiary—her insecurity and dutiful hesitations were falling steadily before the onslaught of her desires. Though he needed her to submit to him, he never wanted to inhibit her from telling him what she wanted.

Her lips moved, as if she were trying to say something. "Tell me," he whispered.

"Don't you want...?" Genevieve blinked back some tears, afraid that he would disapprove.

"To make love to you again? Desperately!" he answered. "I only feared you were too sore. Are you sure, darling?"

She choked out a half-laugh, half-sob, hiding her face in his neck, which for once he allowed. She needed comfort and reassurance. Their society's hypocritical idiocy meant she took a great risk exposing her desires to him. He'd told her that she couldn't be too wanton, but Genevieve found it impossible to trust other people's reassurances.

Many men, most probably, would disapprove of their young wife eagerly seeking out her own pleasure. Too many of them would heartlessly make her feel rejected or humiliated, inflicting a wound that she might never recover from. It would be the goal of his life to make sure Genevieve never felt a moment's shame for any desire of hers. He nibbled her ear and murmured, "Should we then?"

She nodded—he could feel the heat flooding her cheeks. He wished he could put her on top, which would allow her to control their pace and stop if she felt pain, but he sensed it would leave her feeling even more exposed.

Instead, he shifted them so she was beneath him on the divan. Genevieve ripped his shirt over his head, obviously close to frantic. He kissed her deeply as she threaded her fingers through his hair. He moved his hips against her, nudging her legs apart. She reacted immediately, spreading them and pushing against him urgently. "Please," she begged.

He was lost.

Chapter Fifteen

Genevieve was out of her mind, but the empty ache was more than she could bear, and then touching Damian and sensing his desire.... She thought she would die if she couldn't have him.

"Tell me if you feel any pain at all, darling," he said hoarsely and thrust into her.

"Oh Gods," she screamed.

There was still a little soreness, but nothing like the pain from last night. And the pleasure! Last night she'd been surprised by it, but now she realized she'd only had a small taste. It was so different too in daylight. Now she could see Damian. She loved the way he looked: the hard muscles of his chest and arms flexing, the way a lock of his hair fell over his forehead as he pulsed into her, the strained expression on his face. She understood that his pleasure was equally intense.

She wanted desperately to touch him again, but now she was afraid. Before, he'd kept her hands bound— perhaps he did it to make sure she wasn't too forward—or worse, there was something he disliked in her touch— perhaps she wasn't doing it right. The thought was horrible, but only confirmed assumptions that were always close to the surface for her.

But she had no chance to dwell on such depressing thoughts. Damian had been watching her and grabbed her chin firmly, forcing all of her attention back to what he was doing. His eyes narrowed and suddenly he adjusted his arm, arching her back, which brought her breasts up to his mouth.

Genevieve instinctively raised her hands to push against him, cover her breasts—anything to protect herself. Damian instantly stopped moving and pulled out. He snarled fiercely and grabbed both her wrists. Within seconds they were tied together and tethered to the leg of the divan.

"Damian no!"

"I will tie your hands any time you try to stop me from giving you pleasure, Genevieve," he said sharply.

He pushed in again, but was barely moving. Once again, he arched her back until her left breast was at his lips. He licked slowly and then blew on it, causing her to try to squirm away.

"Hold still," he ordered. "In this room, these breasts are mine."

He gripped her even more tightly and took her whole breast in his mouth. She groaned, jerking frantically, pulling at the bonds.

"Good girl—take the pleasure," Damian said with her breast still in his mouth. "If I had more patience, I would make you come like this over and over again."

Genevieve cried out, not sure she could bear the intense sensations. Damian took pity on her and switched to the other breast, repeating his treatment. Finally he lifted up. "That's all I can manage for now."

At last, he began to thrust again, slowly at first but building steadily. Thank Titania, for now she was as desperate to come as he was. As the pleasure built, she lost all control. Bizarre sounds came out of her mouth, which would have mortified her if she'd not been frenzied with desire. She pulled again on her trapped hands.

It made no sense, but she couldn't lie to herself: this feeling of helplessness, of being so thoroughly at his mercy, brought intense spasms between her legs. The sight of her struggling made Damian's eyes shimmer with lust, and his thrusts became more forceful. His whole chest was covered with sweat, and his face was twisted with concentration.

"There's my girl," he snarled. "Come for me now, Genevieve."

His words worked like a spring, propelling her over the edge into ecstasy. He followed her over, slamming her almost too hard, until finally he let out a rough yell. "Genevieve, Gods, yes!"

They lay there panting for some time when he slipped out and quickly undid the ties that held her hands. This time there were red marks from her crazed struggling. Damian looked at them carefully as he always did, rubbing them and then giving her a little kiss. "Wait here," he said softly. He pulled up his loose pants, which he'd not fully removed and slipped through a door she assumed went to the dressing room.

He returned with a cloth, a jar of salve, and over his arm a filmy, white nightdress. To her mortification, he forced her to lie still while he gently cleaned between her legs. Afterwards, he helped her sit up.

"Arms up," he ordered and slipped the dress over her head. It was little more than a sleeveless shift and didn't even reach below the knee. "Do you like it, darling?" he asked, giving her one of his treacherously bland smiles.

Genevieve narrowed her eyes at him. It was beautiful, the skirt made from the finest silk with a placket of exquisite—and very expensive—lace over her breasts, gathered with a blue satin ribbon. It was *not* one of the pieces she and her mother had sewn for her trousseau. Her mother would faint if she knew Genevieve was wearing something so... revealing.

She couldn't imagine anyone making, let alone purchasing, something so fine and expensive that could not be worn outside the bedroom—or in the bedroom, for that matter. Though she'd been unclothed since the bath, somehow the dress made her feel indecent. The lace showed as much as it hid her breasts, and the fine silk was so sheer, the dark hair between her legs was plainly visible.

She was distracted by Damian's carefully applying the salve to her wrists. He was shaking his head. "Is something wrong?" she asked.

"No—there was a little chafing though," he said. "I'll be back in a moment." He left the room, locking the door of course, and returned a few minutes later. "I have something for you. With these, there's no chance of your pretty wrists getting marked."

Genevieve's face went crimson. He was holding out a pair of cuffs—not the ones she'd slept in. These were made of moss-green leather, lightly sueded and soft as well-washed flannel and lined with padded dark blue silk. Each cuff had two small gold rings, one on each side, and an odd-looking buckle, also gold. She could tell that the workmanship was extraordinarily fine. She wondered that she couldn't stop staring at them, but there was something spellbinding about their appearance. They were beautiful, though it mortified her that she thought so.

Damian moved closer, looming over her seductively, and whispered in her ear, "These are yours, Genevieve.

They are specially made for you, and whenever you are in this room, you will wear them."

"Damian, please, no..." she pleaded.

"Yes, Genevieve," he said, his eyes heavy-lidded with desire. "I have no doubt that just the sight of them will soon be enough to make you mad with desire—and me as well. Hold out your hands, darling," he said soothingly.

She couldn't resist him, though she was sure she should. He took each hand and gently buckled on the cuffs, giving her a wicked smile when they were on. "No touching them, Genevieve," he said firmly. "I decide when they come off."

Genevieve's face flushed for what must have been the thousandth time, and her breathing stuttered. They'd just been intimate—how could she be thinking of *that* again? But her desire crashed just as quickly as she wondered again if he disliked her touch. To her annoyance, he was watching her carefully as usual.

"What is troubling you, Genevieve?" Why couldn't she control her expressions! "Whatever it is, darling, you won't make me angry—I give you my word."

"I want to touch you," she whispered.

Damian's smile was surprised. "I'm glad you do, love. I am your husband after all."

She took a deep breath of relief—he sounded completely sincere.

"You thought I wouldn't want you to?"

Genevieve blushed again—this was so hard to talk about. "I thought perhaps you didn't like it—you bound my hands...."

He laughed and kissed her warmly. "You dear, insane girl! That is emphatically *not* the reason. I'm afraid, darling, that there is almost nothing I find more arousing than the sight of my bride bound for my pleasure—and hers. However, I did it just now because you need to become accustomed to accepting my touch—your instinct is to fight me, and I won't allow it. If you knew what the sight of you in those cuffs did to me...." He shivered dramatically. "I'll show you later. But for now, time for chores. It's wonderful having privacy, but it means we have no servants for the next few days. Would you mind helping me change the bed-linens?"

Genevieve almost laughed. She did not grow up in a house with servants who did such things. Together they pulled the linens off the bed. Of course, Damian must hold out the part that was stained with her virgin blood with an arrogant smile.

After the sheets were off, he suggested they air the bed. He opened the casements, letting in the fresh summer air. She followed and looked out the window.

Their room looked out over a garden, a few acres large, with a gurgling fountain at the center, surrounded by white benches. Fanning out in a star pattern from the fountain were diamond-shaped beds with hedge borders that could barely contain the lush herbs and flowers growing within. The whole garden was enclosed by high brick walls with vicious-looking spikes on top. But the harshness was greatly softened by a plethora of flowering vines and a white pergola overflowing with bougainvillea, which ran the length of the far wall.

The garden surprised her, probably because it seemed so classically pretty. It was feminine, she realized, in marked contrast to all the stone and dark colors of the house—at least the one room she'd seen—which seemed so relentlessly masculine. On that June morning, her wedding morning, she couldn't imagine a more lovely, peaceful spot. She started when Damian wrapped his arms around her, kissing the top of her head and down her neck. "It's lovely," she murmured.

"It's yours, darling—your domain."

"What does that mean?"

"It means that you may redesign it in any way that you please. I will introduce you to the castle groundskeeper in a few days if you like. And when you desire peace from the overbearing males you share a house with, you need only say the word, and you will be left undisturbed. The walls have no gates and are warded so it is as safe as the house."

"This room is your domain," she said after a minute.

"Yes darling. You share it with me, but this is my domain." The idea evidently sparked his arousal, and he pulled her in and began fondling her.

Genevieve pulled away, not wishing to be distracted by his kisses. "And if I wished to make some change?"

"Just ask. Anything you need—I want you to be comfortable here, love," he answered, giving her an amused smile that just irritated her. He wasn't obtuse—he must know what she was trying to ask. Behind his relaxed expression he was watching her closely. He did that often, she realized. She wasn't sure how she felt about that—he seemed almost too clever at guessing what she was thinking. It gave him even more advantage.

"You used the word domain, Damian," she said, pressing the point. "Is there a room in the house that is mine—my domain—or is it only the garden?"

"Yes, of course," he laughed. "There are several rooms set aside for your use. If you wish to make any changes to them, I will arrange for it. The cost is not a problem."

She shook her head. Clearly money was a very different matter for the Black family, but she didn't want to address that question now. "But not this room."

Damian's eyes got that dangerous glint. "I told you already: I decide everything in this room, Genevieve."

There was the crux. There was a world of meaning contained in Damian's word, *everything*. She sensed that she was only beginning to grasp its implications. "May I see this room of mine, then?" she asked, knowing she sounded petulant, but truly he was exasperating!

"Not today," he said. "I think it's time for lunch. I'll see what they've brought for us." He held her chin, leaving her in no doubt that she was not allowed to leave the room.

She bit her lip, angry with him and annoyed that the muscles between her legs clenched. How was it that her treacherous body became aroused by Damian's despotic side? She stayed by the window, enjoying the light breeze that played over the "dress" he'd chosen for her.

Damian returned within a few minutes, bearing a tray laden with plates and a covered casserole. It smelled heavenly. She really was hungry for more than the tarts and cherries he'd taunted her with for breakfast.

He nodded towards the table near the windows. She sat while Damian set the tray down on the coffee table and went out again and returned with a bottle of white wine and two glasses. He piled two plates with a delicate dish of creamed chicken baked over rice, dotted with fresh June peas, and some doughy rolls with an excellent cultured butter. He then poured them each a glass of the bright yellow wine, which proved to be nicely chilled and deliciously floral.

Genevieve was relieved that Damian did not feel it necessary to scrutinize her eating the way Derek did. They were both hungry from their activities and for several minutes were too busy eating to make conversation. But again, Genevieve did not find the silence uncomfortable. Every time he caught her eye, Damian gave her an affectionate smile or blew a kiss, which made her giggle.

Genevieve had never imagined she would love being married so much, but she did. But even more extraordinary to her was that Damian was so clearly happy. She made him happy. It had been many years since she could think of herself as anything but a burden and a source of misery to those she loved. As she sat with her husband, those feelings seemed somehow irrelevant to her new life.

After lunch, Damian removed the dishes to the mysterious depths of the house, returning with fresh sheets. They remade the bed, and Genevieve wondered at how enjoyable it was to do such homely tasks with him. But of course, once they'd finished, he got a look in his eye that she had learned signaled that he felt amorous. He came around her and nibbled her neck, lightly brushing her breasts through the silk dress until her desires easily equaled his.

"Perhaps we should continue our lessons," he murmured. "My bride has proven herself a very apt pupil so far. You mentioned you wished to touch me."

"Yes!"

"Ask me to teach you."

"Teach me!" she said laughing. She was discovering that she loved these lessons.

"Very well, darling. We will continue our game of the barbarian and his captive. One of the captive's duties is to rub her master's body with oil each day." He went into the bathing chamber and returned with a glass bottle and a fresh towel. He pulled the spread down and laid the towel over the mattress. "First my captive will help me off with my shirt," he said.

She made a wry smile, but obeyed, going up on tiptoes to lift the shirt over his head.

"My captive does not wear clothes with her master," he said and whisked the silk shift over her head before she could object.

He gave Genevieve the bottle of oil, climbed up on the bed, and lay on his stomach with his head resting on his folded arms. The bed was too high for her to reach him, so she had no choice but to climb up after him. She unstoppered the bottle, poured some of the oil onto her hands, and put the bottle on the bedside table. The oil smelled lightly of jasmine, which she decided was a very sensual scent.

When she hesitated, unsure what she should be doing, Damian drawled out in his version of the mighty barbarian, "You may begin, slave."

He glanced over his shoulder and gave her a merry smile, well aware of his own absurdity. Genevieve giggled, deciding she liked this game very well. There was nothing for it but to start, so she slapped her hands down on the middle of his back, grimacing that her touch was not exactly seductive.

She quickly became preoccupied by the problem that his skin absorbed the oil too quickly. She reapplied it to her hands twice, and finally poured it directly on his back, which caused him to shiver. Once there was plenty of oil, she began sliding her hands up and down the length of his back.

Damian lay quietly, seeming quite content, which helped her confidence. She'd never even seen a man's bare back up close before. His skin was lightly browned—he'd spent time in the sun without a shirt. Her thighs squeezed involuntarily when she pictured it—she wondered if he would ever do such a thing when she was present.

Even lying in this relaxed pose, Damian gave off an aura of coiled power. His forearms in particular proclaimed his strength. They were twice the size of hers—no wonder he subdued her so easily. She didn't even try to pretend the idea didn't excite her.

She soon forgot she was naked and straddled him to get better access to his shoulders. She couldn't resist the chance to plunge her hands into the roped muscle. She began kneading and soon found a hard knot of tension. She went to work softening it as Damian let out a purr of pleasure. "That feels so wonderful, you can't imagine."

Delighted, she began rubbing in earnest, reveling in the subtle scent of the oil, which became stronger as it was heated by the warmth of his skin. As she reached again for the oil, Damian turned over pulling her to lie against his chest. It was sprinkled with dark, wiry hair that tickled and abraded her breasts in a way that made her gasp. There was no missing his aroused state.

He gently touched her cheek. "Pull my pants off," he ordered softly.

Genevieve didn't hesitate: she was done with being lady-like.

Chapter Sixteen

By the end of Genevieve's first day of being married, spending the day locked in her room did not feel like a trial. She'd lost track of how often they'd made love, her soreness not able to compete with her desires. Her modesty likewise fell easily before Damian's demands, and when they took a quick bath before retiring for the night, she could even laugh that only this morning she'd felt mortified at the idea of being unclothed in front of him. Indeed, as she curled against his chest sleepily in the warm water, she decided she never again wanted to bathe alone.

Tired as she was, though, she didn't fail to notice the gleam in Damian's eye as he was helping her dry off. She discovered the reason when he fetched her nightdress—he'd not even let her enter the dressing room yet. She stood stiffly as he slid it over her, but when he took her hands to replace the green cuffs, which he'd removed for the bath, she wrested her hands away. "What are you doing?"

"You know the answer to that, darling," he said silkily, grasping her hand again.

"You mean to bind me to the bed?" she demanded. He gave her a sultry smile in answer. "No!" she said outraged.

"In this room, Genevieve, you obey," he warned softly.

"Are you always going to ignore my wishes?" She suddenly felt how exhausted she was, and before she could stop them, tears of frustration sprang to her eyes.

He looked at her thoughtfully and then pulled her onto the bed and settled her in his arms. For a moment she thought he'd given up, but it appeared he was arranging his thoughts. "I'm going to ask you a few questions, darling." She nodded. "The first one is this: if you truly disliked something I did—if it gave you no pleasure at all, or left you feeling humiliated or frightened—would you keep silent?"

"No!" The very idea offended her.

"And thank Titania for that," he said feelingly. "Second question: last night if I'd asked your permission before tying you to the bedpost and taking your beautiful sex with my mouth, would you have said yes?"

Her sharp red blush was answer enough.

"Final question: do you think that I could not tell the difference between a true, urgent refusal from you and, say, the kind of objection you made when I ordered you to come a second time as we made love last night?"

"No," she said grumpily, though it comforted her that she knew he would instantly be able to tell the difference.

"Genevieve, please attend, because this is very important. If we are playing, making love, and you are still experiencing pleasure, if your refusal is driven by frustration or village modesty or testiness then I will likely disregard it. If your refusal is driven by fear or distress, I will always, *always* stop immediately. Do you trust that I speak the truth?"

"Yes."

"Thank you. Now, let's assume that you have an objection to something, but it is not a matter of distress, not urgent. That is fine and you should tell me, but such discussions will not take place during our play, but after we are finished. If the objection is serious, I will consider it. But Genevieve, I would counsel you to think carefully about any objections you make."

In a gentler tone he said, "Certain things, such as my binding your hands or spanking you if you are very disobedient are *not* subject to debate. You must understand that they are part of what it means to be descended from Declan. It is not merely a taste or a liking for us, but a very powerful drive."

"You mean that it will always be like this?" she whispered.

"Almost always, yes."

She rested her head against his chest, silently pondering what he'd told her as he rubbed her back.

"That's what the heartwood box is for. It wasn't for the village. Titania did it for Declan, so he might find someone...." She didn't know how to finish.

Damian looked at her in utter amazement, as if he were deeply moved. "Yes, that is why, you clever girl. She did it for his descendants. Those girls whose boxes turned black could find pleasure submitting to their mastery; they would not break under their demands." Damian's voice cracked slightly as he asked, "Do you regret that you are one of them?"

"No!" she said, half laughing, trying to keep the tone light. "I wouldn't mind getting my way at least once—or perhaps being allowed to see my new home. But no, I've no regrets."

She closed her eyes—she never would, so long as Damian did not.

"I know I've been ruthless with you—we have only the four days alone here. Once they are over, I promise I won't be so tyrannical. And Genevieve, never forget, the things we do are always meant to give pleasure to both of us. They are never meant to frighten you or crush your will. And the other side of informing me if you have an objection is that you are always free, more than free, *required* to let me know what pleases you—what you desire. I wasn't joking about it being impossible for you to be too wanton. All of that rot about virginal brides and shamefaced modesty—that sort of village rubbish has no place in our bedroom."

She looked at him skeptically. "Damian, you talk as if a girl mustn't be a virgin when she marries."

"Well, to be completely honest, I'm very pleased you were a virgin. Being the one who first possessed you fills me with such an unholy satisfaction, it is almost savage. But that has nothing to do with whether you were pure and modest or a good girl. Thank the heavens you are none of those things! And if you hadn't been untouched, I wouldn't have thought less of you for it. It is practical for a girl to delay lovemaking until she can find a reliable man lest she get pregnant and be left on her own with a child—practical, not moral. If it were truly a matter of morality, it would be expected of males as well, which it is not."

"You were not a virgin—before our wedding." She didn't phrase it as a question. She knew it was impossible, that boys were not expected.... But she suddenly wondered about the other women he'd been with. He was watching her closely. She tried to make an unconcerned smile, but it didn't fool him.

"Genevieve, you understand that there are women who are willing to accommodate men, who don't expect marriage...."

"You mean for money—yes, I am aware there is such a thing as whores, Damian." She wished she didn't sound bitter, but she couldn't help it.

"Well, I'm glad to hear that my little bride didn't grow up completely wrapped in cotton-wool. In truth, I don't use that word because Declan would thrash me unmercifully if I did—there is almost nothing that would make him so angry."

Genevieve swallowed, chilled at the thought of Declan's anger.

Damian took her chin and forced her to meet his gaze. "Genevieve, no one would ever punish you for breaking a rule you knew nothing of. It is different for a man who has made use of such women to speak of them like that—with contempt. Declan believes very strongly, and raised us to believe, that all women should be treated with respect, and those driven to such straits are if anything owed *more* consideration because they unfairly bear all the blame for a sin that requires both a male and a female to participate."

She made a shaky nod.

"To address your implied question, I was not a virgin, nor have I been for some time. I thank the queen of light for it. Indeed, you could spare a moment's pity for the poor woman who initiated me and suffered having her breasts slobbered over and pulled about like taffy, all for the fifteen seconds of pleasure I was able to give her."

Genevieve snorted. Damian gave her a ridiculously wounded expression. "Cruel girl to laugh at my humiliation! I think it was at least a year before I was able to last more than a minute." Brushing her hair away from her face, he said seriously, "I can say this of my past, darling. I treated every woman I was with as well and fairly as I could under the circumstances. I swear upon my honor that I never formed any attachments—not so much as a schoolboy's crush. And Genevieve, I will never, ever cheat on you."

She leaned over and kissed him gently on the lips. "Thank you, Damian. I would never cheat on you either."

He gently stroked her cheek. "I know you are incapable of deceit, Genevieve," he replied. "Now hold out your wrists!"

"Damian, you're not serious!"

"Genevieve, there is nothing on this earth with greater power to arouse me than the sight of you bound and helpless in my bed," he explained as he buckled the cuffs onto her wrists.

Genevieve couldn't help but feel her own desires stirring as well. He pushed her down onto the bed and reached for the chains and attached them to the gold rings on her cuffs. He kept them loose so that her arms might be comfortable, but she was well and truly bound there.

From the smile he gave, she couldn't doubt the truth of his words. He leaned down and whispered in her ear, "And we both know that it arouses you as well, so for the next three days, and whenever the mood strikes me, you will submit to this."

Chapter Seventeen

Finally after breakfast the second morning, Damian announced that Genevieve would be allowed to see the house. For the first time, he opened the other small door, revealing a large dressing room. "Get dressed," he whispered and then rubbing her rear said, "No drawers, darling. Put on nothing under the dress."

"Damian, I can't do that!" she protested automatically, realizing it was a little absurd after the things they'd done.

"Try disobeying and see what happens," he said hopefully. More seriously he added, "It's only us—no one else will come near the house."

She grunted and went into the dressing room, which was the size of the bathing chamber. One side was filled with her things, which had been delivered during the wedding celebration and put away by some helpful soul, and the other half was full of Damian's things. She ignored the new dresses she and her mother had prepared as a trousseau and selected an old favorite, a plain, light-blue muslin dress, well washed and soft. Thank Titania she no longer had to wear white.

Once she'd put it on, she couldn't resist the chance to examine Damian's things. His side of the dressing room bore traces of his scent, definitely oakmoss, which had an instant effect on her. She ran her hand over the shirts and trousers, looked at his uniform jackets, at the row of tall leather boots, shined to soldierly precision—it was all so masculine, she thought.

Then she laughed at herself: what else would it be?

Before she left, though, something caught her attention. Lying on the shelf below Damian's coats was a leather riding crop. For some reason Genevieve froze when she saw it. It was nothing, she reminded herself. He was a rider; of course he would have a crop. He must have forgotten to leave it in the stable as he came in one day. Oddly it didn't look used, and there was something about the handle....

Suddenly she felt dizzy and swayed. To her surprise, strong hands gripped her, preventing her from falling. It reminded her of when Damian caught her the day they met—at the picnic. She gasped for breath, feeling her chest tighten. Suddenly she was seated with her head hanging down below her knees as Damian massaged her neck. She kept telling herself it was absurd, but she was finding it impossible to calm down.

How could she behave like this!

Genevieve's face was white as she sat up. Damian felt little better himself. He'd taken the crop from her heartwood box and left it lying in the dressing room as if by chance, wondering if she'd even notice it. He wanted a distraction while he was showing her the house, lest Genevieve become angry about the way it was designed.

If he'd known she'd react this way....

He cursed himself again for being unprepared. Promising to return in a second, he fetched a glass of cold lemon-water from their room. She gulped it down, her face desperate. "I'm sorry.... I don't know what came over me.... I'm sorry." Her continued glances at the crop gave the lie to her words.

"Genevieve, you're apologizing," he said gently.

"Because I *am* sorry, Damian!" she cried out. "I don't know why I act this way." In a small voice she mumbled, "It makes me so ashamed."

He knelt and took her hand in his. "You will learn, darling, as you come to know me better that there are things that I think you should apologize for, contritely: lying, putting yourself in danger, not taking care of yourself. And then there are things that need no apology— ever. I would know what you are feeling, at all times, Genevieve. And truly, darling, I like that you lose composure—not that you're distressed, but that you don't hide it from me."

"I don't understand why I feel these things," she said.

Wise girl. She grasped that her distress came from a hidden place within her, full of desires that frightened her.

"Fair enough," he said. "But that is different from feeling you have done something wrong requiring my forgiveness."

"I can't bear that idea."

Damian gripped her tightly to him, wishing to hide his own face, which had blushed as red as hers usually did. He was forced to admit to himself that part of the reason he'd left the crop out was to test Declan's theory. He should have known his sire would never have spoken if he weren't certain. With Damian, the crop aroused fear, not desire. But putting aside the trouble about that blasted crop, he hated that Genevieve feared losing his love.

When he felt better composed he gripped her by the shoulders and kissed her nose affectionately. "Darling, is it possible that your fear of my anger comes from you and not me—from some fear you carry with you, rather than something I've done or said?"

Genevieve shrugged, looking tired and irritable. His suggestion meant nothing to her. Well enough. Time to move on. "Are you still up for our tour of the house?"

That roused her. "Yes!" she said snappishly. "I am ready to be released."

He kissed her forehead, helped her to stand, and said, "Hold out your wrists."

Genevieve looked about to explode but settled into a scowl when he took her right hand and unbuckled the cuff, followed by her left. "I told you, darling, only in this room."

He tossed the cuffs over to the bed. He debated leaving the crop where it was but then decided it would serve the purpose he'd intended. Appearing casual, he picked it up and slashed the air a few times, the way all males fooled about with riding crops. He gave her his blandest smile—causing her eyes to narrow with adorable suspicion—and finally unlocked the door to their room.

Damian gave her a highly edited description of the property, preferring to leave Genevieve to discover the house's distinctive feature—perhaps she would notice, perhaps not. Their wing, the back half, had been modeled after the private apartments of Queen Titania to provide the queen maximum protection and privacy without requiring the invasive presence of guards.

As far as Damian was concerned, the front part of the house was nothing but a decoy, though of course it had not always been this way. The front followed the design of a traditional manor house, with a curved drive leading up to a large columned portico covering a grand entrance.

Once inside, one found the expected entrance hall, with an elegant marble staircase leading upstairs. On the first floor there was a formal receiving room and dining room, the master's study and a library. Upstairs there were lavishly decorated bedrooms that his brothers would use and on the third floor, the expected servants' chambers, though he'd decided that no servants would live in the house.

But except for a single, heavily reinforced door in the kitchen pantry, which was now disguised by shelving, there was no connection between the front and Genevieve's half.

If Damian had his way, Genevieve would never enter the other part of the house—would barely know it existed.

When his parents were alive, the two sections had been left open to each other. There had been a lull in the hostilities with the Reavers for some years, which must have led to a relaxation in everyone's vigilance. His mother, the most gentle, sweet-tempered woman who ever lived, had used that part of the house and even received guests there.

It had been two "guests," really Reavers in disguise, who had violated the laws of hospitality to murder both his parents, and would have murdered two-year-old Derek as well, but for Declan's unexpected arrival.

Damian, with Declan's concurrence, had decided that no one but the family and a handful of trusted servants would ever enter this house—and Declan had laid wards to make sure of it.

Damian did not anticipate any objections from Genevieve on that topic today, nor any about a part of the house she had no reason to enter, but in fact, her half possessed another feature that she would notice soon enough, and he knew well that it would require all of his authority to make her accept.

Damian wouldn't stop with that infernal crop—swishing it through the air, making it whine, playing with it. When she tried to go through a door that led to a closet, he put the crop in front of her as a barrier, drawing it up so it scraped her breasts. She thought about grabbing it from him and breaking it across her knee, but something in the idea repelled her. She didn't want to touch it, think about it, but Damian was being so distracting.

She was having trouble paying attention to her new home. It was the bride's house, he explained, but had stood empty for more than twenty years. Damian emphasized how safe the house was: Declan had laid spells protecting it from fire or any kind of attack—wards he called them. They would live here instead of the fortress where all of their soldiers and retainers lived.

From his tone, he made it sound like a cottage instead of an enormous manor house, though only the four of them would actually live here. He pointed out two empty bedrooms on their corridor and added, "for now," with a wink that told her he was thinking of the children they would have.

There was one other furnished room on the corridor, which to Genevieve's surprise contained only a narrow bed and an enormous rack holding what seemed like an army's worth of grisly-looking weapons. She looked at him in inquiry, and Damian explained that those times when he must be absent, Derek would sleep in that room. Genevieve just stared in astonishment.

"I know he's difficult, darling, but I promise he won't bother you at all."

"In the first place, your brother has demonstrated that he has no compunction about bothering me—or have you forgotten every meal I've shared with him? In the second place, why on earth would Derek leave his own bed to sleep here?"

She was discovering that Damian had a tendency to pretend obtuseness when he preferred not to explain yet another of his family's infuriating customs. It didn't help her temper that he would not stop fiddling with that crop.

"You will be protected at all times, Genevieve," Damian said in his iron tone. "That is not subject to debate."

"Protected or guarded?" she muttered sullenly, remembering the way Donal had sat outside the door to her room—while she'd been locked inside!

She was startled by a little snap on her buttocks, which elicited an embarrassingly shrill yelp. He'd hit her with that blasted crop!

"Temper, darling," he said, his eyes blazing with humorous challenge. "And the answer is both—I must always know where you are and that you are safe."

Damian had a hungry expression on his face, as if he yearned to hit her a few more times with that... that... thing in his hand. Her breathing shallowed. "Shall we continue?" he asked blandly, offering her his arm.

They continued down a narrow stair, which opened into a square room, twice the size of her parents' parlor, completely empty of furniture. Apparently, the Blacks had rooms this size to serve as vestibules or anterooms. On the wall facing the staircase was a set of oak double-doors, and on each of the adjacent walls was a regular door.

Damian opened the right-hand door to reveal a wood-paneled dining room that was reassuringly small and cozy. Though the room was larger than her parents' dining room, the round table was smaller, seating only four comfortably. A dish hutch against the far wall held ordinary Blue Willow china that might be seen in any house in the village.

Genevieve breathed a sigh of relief. The idea of being a great lady was so outlandish, she had never even contemplated it, but certain offhand remarks and frippery like that nightdress made it clear that Damian had vastly different assumptions about money than her family. She'd half feared she would be eating every meal in some enormous, majestic hall at a table that seated twenty.

Next on the tour was the room opposite the dining room, which Damian called the "study." The walls here were plain stone and covered with tapestries featuring gruesome scenes of soldiers battling demons. The room was dominated by a large, carved desk. Because one must face it as one entered the room, just being in there made her feel like a guilty schoolgirl being called to task by a teacher. The room was obviously masculine, and she knew instinctively that this was not her domain. She was relieved to exit.

That left only the double-doors. Luckily, Damian seemed to have put down the crop. He looked a little nervous as he threw open both doors with a slight flourish. Genevieve stepped inside and was stunned. Too many details were bombarding her, but they all gave her the same message—hers.

The room was in two parts—a sitting room that connected to a glassed in conservatory. The sitting room was plastered instead of stone, with nary a tapestry in sight. Two walls were covered with bookshelves. Plump chairs and sofas were set in front of an ordinary (to her) hearth, which unlike the others in the house was decorated with pretty delft-tiles instead of gigantic rusticated stones, and was three feet instead of seven feet tall. Opposite the hearth, there was a deep bay window with a long, cushioned window-seat that could be curtained off—the perfect place to curl up with a book on a stormy day.

If she'd tried to imagine a perfect room, somehow it would look like this. Even the walls—they were painted moss green. In fact, it was precisely the shade of the quilt in her old bedroom. She'd always thought the color soothing but also mysterious—the color of some hidden nook in a forest where she could hide or daydream.

She noticed then the scent of fresh paint and looked at Damian in amazement. He seemed slightly abashed. "I'm sorry about the smell. It was only painted two days ago." He went to open the doors leading out to the conservatory. "Blame Donal. He noticed the spread on your bed, and I kid you not, after breakfast that morning said I must have the room painted this shade. The scoundrel actually cut a piece from your quilt so our men could match it. I'd thought to leave it empty so you could decorate it, but Donal overruled me. He rode up here the night before the wedding and told the steward what furniture should be moved in. I did suggest the rug and the desk, but you can change them if you wish."

She looked at the rug, and her heart leapt—she loved it. It was a plush Persian carpet, obviously quite old and large enough to fill almost the whole room. The mix of dark blues, oranges, and greens on a mostly red background perfectly complemented the green walls.

The desk too was wonderful: it was an old apothecary's table, crafted from a lovely rose-wood, filled with a multitude of little drawers—practical but somehow whimsical as well. And unlike the massive pieces in Damian's room, which were so heavy they must require a dozen men to lift, this desk looked light enough that she might have it moved to the conservatory without feeling hopelessly troublesome.

To her dismay, her eyes were tearing up—why must she do this!

"Darling," Damian said, taking her in his arms. "Why the tears? You won't hurt my feelings or Donal's if you wish to change it—not in the slightest. The cost would be trifling, and the work could be done in a day. Do you believe me when I say that my dearest wish is for you to make the room exactly how you like?"

Genevieve let out a shuddering breath and put her hand up to his mouth. "It's perfect, Damian—so perfect. You can't imagine.... Thank you so much. I don't want to change a thing."

As usual she felt mortified for allowing herself to be so overset. How could she explain what the room meant to her? It barely made sense to her. Just being in here was like suddenly discovering that she'd been trying to live without something vital, as if she were an ocean creature who'd been trapped in a small fresh-water lake its whole life and was suddenly thrust into the sea and finally understood that it couldn't truly live without the cold, salty vastness.

This room felt like it was *hers*—like she belonged there. She loved her parents so much, but the relentless cheer of their cottage often made her feel like an ill-omened interloper. She'd kept her own room empty to provide some relief from all the pink and yellow, but she realized now that the sterile white walls offered no actual sustenance.

"Donal picked the shade?" she asked shakily. How could he guess such a thing? His comment about being an oracle was no jest. But in a way she wasn't surprised. With Damian, with Donal, even with Derek, within minutes she'd already felt like she knew them better than the people she'd known her whole life—like they all possessed some instinct that made them instantly recognize each other as kindred.

She took a great breath and shook her head sharply, trying to throw off this absurd mood before she made a complete scene. "As usual, I'm a watering-pot. I think it's making me thirsty."

Damian let out a startled laugh. He pulled her in for a tight hug. "You dear girl... Genevieve, you've no idea—what you bring to this house...." She looked at him and to her surprise, he seemed almost as affected as she was. "But my bride is thirsty. Why don't you explore while I fetch us something?"

She tried to offer a polite protest, though really she wanted to explore her "domain" according to the ways of the Blacks. Damian pinched her chin and left.

Genevieve stepped into the conservatory, which was large enough to hold a small dining table with four chairs, a double-width lounge chair that could be lowered to create a daybed, two other armchairs, and assorted small tables. All the furniture was wrought iron, with blue-and-white-striped cushions that looked brand new. There were potted date palms that provided some shade, along with orange and lemon trees that smelled heavenly.

She wondered what it would be like to sleep the night in here—could one see the stars? Even better, the date palms told her the room must be heated somehow: how magical it would be to sit out here during the winter watching the snow swirl all around, but feeling safely warm and comfortable.

But today was no stormy or snowy day, but a perfect June morning, gently warm with mild blue skies. Much as she adored her new rooms, the garden was calling to her.

Chapter Eighteen

Genevieve quickly realized the garden was so big, it would take weeks if not months to discover all its beauties. But she spent the next twenty minutes contentedly wandering the paths, reveling in being in the sun, hearing the soothing buzz of the summer insects mixed with the soft breeze.

She was no gardener to recognize all the different flowers, but at least one of the people who had planted this garden dearly loved herbs. At least seven different types of thyme were growing in unruly sweeps; there were beds full of basil, sage, tarragon, chives with their whimsical purple buds. A row of lavender ran the length of one of the walls; beds were enclosed with tall hedges of rosemary.

Best of all, in the sunniest spot in the garden was a huge bed just for her favorite, mint—and not just peppermint and spearmint. She saw apple, bergamot mint, and pennyroyal varieties as well.

Everything grew in such abundance, she could pick a generous bouquet every day and feel no guilt at all. Genevieve immediately set about picking a bouquet of lavender for their room, and that was how Damian found her some minutes later.

He'd brought a tray filled with jam tarts, biscuits, and a large Colby cheese, along with a pitcher of lemon-water, to which she could now add different types of mint. She practically clapped when she saw he'd brought a blanket—she'd never dreamt she'd love picnics so much.

Damian spread it out in a sunny part of the lawn, and they both lay down, nibbling the food, teasing, but really just spending time together.

Damian mostly talked, explaining how he and his brothers had been raised by Declan in the castle after their parents' deaths. Genevieve sensed that though at the time it had been a horrible tragedy, grief had long since mellowed into a gentle sorrow. Their childhood had been a happy one. Though Declan had insisted they train very hard, he'd made sure there was plenty of time for sports, reading, riding, and in Donal's case, endless pranks.

Damian told hilarious stories of Donal's ongoing war with Roderick, the castle's irascible cook. It seemed she'd not been far off when she thought he looked like a child stealing tarts from a tea-tray. So far as his family could tell, Donal set himself the goal of causing mayhem in the kitchen at least once a day, though Roderick would thrash him unmercifully when he was caught. Declan had finally been forced to double the cook's wages to keep him from departing.

"And you were not a party to these raids on the kitchen?" she asked.

"I've stolen my share of tarts and felt the snap of Roderick's great wooden spoon," he said, laughing. "To be honest, though, my passion was for riding. I was a lazy devil when it came to books, but any time Declan gave us an hour's leisure, I was on my horse."

"What of Derek? Somehow I can't see him stealing fruit-tarts."

"No—Derek's passion was for hunting. He was probably the only one of Declan's descendants never once to be thrashed for stealing from the kitchen. But he was much the same as a child as he is now, surly and unsociable. I think Donal would have taunted him to madness, but Derek has the devil's own temper and he's vicious with his fists. As Derek is not a source of jam-tarts, Donal soon learned the amusement of provoking him was not worth the beating he'd inevitably get."

Genevieve laughed, but she sensed something in Damian's tone—he loved his brothers deeply and felt protective of them. Her coming would make a great change for them: they would live in a new house; all of their usual arrangements were being disrupted. She couldn't help worrying about them, especially Derek. Donal struck her as able to find cheer wherever he looked, and not even Genevieve's self-doubt could stand against his sincere warmth. But Derek....

She shook it off and turned back to Damian, who'd sat there for a whole entire hour without once restraining her hands, fondling her breasts, or driving his tongue into her mouth. She almost laughed at herself for the pang she felt—perhaps she wouldn't mind just a bit of that.

But though she felt a lingering desire, for the moment she was content to let it recede a bit. There was something to having it not be quite so clamorous. It allowed her to enjoy another side of Damian, or at least a different way of spending time with Damian. And much as she loved the sensual "play" as he called it, she loved this easy companionableness almost as much. It had been many years since she'd had anything like it, and it made her unspeakably grateful that she would have it with her husband.

Suddenly it was on her lips to tell him she loved him, but she forced down the impulse. A familiar, cruel voice pointed out that they'd known each other a grand total of four days, were still little more than strangers to each other. He might think her needy or easy in her affections for proclaiming her love so quickly. He might feel uncomfortable if (Titania forbid) he couldn't in honesty return the sentiment.

Another, more recent voice said she was unfair to him. Damian was no cad to humiliate her for feeling affection. He'd consistently shown respect for her feelings. And for all his annoying domineering, she saw how he'd been gently and steadily trying to do away with her fear so that she might feel safe telling him her desires.

But it was too hard: the cowardly voice was too long-standing and tenacious. She blushed when she realized he'd been watching her. His knowing look made her wonder how much he guessed of her thoughts. "You dear girl," he murmured.

She didn't confess her love, but she found the courage to reach for his face. He seemed pleased and held still for her so she might explore. She drew three of her fingers over his forehead, up to the line of his hair, pushing back the lock that always seemed to be falling over his brow— she loved that lock. He obligingly closed his eyes so she could draw a featherlight stroke over his eyelids. She traced his ears, caressing the baby-soft lobes, over to the still-strange scratchiness of his cheeks.

They'd both been lying on their sides, propped up by their elbows. When she finished, Damian lay down on his back, inviting her to lay her head on his welcoming chest. Genevieve couldn't resist. He pulled her in with his arm and after a moment's hesitation, she laid her hand over his heart, wondering if he would guess what she was too afraid to say.

For a long while they just lay like that, without speaking, enjoying the gentle warmth of the June day— she loved that she could do this. After a while, Genevieve said lazily, "This is the most beautiful garden I've ever seen. I think I shall live out here in the warm months— that is," she looked up nervously, "I don't mean to be idle. If there are things I should do—duties...."

She wasn't even sure how to ask. Many of his remarks had made clear that unlike her mother, she would not be responsible for the cooking and cleaning.

"I *can* cook a little," she said gamely. "Nothing like mama, I'm afraid. Where is the kitchen, by the way? You never showed it to me."

"Not today, love," Damian said, giving her a little smile.

The change in his expression was very slight, but Genevieve was becoming more sensitive to Damian's smiles, and this was the one he saved for his most despotic assertions of authority. It should have been inconsequential, because in truth she didn't feel any strong curiosity about the kitchen, but she looked at him suspiciously. It was consequential to him.

What wasn't he saying?

It came to her suddenly. "Where is the kitchen?"

The antechamber had three doors in it, for the dining room, the study, and the sitting room. This room gave out to the garden, and the other two rooms had no doors that she could recall. How was that possible? Both his brothers would live here, and yet she'd seen only the small bedroom that Derek would use when Damian was absent—where were his brothers' rooms?

Damian was giving her a smile that was all challenge. Genevieve stood up and walked back to the house. A quick look told her there were no other doors in her sitting room. She checked both the other rooms—no doors. There was a door below the staircase in the antechamber she'd not noticed before, but it led only to a small water closet.

Damian was standing by the double doors, watching her. She turned on him. "Explain this to me!"

"Explain what, love?" he said softly.

"Don't be obtuse!" she growled through her teeth. "Where is the door? How do I leave this house?"

"You don't," he said with the same velvet softness. "Not until we have settled matters between us, including your rules."

"My rules?"

"Yes, Genevieve, rules."

"I suppose I must have your permission to go out then?" she said with maximum scorn.

"No," he responded. "You may not go out at all unless one of us is with you."

"One of us?"

"Me or my brothers."

"Your brothers!"

"Yes. When I am absent, they have charge of you."

"Your brothers have charge of me? Damian, I'm a grown woman."

"You're a *married* woman, Genevieve," he warned.

"My mother is a married woman. She does not have to beg permission when she leaves to do the shopping."

"What happens in your parents' house or any other house is irrelevant. You are my wife, and I am the one you must obey."

"Damian, I've not asked permission to go out since I was nine years old."

"I know, darling, and I realize it will be an adjustment for you," Damian said, sounding eminently reasonable, though his words were anything but. "You will be permitted to visit the town and invite friends to the castle."

"To the castle, but not to the house!" she sputtered. "Not to my house."

"No one outside the family may enter this house. That's my final word," he said, his temper showing signs of fraying. "The bottom line is that you are my wife now, and you must accustom yourself to having less freedom than you enjoyed before."

"Not less freedom, no freedom!" she burst out, utterly outraged. Many odd details of the past few days with him suddenly made a sinister kind of sense. "This was the plan from the beginning—locking me in my room, making sure no one spoke to me. This is what you didn't wish me to hear, isn't it! That after marrying you, I would be locked away inside an eastern hareem. And I actually worried I might deceive you! You spoke the truth that night. You were the one deceiving me!"

As she said the words, she realized she'd gone too far. She could tell from his expression that he'd lost the battle with his temper. She backed away, not frightened precisely, but wary. "As you will it then, Genevieve. *No freedom*," Damian said silkily, stalking closer, caging her in between the wall and the stairwell.

When he struck, it was tiger-fast. Once again she was over his shoulder, being carried upstairs. "Though I believe you will find that there is a difference," he explained, his voice showing no more strain than if he'd been carrying a kitten not a grown woman. "I *would* be willing to allow you some freedom, darling, but only if you acknowledge that it is mine to grant, and that I may take it away again at any time. And beware how you goad me, bride, lest I decide to ignore your wishes entirely. Were I only to consult my own preference, you would remain locked in this house, completely sequestered from all but me and the men of my family."

They had reached the bedroom.

"And" he said, lowering her down on the bed, "when you defied me, you would remain chained to my bed until you saw reason." There was nothing playful in his tone.

"Damian don't you dare!" she screamed.

He let go, and she rolled to escape, but it was apparent from his mocking expression that he was merely taunting her. He caught her before she could touch the floor and used his knee to hold her in place while he buckled the cuffs back on. This truly was humiliating.

"This is no game," she yelled savagely.

"You are right, it isn't." He attached the chains and pulled them tight. "You will stay here until you give me your solemn promise never to leave this house without proper permission and without one of us to guard you. I will give you some time to think on your choice."

And with that, he left the room. She heard the click of the lock, and a second later the sobs started.

Chapter Nineteen

D amian leaned against the wall outside the door to their room, confounded by what had just happened. How on earth had he botched that so thoroughly? Her defiance had triggered some primitive instinct in him, and all he could think was that he would bring her to heel. Declan had warned him of this—and strongly counseled against giving ultimatums. What would he do if she refused him? He'd left himself no way of backing down without looking weak or admitting that he'd been acting like a bully.

Not that he had any compromise to offer her—not on this. He should have just told her about the Reavers, but he'd wanted her to acknowledge his authority over her. It was for her to obey him, whether or not he chose to give a reason for his command! She may have had this freedom at her parents' home, but she had married into the Black family. If he chose to restrict her to the house or lock her in their room, he expected her to submit gracefully!

And he knew even if the Reavers were not a threat, he would never have allowed her to come and go as she pleased. Neither he nor Derek could live with the anxiety of worrying about her. But this went beyond worry too. He wasn't worried about her safety in the garden or the sitting room, but he'd still locked Genevieve inside their room. Just the thought of it made him shoot impossibly hard.

And not only him: he recalled the way her eyes glazed when he told her he'd consider letting her out in a day or so. He didn't want her to feel like a prisoner, like she had no freedom—this truly wasn't about crushing her will or leaving her cowed. He adored the outraged glint she got when she demanded he let her go. But it was her temper to be excited when he exercised mastery, and when she yielded despite herself, he thought he would go mad with lust.

That was his mistake: he'd made it a question of brute force, when he should have talked to her openly. Her protests were legitimate and completely understandable. While it was his right as husband to make decisions like this, it was only fair that they be discussed.

That's what they'd done so far, he realized. They talked and negotiated, made sure at every point that both of their views were taken into account. Though he'd dominated her, until now he'd not acted as if her will was unimportant. And unquestionably, Genevieve had known incredible pleasure surrendering to him.

His heart ached when he thought of her expression when he showed her the sitting room, when she said how perfect it was. Genevieve belonged here. The last thing the house should ever feel like was a prison. She needed a haven—a home. Truly, he had botched this. The worst was he had no idea how to repair the damage. Unfortunately for Damian, the fates would not give him the chance that day.

"Damian!" a voice roared from the bottom of the stairs. It was Donal, and Damian knew immediately that disaster had struck. His brother appeared a moment later out of breath. "They ambushed us—lightning strikes from the north and the west, right over that bloody cliff. Our men fought brilliantly, but they couldn't hold the lines."

"Where is Derek?" His first thought was for Genevieve's protection.

"He's bringing Nightshade—he's right behind me—I'm to take you to the rallying point."

At least Derek was close. Damian had no idea how to face Genevieve, so he played for time by entering Derek's little room and began putting on one of his uniforms—all three of them were the same size, thank Titania.

As he pulled on the pants, his mind struggled frantically for some way to repair this quarrel in the time he had. What would she think of him for leaving so abruptly? Would she feel betrayed—or worse, abandoned? It was too horrible to contemplate.

"Donal I need five minutes—I need to speak to Genevieve!" he said desperately.

"Damian...." Donal was pale. "The gate was breached."

Damian's stomach sank. "How many?"

"Possibly twenty demons. Declan ordered Derek to take Genevieve into the hills. That's why he's bringing Nightshade."

"Damnation!" he hissed, grabbing down weapons from Derek's rack. The protections of the house would hold back the Reavers, but no Fae ward could keep out a demon. "Donal, you need to stay with her."

Donal stared at him like he'd gone mad. "Damian, Declan told me to...."

"Donal!" he growled. "We just quarreled, ten minutes ago—in a fit of insanity I tied her to the bed. I need you... Derek can't... I need you to make this right," he said desperately, thinking of Declan's request to Donal at their wedding.

"Damian, we must get to the gate." If the demon gate fell, truly all would be lost. Demons would pour into their world, raping any woman of childbearing age and slaughtering everyone else.

"Just five minutes, Donal!"

"You were followed!" Derek roared, coming up the stairs. "I took out four, but the rest ran into the brush."

There was no time for anything else. Damian and Donal sped off down the stairs.

Chapter Twenty

Genevieve lay on the bed, swinging wildly between misery and rage. The fluctuations were making her head ache. How had such a perfect moment gone so sour? She'd been so happy, but was it all an illusion? Was she now married to a bully who would use force on her anytime she disagreed with him? She had no idea what to think.

She was startled by the door flying open. It took her two seconds to realize that it wasn't Damian but Derek! In her room! While she was chained to the bed! Thank Titania she was dressed.

Derek showed no surprise at her state but walked up to her, unsnapped the chains from the cuffs, and pulled her up. "Get your boots!" he ordered. He was dressed for battle, with a sword strapped to his back, an axe at his waist, and braces on his arms, which held a dozen small knives. "What are you doing here?" she demanded.

"No questions! Get your boots!" he snapped out as he threw open the dressing room door and returned with some of her dresses and a cloak.

Genevieve was furious. "Are you mad! Where is Damian?"

Derek grabbed her arm, twisted her around, and slapped her buttocks twice. He gripped her chin and said icily, "No questions—get your boots."

Genevieve shuddered under his granite-hard gaze—what was it with these Black men! All defiance evaporated, she sat on the edge of the bed as he tossed her stockings at her. Mechanically she pulled them on and slipped on her boots, letting out a slightly hysterical laugh when she wondered if she should tell Derek that per Damian's orders she wasn't wearing drawers or a petticoat.

When her boots were on, Derek took her hand and pulled her towards the door. "No! Where are you taking me?"

She couldn't fathom why Damian would send Derek for her unless he'd been so outraged by their quarrel, he'd decided to expel her from the house. No matter how angry Damian had made her, she didn't want to leave him. Couldn't they at least discuss their differences? How could Damian get that angry with her?

She couldn't control the rising panic and started screaming and thrashing wildly. When she ignored his orders to stop, Derek shoved her against the wall, clipped the cuffs together behind her back, and tied a cloth over her mouth. He heaved her over his shoulder and carried her down the stairs into the dining room, where it turned out the dish-hutch concealed a door. They moved so quickly she caught only glimpses of the deserted kitchen before they were outside.

A huge black horse stood saddled and waiting—Nightshade. Derek laid her over the front of the saddle as if she were a sack of grain and then mounted up behind her. Something tightened around her waist—he'd tied her down—and just like that, they were galloping away at a heart-stopping pace.

Genevieve was stupefied: she could make nothing of her predicament except that she'd been kidnapped by her new brother, who was carrying her away from her husband on this otherworldly animal. With her face pressed against Nightshade's flank, she could see almost nothing of the terrain, but it was clear they were climbing.

Every part of her ached from being bound in this unnatural position. But to her utter humiliation, as she fought for the thousandth time against the cuffs and the rope that tied her down, she felt a warm tremor between her thighs.

No! That was impossible. It was merely an effect of the constant jar of Nightshade's movements, but she couldn't help rubbing her thighs together and squeezing the muscles of her sex trying to get some relief. One of her legs flailed out, accidentally kicking some of the bushes that lined the road, which produced a sharp slap on her buttocks. "Keep still!" came Derek's angry order.

Genevieve's rage was sharp and lucid, invigorating under the circumstances. It completely did away with fear and luckily distracted her from her less acceptable sensations.

After that, time passed in a haze—she knew only that it was late afternoon when the horse finally slowed. Derek was off in a moment, slinging her over the horse's side. He removed several bags from the saddle and then whispered in Nightshade's ear, "Run fast, lose them, then find Declan."

The horse practically vanished down the narrow road. Derek knelt and put his hand to the ground. With a quick curse, he pulled her off the road, moving sideways through a very narrow path that had been cut through the brush. He went about thirty feet, before he shoved her face down beneath a dense mulberry and to her astonishment, threw himself on top of her.

Holding his hand across her mouth, he whispered so low she could barely hear, "You must be absolutely silent. Reavers are behind us."

Genevieve chilled. In a thousand years she wouldn't have suspected such a thing. In the village, the Reavers were the stuff of frightening fireside tales. The half-human offspring of women who'd been raped by demons, they were fiends who murdered their own mothers and anyone else they could find: children, the aged, male, female—none were spared their rampages.

Derek kept his hand on her mouth and rested his head against the back of hers, pinning her so that she couldn't move at all. Two minutes later, she heard it: the sound of horses and brutal shouts in some unknown language.

The sounds died off, but Derek's only movement was to retrieve a small vial from his pocket and pour some liquid over both of them. Then he lay perfectly still. Minutes passed, the light dimmed, the air grew even more chilled, and still he kept her there.

Perhaps ten minutes after they heard the horses, Derek tensed, nuzzling her in warning. Soon she caught the sounds, these ones on foot. She realized that it was a second wave of pursuers who followed to try to catch them as they broke cover. These did not stay on the road but fanned out into the bordering wood. Her stomach clenched as the sounds came closer.

The footsteps were only a few yards away when Genevieve heard a flurry of growling that caused a rivulet of cold sweat to snake down her face. Nothing human could make that sound. Genevieve's heart nearly stopped when a pair of bright red talons, larger than a man's foot, appeared at the edge of the bush. She was three feet from an actual demon.

Thank Titania, Derek remained utterly motionless, which somehow helped her find calm enough not to react. The feet prowled about for what seemed like an eternity, during which she was certain an enormous bloody claw was going to slice right through the bush, Derek, and then her as easily as softened butter. But then, miraculously, the talons moved away again.

She was convinced it was a trap, but after ten minutes Derek shifted off of her. He undid her bound hands and then untied the cloth in her mouth, patting her lips in reminder that she should remain silent. He helped her roll to her side and held up a canister to her lips. She drank greedily.

Pulling her head in to his, he said very quietly, "There is a hideout not far. Keep quiet."

Derek slipped out through the branches without making a sound though he was twice her size, but Genevieve was as loud as a bear blundering through a briar patch as she tried to extricate herself. Luckily for her sanity, Derek showed no alarm. He must be certain that for now the two of them were alone. There was something about Derek that defied mistrust. He seemed incapable of even harmless deceptions. Genevieve couldn't help but feel reassured, though she was still furious.

He pulled out a grey-green cloak and put it over her shoulders, pulling the hood up so that her hair was completely covered and her face was shadowed. He put another on himself and then nodded for her to follow him. In the failing light, Genevieve couldn't discern anything distinctive enough to be a landmark. The trees and rocks were so many vague outlines, but Derek moved without hesitation, as silent and graceful as a large cat on the hunt.

An old path went up the mountain, bordered on either side by dense brush. They climbed for a quarter mile, when Derek stopped and pulled back the branches of a tall thorny shrub. Behind it, a subtle path had been cut, giving them just enough room to move quietly, but next to impossible to see if you didn't know it was there.

It led them away from the main path until they'd gone high enough to reach the pine strands where no paths were needed. He pulled her at a jog then, running in and out of the trees, stopping every so often to listen.

Finally, when they'd travelled another mile, up and east, he stopped and pulled her over to a tree. He took out some tool and knelt down. He was digging a hole, she realized. He stood up again and whispered, "Go."

"What?"

He pushed on her shoulders so that she would bend down. "Go—make water."

Genevieve almost fainted with embarrassment. "No," she hissed, trying to stomp away. She was not doing *that* in front of her husband, let alone her husband's brother.

Derek's eyes blazed. He gripped both her arms and pushed her against the tree. "Now!"

"Get your hands off of me, you oaf!" She was sick to death of being manhandled by the men of this family.

"Think carefully, Genevieve," he whispered sneeringly. "Do you really wish to do this with your hands bound?"

Genevieve swallowed at the threat. Unfortunately the same qualities that made Derek seem incapable of deception also made him seem unlikely to bluff. It helped her compliance that she did in fact have to "go," badly.

"At least turn your back," she growled furiously.

He smirked and deigned to make a quarter turn away from her. She crouched down, gripping the tree with one hand, trying to pull her skirt out of the way with the other.

She hated going outdoors!

It took a good half-minute to even start with her infernal brother standing right there, but finally she released her stream. She experienced yet more agonies of mortification when it seemed to take an impossibly long time to finish.

When she stood again, Derek handed her a wad of paper. By now she was ready to kill him. She grabbed it furiously while he again made a show of turning away so she could pull up her skirts and clean herself. He nodded that she should place it on the spot she'd just gone in. He seemed about to cover the hole, but she grabbed the trowel from his hand and stooped down to bury it herself.

She returned the trowel and he walked ten steps away and dug his own hole—so it seemed only she was not allowed any privacy! When he was done, he took out another vial of liquid and poured a little on each spot. She guessed it was to disguise any scent.

They then continued east across the mountain another half-mile when they reached a large hill that was dotted with rocks and massive boulders. Winding in between two man-sized stones, they reached another pile of brush, which turned out to be attached to a wooden door. Derek pulled it back, revealing a small triangular opening in the rocks, barely three feet across.

He motioned that she should wait and then climbed in feet first on his stomach. He reached for the bags, dropped them down, and then nodded that she should follow him. He guided her until she'd climbed down enough to be fully inside the opening. Then he climbed up so that he was standing over her with her back against his chest. He reached out and pulled the little door closed, leaving them in utter darkness.

Keeping his arm tightly around her waist, he helped her feel her way down the ladder, which descended about twelve feet into the ground. "Don't move," he said, his voice closer to normal, and then moved away. A minute later there was a scratch and a flicker of light and then the steady light from an oil lantern.

Genevieve was astonished to find herself in a sizable underground room that looked like it had been stocked with necessities and even a few comforts so that two people might live reasonably well for years. The packed earth floor was covered with thick woven mats; wooden shelves along three walls held lanterns, blankets, clothing, weapons, rope, jars with all manner of preserves, metal food tins, even bottles of brandy. Below the shelves were five large barrels she assumed were filled with water. Against the fourth wall was a narrow cot.

Now that they seemed safe for the moment, she stared at Derek, waiting for him to offer some explanation. He was scowling fiercely. "Why were you tied to the bed?" came his blunt question.

Genevieve couldn't help laughing—of all the things he could say! Was there ever in the history of the universe a more infuriating man?

"Hello Genevieve," she said sarcastically. "I am so sorry for snatching you from your bed and throwing you over the back of a horse, bound and gagged. I suppose you want an explanation: you'd never have guessed but Reavers were after you! Not to mention a bloody demon!"

Derek gave her one of his glares that was supposed to leave her cowering, but she merely folded her arms and glared back. She was past all patience with the men of this family. His gaze shifted then to something more assessing. "Did you refuse to stay put when you were told?"

"It is none of your business," she bit out.

That produced a loud snort. "I've been charged to protect you. Anything that concerns your safety is my business. When did you last eat?"

"I have no idea—some time before I was tied to the bed by my husband and then kidnapped by his brother."

Derek's eyes narrowed at her insolent tone. He said nothing but removed some wrapped packages from the saddlebags that looked all too familiar. "So help me, Derek, if that is a tongue sandwich!" she cried, her voice shaking.

"Don't push me, Genevieve," he warned back. "I'm within a hair of taking over my knee as it is." Recovering his temper, he pointed to the shelves. "There is all the food and water you could need to survive, lamp oil, extra blankets. I put in some books, drawing things. I didn't know what your pastimes might be, so I just guessed."

He pulled her around the far side of the cot where the wall ended, creating a small alcove. On the ground was a deep, narrow hole with a pile of dirt next to it, a bucket for water, and bottles of distilled pine oil. "The less we use that the better, but it will do for now. The others know where this place is. Someone will come if I can't get back."

"If you can't get back? Where are you going?"

"I must go hunt down that demon," he said as he grabbed yet more weapons from the shelves.

"When are you coming back?" she cried, ashamed of how shrill she sounded, but even Derek's company was preferable to being abandoned in this cave.

He moved swiftly towards her. "Do you want me to come back, angel?" he sneered.

Genevieve would never understand what came over her, but her hand darted out smacking him hard across the face. There was a moment where they both stared at each other, Genevieve as surprised as Derek was.

When Derek moved, it was almost inhumanly fast—truly he was Declan's descendant! Within seconds he had her over his lap, her wrists gripped behind her back. There was a click, and she realized he'd bound her hands together with those bloody cuffs. He flipped her skirt up, revealing her lack of drawers.

"Twelve," he growled, and then his hand smashed down.

Genevieve was so shocked by the pain, she could only let out an inarticulate cry. Blow followed blow while her eyes smarted with tears, and her brain tried and failed to make sense of the agony. These were a million times harder than Damian's playful little slaps.

But even as she felt in danger of being driven mad by the pain, to her horror, the muscles between her legs clenched, and she could feel the wetness pooling as her desires soared. With the next smack of Derek's hand, she made a sound that was closer to a groan, as pain and pleasure seemed to writhe in and out of each other.

She realized he'd stopped. He rubbed her buttocks soothingly and then unlocked her hands and pulled her up. He tried to cradle her in his arms, but she shoved away from him furiously, elbowing him sharply in the side. "You continue to goad me?" Derek demanded incredulously.

"I hate you," she screamed, hating herself more.

"You can't stop, can you?" he murmured.

Genevieve thought she would faint as his usual forbidding scowl melted and was replaced by something smoldering with dark promise. Thankfully, after a minute he seemed to shake it off. Back to business, he gripped her by the wrist and reached behind the cot and pulled up something, which he clicked to the ring on one of her cuffs. It was another chain!

"I presume Damian told you that you are strictly forbidden to touch your bonds. You can't escape them, and I will know if you have tried to tamper with them. I may be gone a day, perhaps two. While I'm gone, think about what you want, Genevieve. If you keep provoking me, I will give you what you crave." He sounded as desperate as she felt. "And next time, I won't stop until you are sated."

With that, he disappeared up the ladder, closing the hatch behind him.

Genevieve was left in a state of shock. She mechanically opened the package he'd left for her and let out a shrill giggle. The cursed scoundrel really had packed her a tongue sandwich. With a shriek of rage, she hurled it against the far wall.

She'd reached her limit. An instinct of self-preservation warned her that she could not stay here—could not trust herself with Derek. She frantically attacked the cuffs, trying with her fingers and teeth to pull them off. Damian had simply buckled them on and off, but when she tried, she found there was some mechanism that made them lock. Likewise the chain proved stubbornly bolted deep into the ground. She would have searched for a knife to cut through the leather, but the chain didn't stretch far enough to reach the shelves that held the weapons.

She was well and truly trapped here.

With that realization came exhaustion. She could either start screaming hysterically or go to sleep. She opted for sleep. She turned the lantern to its lowest flame and sat gingerly down on the edge of the cot, fumbling to untie her bootlaces. Apparently she was too much her mother's daughter to get into a bed wearing shoes, which had been a high crime in their cottage. Heaven forbid she do it in this underground prison, chained to a cot, while impossibly aroused by her new brother-in-law's spanking?

Bizarre-sounding laughs gurgled up as she pulled off each boot and neatly placed it by the side of the cot. She'd have to ponder that one. Fortunately, before she went utterly mad, Genevieve curled up on the cot and allowed sleep to claim her.

Chapter Twenty-one

Genevieve slept surprisingly well despite her recent turmoil. When she finally woke, she sensed that she had slept well past her usual time, though there was no way to tell in her underground prison.

She was alone. Thank goodness the lantern was still flickering. She got up before her only light completely sputtered out. The shelf held a row of lanterns, along with twenty bottles of oil, enough to light her parents' cottage for a year. Though it made her feel profligate, she lit three lanterns, which left the small space bright enough that she could have done fine lacework if she'd wished.

She made use of the "hole," trying to ignore the lingering burn on her buttocks. She poured the pine oil a bit too liberally afterwards. It didn't surprise her that Derek would push for them to go outside whenever they had the chance since the primitive necessary would eventually begin to stink. Afterwards, she drank some water and forced down a few biscuits before her stomach rebelled.

Thus began an endless day trapped alone in this sunless cave with no idea of how long she must stay. If she'd been the good girl her parents had tried to raise, she would have read or sketched, but Genevieve was in too great a tumult to do more than pace restlessly as far as her chain would allow until she felt lightheaded. She then curled up on her cot, only to begin the cycle again when that became intolerable.

Now that there was nothing else to distract her, her thoughts divided pretty evenly between Damian and Derek. Every attempt to make sense of her quarrel with Damian made her head ache. She was stunned that he could get so angry that he would leave her without a single word. She wanted to scream at the unfairness of it. The very first time she'd fought back against his tyranny, he'd *abandoned* her.

She ranted out loud that she was better off without him if this was how he would treat her. Clearly he wanted to lock her away in that prison of a house, leaving her to wait for those moments when he could spare her some time.

But then she would remember everything that had passed before the quarrel: lying in his arms in the bath, his wicked games, their morning in the garden where he regaled her with tales of Roderick the cook. She'd been happy. When she thought of the beautiful room he'd prepared so thoughtfully, she desperately wanted to reconcile matters with him. Surely it must be possible!

Then an evil voice sneered that she was a fool to be surprised that he would leave her. Had she really thought she could win his love? Why on earth would her marriage be happy when all she'd done for the past four years was make everyone around her miserable?

A week ago, such thoughts would have precipitated one of her attacks where she would lie in a darkened room, curled on her bed, gripped by despair. But today rage at one Derek Black was enough to drive her from her cot.

She crossed and recrossed the floor of the cave as she contemplated her endless grievances against him: the spanking, the sandwiches, the ride on Nightshade, making her "go" outside in front of him! Just the sensation of the cuff on her wrist made her shudder with rage. She yearned to slap his face again! She barely ate, relishing the hunger pangs, knowing her skipping meals would anger him past all endurance.

When hunger and emotional exhaustion finally caused her to sink into a kind of half-sleep, she was assailed by strange images of Derek standing before the great desk in the study, flicking that wicked crop of Damian's, thinking to take her to task for some misdeed while she spat at him, relishing his explosion....

She slept long and hard and would have slept longer, but some instinct managed to penetrate the thick blanket of slumber to warn her she wasn't alone.

She jerked her eyes open to see Derek, silently removing each weapon and carefully cleaning it before putting it away. Even from the cot, she caught an aroma of sulfur and knew he was fresh from the battlefield. His weapons stowed, he began to undress. He removed his jacket and then gingerly removed his shirt, revealing a long bloody gash, which stretched from his chest half way around his back.

"You're wounded!" she said, jumping up, only to be held in check by the chain. "Let me help you, Derek."

Unfortunately, she'd not counted on the effects of hunger combined with standing too quickly. She swayed dizzily and might have fallen but for his arm gripping hers.

"You're dizzy! When did you last eat?" Derek demanded furiously. When she didn't answer right away, he shook her. "Answer me now, Genevieve!"

"Yesterday... morning I think," she said through her teeth, all worry over his wound evaporating like mist under a scorching sun.

Derek clenched his hands, breathing in and out as if to keep control. "You disobey me at every turn. Genevieve, have you any idea.... What use is my staying away if the moment I return you begin baiting me?"

"*I* am baiting *you*?" she choked incredulously.

"From the day you met me! Did you think I would not react?"

Genevieve let out a loud wail as she picked up her boots and threw them at him and then threw herself, pounding him with her fists.

Derek caught her hands and cuffed them together behind her back. He sat on the cot and pulled her over his lap, flipping up her dress. He delivered five sharp slaps and then forced her to her knees, tightening the chain until she couldn't move at all from her spot.

"Now you will stay! If you provoke me further, Genevieve, I will give you a real spanking, and this time I won't go easy on you!"

Her rear end burning brutally, Genevieve sobbed silently. It shouldn't be possible for another person to make her this angry. Even during the worst moments over the last four years, she'd never actually had an argument. Her parents were as far from irascible as human beings could be. The closest either of them got to anger was a mild querulousness, her mother when someone tracked mud in the house, her father when he misplaced his pipe. Watching Derek's awkward attempts to bandage the gaping *claw mark* on his back, she shuddered from helpless rage.

When Derek finished his treatment, he went behind the alcove. She could hear sounds of splashing. The crying had left her desperately thirsty as well as dizzy from hunger, but she would rather expire than ask Derek for anything.

He emerged his hair damp, all traces of blood gone. The washing seemed to have calmed him slightly. Genevieve tried not to stare, but he'd not put on a shirt, and she found herself riveted by the sight of his broad shoulders and the sharply defined muscles of his arms and chest.

He caught her staring and snarled, "You're about to collapse." He pulled out more packages from the saddlebags and unwrapped a sandwich, using a knife to cut it into small pieces. He knelt in front of her and held a piece to her lips. Of course it was tongue.

It was all too much.

"Please Derek," she sobbed pathetically. "Please, can I have something else?"

He held her chin forcing her to meet his gaze. He nodded very deliberately, conveying that she'd chosen the right approach. "I'll give you something else if you promise to answer my questions—truthfully."

She nodded, past caring what she was agreeing to. He put the sandwich aside and went to the shelves and spent some time opening the tins and jars there. He returned with a plate piled high with stewed fruit, biscuits, nuts, and strips of dried beef. "Every bite, Genevieve. Don't test me again."

Too hungry to fight, Genevieve obediently ate every bite he fed her, gratefully drinking down the glass of water he offered. He was utterly intent, watching everything, but communicating almost nothing. When she finished, he stroked her cheek almost... tenderly. It was the first kind gesture she'd had from him. She feared she was dangerously close to hysteria.

He didn't take his eyes off of her as he quickly devoured that cursed sandwich. Once he'd eaten, he cleaned up the remains of their meal and then sat down on the cot, making no move to free her. "Tell me why Damian chained you to the bed," he said softly.

Of course he would ask that! But she'd given her word to answer his questions. "He showed me around the prison that is my new home and informed me that I was not permitted to leave the house unless one of you is with me. When I protested, he tied me to the bed."

"You vowed at Titania's Altar to obey him."

"So I am to have no freedom whatsoever?"

"You will have as much as he chooses to grant you and no more. Be thankful Damian is so lenient with you."

"Lenient!"

"If you were my wife, you'd *never* leave the house but on Titania's feast day," he growled.

"You're not serious!" she protested.

He came closer until he was kneeling in front of her. That savage, hungry expression was back. "I am completely serious. If you were mine, then you belong in my house. I prefer you to remain—that is all you need to know."

"That's absurd," she said breathlessly. How could such outrageous words cast such a spell?

"Genevieve, so help me, if you were mine, you would know every second of every day that my will is yours. I would not tolerate any hesitation, any arguments from you. If you disobeyed me, I would tie you down and spank you until we both were sure the disobedience would never be repeated. If you were difficult over your eating, you would take your meals on your knees, blindfolded, with your hands bound behind your back."

"I would leave you—I'd never let anyone treat me like that."

"You say that, Genevieve, but it's not true. You can't hide from me. I know my words excite you—just like I know those cuffs you're wearing came from your heartwood box."

"What are you talking about?" she demanded, becoming alarmed.

"They are Fae-made—the workmanship is unmistakable. They could only have come from your box.

Did you try to remove them despite being forbidden? Answer!"

"Yes," she said through gritted teeth.

"Wise of you not to lie. They have been specially charmed so the wearer cannot remove them. If you know the trick, it takes but a second to lock or unlock them, but if you don't, they are virtually unbreakable. They also make it obvious when someone has tried to tamper with them. You can wear them comfortably for days, with no risk of chafing, and at any time, the rings can be locked together if you misbehave. They are the perfect restraint, and they appeared in your heartwood box. Have you guessed why?"

"No!"

"The answer is: they were in your box because one of the deepest wishes of your heart is to be bound by your husband."

"It's not true, you bastard!"

"I've warned you, and yet you continue to provoke me. You clearly wish for me to discipline you. No doubt I would find something in your box to satisfy your need. I can think of many possibilities: a wooden paddle? A hairbrush? A leather strap? No? Perhaps a riding crop then?" He clearly noticed some reaction because he seized on it immediately. "You've fantasized about a riding crop?

I can think of many things I could do with that—do you want me to tell you about them?"

"No!" she cried out.

"Shhh, easy, little one." He came closer and kissed her forehead comfortingly. "Your box turned black—these desires are part of you. You need to stop fearing them—or feeling ashamed that you have them. You promised to answer truthfully. You are no liar, Genevieve, so don't lie to me now. Do you want me to tell you what I would do with the crop?"

His voice was so gentle, she couldn't fight him. "Yes."

"Good girl. A riding crop does not work well for regular discipline—for that I would use a paddle. A crop is a very sensuous tool, as effective at giving pleasure as pain. Nothing works better for interrogation. If I wished to use a crop on you, I would have you standing naked in the middle of the room, your hands bound and stretched tightly above your head, your ankles cuffed to a bar to keep your legs apart."

He stood as he spoke, circling the room, watching her as if envisioning what his words described.

"A crop is very visual, so I would leave your eyes uncovered. Then I could circle around you, using the crop to rub up and down your thighs, across your stomach and breasts, until you were even more aroused than you are right now, giving you occasional reminders of what I

234

could do with the handle. I would ask you questions, and when I got a disrespectful or unsatisfactory answer, a slight flick against your breasts or your sex, or a harder strike against your back or thighs or buttocks, would ensure that you maintained a properly submissive attitude."

Genevieve shuddered. Everything about Derek had changed. All signs of harshness and ill temper had melted away. His eyes seemed to glow with raw desire. Even his voice had changed, becoming rich and seductive, his movements fluid and cat-like.

"Are you aroused by what I just described, Genevieve? Answer me truthfully."

"Yes," she gasped.

"Good girl. I can continue—you just need to ask."

She swallowed, her voice suddenly gone. "Please."

"Please what?'

"Please continue," she said, mesmerized.

He smiled, running his fingers through her hair. She squeezed her eyes closed, wondering if one could die of lust.

"One morning I would open your box and find something very special indeed, and before I'd even unlocked the chains that bound you to our bed, I would dangle it before you. It would not appear much, just a small ball with leather straps that buckled, but even before you knew what it was for, you would see in my eyes that I was going to demand the most complete submission from you yet.

"As soon as you'd eaten your breakfast, I would order you to kneel before me and hold open your mouth. I would place the ball in your mouth and then buckle the strap tightly around your head, making it impossible for you to speak. And then, Genevieve, I would send you about your usual activities. You would walk in the garden alone, read in your sitting room with no one to see or stop you, and yet you wouldn't touch the gag, because I had forbidden it.

"At various times during the day you would hear a bell ring warning you to kneel down and keep your eyes lowered. Someone you couldn't see would come and tie a blindfold over your eyes and bind your hands behind you. Only then would the gag be removed so that an unknown hand could give you water or food. You would not be allowed to say a single word then or face three more days wearing the gag. When you'd had your water and food, the gag would be replaced, your hands released and the blindfold removed. Again you would keep your eyes strictly before you, knowing that you would never learn who was the one who had just fed you.

"Finally after an entire day wearing it, you would kneel before me in your nightdress, and I would remove it and put it back in your heartwood box, safe for the next time I chose that you wear it. And every second of that day, every time you yearned to speak but couldn't, you would remember that it was my will that you remain silent, and even though you would sob and curse me for putting you through this, the very act of submitting to it would drive you mad with desire."

"You're wrong...." Genevieve swallowed, trying to find her voice, as if just his words could take it away. "I would never desire something like that—I would never do it."

He looked at her with something like wonder. "That's the thing, Genevieve, you wouldn't resist—you couldn't. The pleasure of submitting would be too intense, too intoxicating. You wouldn't fight it at all."

Tears started falling liberally. She felt the lure of his words. She hated him for it, hated herself, but he spoke the truth. The idea of submitting to him like that caused a highly volatile mixture of helplessness, intense misery, and even more intense desire.

"You do know why you've been baiting me, don't you?" he said in that same seductive tone. "You wish me to punish you—more than wish, you need it."

Why wasn't she yelling "no"? But the pull was indescribable.

Gently stroking her hair, he said, "It's all right, Genevieve. I know this is new to you. You don't yet understand these feelings."

"No," she choked. "You're wrong."

"Am I?" He reached behind her, unlocked the chain, and released her hands. "Lie over the end of the cot, angel."

"Derek please...."

"You have been extremely disobedient," he said. "You will not stop baiting me until you have accepted punishment for it. When I am finished, you will kneel and apologize and then give your promise never to leave the house without someone to accompany you."

Genevieve would never understand why she obeyed. She had no sense that her mind had agreed to this outrage, but her body was acting outside her conscious control. Derek pulled the cot away from the wall and then nodded for her to put herself over the edge. Tears were streaming down her face as she heaved herself on.

Her instinct was to curl up on the bed, but Derek gently corrected her. "Too far. Slide down so your buttocks are right at the edge. The cot is low enough for your knees to rest on the floor."

Her face was broiling, but she obeyed, pushing herself down with her arms until her knees reached the floor where he'd placed a thick cushion.

"Genevieve, you won't be able to hold still—I'm going to tie you down so you can't move at all. Do you understand?"

She was past wondering why she would obey him, but her body relaxed as he pulled both of her arms over her head and attached something to the wrist cuffs that held them taut. Next he pulled her dress up above her waist and tucked it in. That aroused a weak protest, but he soothed her and gently commanded her to lie still. A thick leather strap went around her waist, binding her tightly to the cot. Her upper body was completely immobilized, and she could see little of what he was doing.

He moved behind her then, causing her to cry out in fear, but he rubbed her back gently. "I still have to bind your legs. I will tell you before I start."

He buckled what felt like more cuffs around each of her thighs and a moment later pulled the right one very tightly against the leg of the cot, followed by the left one. Derek let out an audible growl as he finished. She was aware that she was indecently splayed before him, but the rational existence where she worried about such things had become hazy and distant.

"Genevieve, it's obvious my earlier spankings were not enough for you. This time I'm going to give you a real punishment, using the paddle. As it is your first time, I will not make you count. If at any time you absolutely can't bear it, say the word 'parole,' and I will stop completely. Do you understand?"

She couldn't answer.

"Genevieve," he said in his iron tone. "What word must you say to make me stop?"

"Parole," she murmured, though she had no understanding of how she'd answered.

A smooth wooden object brushed over her rear, the sensation pleasant, soothing. Then it moved away again. She couldn't help tensing. There was an explosive crack, which she vaguely recognized was the sound of him hitting her body.

"One," he said.

It took her a moment to take in the pain—it was much worse than the night before. So very much worse! She'd no idea physical pain like that existed.

He hit again. "Two."

It was even harder! How was that possible?

"Three." Only three!

Finally her mind caught up enough to produce a guttural scream.

"If you need me to stop, you know what you must say," Derek said, his voice eerily calm.

"Four... five... six... seven," followed rapidly.

With each blow, she determined to say the word, but what came out was only a long howl.

"Thirteen... fourteen... fifteen...."

Finally, she heard him say, "That is twenty."

It was over—thank Titania. She couldn't possibly bear any more.

But then he said, "Do you wish me to stop?"

To her utter horror, her head shook madly, and she croaked out, "No!"

Her speech had failed her when she needed to say the word "parole," but not to tell him to continue! It was no longer in doubt: she really was possessed by a demon!

"Twenty more," Derek rasped. "You need only say the word and I will stop."

Twenty more. The idea was staggering, impossible. She could not possibly endure it, but as he kept hitting, she felt herself sinking deeper and deeper away from the part of herself that was capable of telling him to stop.

The pain had transformed itself into a blossoming, fragrant vine that slipped through her body, filling every part of her with its heady incense. There was nowhere it couldn't go: its roots clawed their way through the packed soil that had long buried those hidden spots of anguish and guilt deep within her. The two pains, one familiar and stagnant, the other new and volatile, meshed and melted together, growing into something fresh and fascinating and vital.

She realized her hands and legs were unbound—he'd stopped. There was nothing but his hand rubbing the back of her neck almost... affectionately and the harsh sound of his breathing.

Then Derek let out a loud curse, and a bunch of things happened. He pushed her onto the cot on her side and then piled blankets onto her until she was weighted down. Not satisfied, he yanked her dress off and pulled her against his bare chest, rubbing her arms, blowing under the blankets. His skin was so hot it burned hers. He must have a fever. It was only then that she realized her teeth were chattering.

"Damn it, Genevieve! Why didn't you stop me?"

The question struck her as silly: he was the one who'd pounded the power of lucid thought from her. "Do you still want the promise?" She'd meant to sound arch, but her words slurred so much she sounded drunk. "Fine," she giggled. "I promise—I won't ever leave without permission. Is that what you want?" When he said nothing, she whispered, "Derek?"

Still nothing.

Right now the pain was muffled and distant, but in a very short time, it would utterly take over. What was she to do with it? Was he really going to leave her alone with it?

Suddenly her beautiful blossoming vine was seized by a toxic, stinking blight of fear. "Derek," she screamed again. "You really do hate me, don't you?"

He clutched her tightly. "Genevieve, angel, hush. Never say that."

"You do," she rasped, her mouth dry. "I thought you wanted it. Gods! I never meant to make you so angry!"

"Genevieve, stop!" He shook her. "I—I could never hate you. You are so beautiful to me—so precious. I have never desired any woman like I desire you. You provoke me to madness! Don't cry, angel."

He began kissing her eyes, her forehead, her neck. When his lips touched hers, she instinctively opened her mouth and reached for him with her tongue. She could feel the shudder ripple through his body. He gripped her harder and plunged his tongue in.

He wasn't wearing a shirt so the blistering heat of his chest burned against her breasts, causing her to arch back. His rigid arousal throbbed against her, maddening her with lust. The pleasure was too intense. It muffled the pain for now, and she instinctively grabbed at it, pushing her hips against his desperately. "Angel.... If you do that.... Gods, Genevieve, forgive me."

Suddenly Derek shifted her body down and lifted her right leg, resting it on his hip. A moment later he slid inside her. "Stay with me, angel, let me help you," he said, and then he began thrusting.

It took mere seconds for her to climax violently. But instead of peaking and waning, the orgasm didn't fade. It made a mocking little dip and immediately began to build again.

It was too much. "Not again, Derek, I can't," she pleaded.

"You took the pain, you will take this," he growled.

"No, I can't, please," she wailed, trying to push away from him.

"You can."

He gripped her hair and yanked her head back, kissing her throat, all the time pumping urgently into her. Though she fought it, the tension was building inexorably, and to her addled mind, her unwillingness only added to the intensity.

"Now angel, come again for me," he ordered savagely. The second climax struck sharp and invasive—glittering shards of pleasurable pain like broken glass. Derek kept pace with her, driving into her convulsively, until he let out one short grunt that managed to hold a lifetime's worth of desire in it.

The tears came the moment he stopped moving. First as a gentle rain, but quickly building to a storm of hoarse, wracking shudders. Derek gripped her, kissing her, murmuring words that soothed but conveyed no meaning to her at all. The door that held back the pain was suddenly ripped from its hinges, and the teasing trickle exploded into a raging river.

For the moment it drove everything else before it, but she was forgetting something crucial and when she remembered it, this river of pain would be nothing to the ocean that would drown her.

Chapter Twenty-two

Genevieve sank afterwards into a strange oblivion where the pain left everything, even itself, vague and indistinct. Her only anchor to solid reality was Derek. If he'd left her alone, she might have floated off into some inaccessible place of pure anguish, but he never left her, never moved except for the gentle rhythm of his breathing, the caress of his hand on her head, with occasional gentle kisses on her forehead. Her brain latched on to his scent of bracing cedar mixed with a hint of homely nutmeg—how fitting that Derek would smell like winter.

She felt nothing but affection for him, except at one point when he tried to get her to drink something cold. Any motion was painful and she slapped feebly at him.

Seconds, minutes, hours—she'd no clue how much time passed until something interrupted them, which she vaguely recognized was catastrophic. A cheerful voice from up in the darkness called down, "You two killed each other yet?" It was Donal. "If you haven't then it's safe to come up. Damian obliterated the Reavers! I knew he was good, but this was bloody genius. They won't bounce back from this any time soon. Derek, if you had seen him, I swear...."

Genevieve couldn't listen to anything more about Damian's victory. It was all she could do to keep from shattering. She remained passive as Derek carefully sat her up, pulled her dress over her head, and put her stockings and boots on. His face was grim, even more than usual, but he was infinitely gentle as he helped her stand and guided her over to the ladder. Walking was difficult, but somehow she managed to lift one leg up to the first rung and then push to bring her second leg up.

After that, the pain caught up with her again, and it was excruciating. She began shaking and sweating, worried she might be sick. She couldn't imagine how she could possibly climb another rung. Derek nuzzled her back gently. "Let me help you, angel—stay still."

He lifted her by the underarms, raising her two more rungs, and then climbed up behind her. Lifting her without the floor to give him leverage proved far trickier. He wrapped his left arm around her waist and pulled himself up another rung. But unlike her underarms, the pressure on her waist pulled directly at the welts, and she cried out. Derek quickly pushed her up four more rungs, realizing there was no way to do this without causing her agony.

When they were close to the top, he called up, "You must pull her up—she's hurt."

Arms reached for her, easily lifting her out into blinding sunshine. Genevieve could do nothing but stand there, clutching her sides, trying to will herself to think clearly again. Suddenly someone was moving rapidly, threateningly towards her, and she instinctively shrank. Damian was before her, gripping her chin hard. She closed her eyes, trying to push away the piece of information that had gotten lost in the pain. He gripped her shoulder to turn her and then yanked up the back of her dress.

And then he let out a roar of rage and launched himself at Derek.

Genevieve had once seen two mastiffs attack each other. The dogs had fought so savagely, the helpless humans watching could do nothing to stop the battle until one was dead, the other mortally wounded. Derek and Damian's fight was every bit as ferocious. Damian looked insane with rage, while Derek appeared almost feral. Though they fought without weapons, their clash was so fast and violent, it was more than her brain could handle. She fell to her knees and let out a keening wail, tearing her hair. Breathing became difficult.

Before she fell over, strong arms gripped her—Donal again!

He nuzzled her cheek. "Genevieve, stay with me, sweetheart. Please, it's not your fault. Declan is here, he'll sort this out."

Declan!

She let out a piercing shriek. He would kill her; he should kill her. She'd destroyed his family. Stars seemed to cascade over her vision, and everything went dim.

Some time later, consciousness returned. Genevieve was leaning against Donal, who was holding something to her lips. She drank down a sweet liquid that tasted of herbs and sunshine. She knew instinctively that it was no human drink. A strange muffled calm flowed over her—as if she were hidden in the innermost part of a large stone house while a terrific storm raged outside. They were speaking around her.

Declan said, "Show me," and then her dress flashed up and down. Just the air brushing against her backside made her wince in agony. Declan said, "I take it you have nothing to treat that?"

Derek answered, "No sire."

"Unbelievable! Sire!" It was Damian. She'd never heard him like that—his voice was shaking with fury.

"Walk to the edge of the trees now!" snapped Declan. "Both of you!"

Declan turned back to her and gave her a kind smile. "Genevieve, listen to me, little one," he said softly. "No one is angry at you. You've done nothing wrong."

She felt laughter bubbling up inside of her. Nothing wrong except cheating on her husband with his own brother less than a week after her marriage. Could there be a greater monster?

"Talk to her, Donal. Don't stop. Get her to finish the draft and see if you can get her promise to do nothing rash."

Donal kissed her forehead. "You mad girl. I swear on Titania's name that we will get this sorted."

The tears started flowing then. Genevieve wanted desperately to cling to his kindness, but there was no part of her that felt she deserved it. Donal held the cup to her lips again. "Time to drink, little sister. That's right, all of it."

When she'd finished, he kissed her nose. He was smiling. He had a glorious smile.

"I'm sure you don't want to hear this right now, Genevieve, but after spending my life going without dessert, being cursed as the devil's own get, and being thrashed daily by my brothers or Declan, *I* am overjoyed that at last there is someone else in the family who causes trouble. Damian is far too responsible, and Derek... well...

thanks to the oversized stick up his rear end, he never broke a single rule during his entire childhood.

"I never imagined one little sister could wreak such havoc—truly you are a miracle! Though I must say, you are still but an imp in training as it were. Fortunately, I am currently at liberty and would be happy to act as tutor. If we joined forces, I have no doubt within a fortnight we could get up enough mayhem to drive everyone in the house stark raving mad."

Genevieve let out a weak giggle. He was truly mad.

"But in return for my help, I must have a promise from you." His tone had gentled. "Genevieve, swear to me you won't try to hurt yourself over this. Please, sweetheart."

Beneath his smile, she could see his concern.

"Please," he whispered, clutching her to him.

Somehow she couldn't refuse him.

"I swear," she said sleepily, feeling the draft take over.

Declan watched as Donal miraculously managed to coax a promise from his new daughter and felt a tiny wisp of hope in what was otherwise a complete disaster. He hated that she felt such fear of him. Though Declan would never touch her, had never touched any woman since his beloved wife's death centuries ago, he understood it.

This strange, extraordinary girl was like a divining rod when it came to the men of his family. Some part of her instinctively sensed the needs that drove them, needs that found an all-too-fertile ground within her. He would never lay a finger on her, but she saw him as head of the family, and that dark corner of her soul that believed she deserved the harshest imaginable punishments fixed on him.

He whistled for Nightshade. Donal stood with Genevieve in his arms. He passed her to Declan and then mounted the horse.

Damn Derek for a fool. He couldn't even seat Genevieve on the horse without putting her in danger of ripping open the welts and risking a serious infection. Instead he gently laid her over the front of the saddle on her stomach. He gripped Donal's arm. "I know she gave her promise, but do not leave her for any reason—not for so much as a second."

Declan watched as the import of his words sank in.

"I would go so far as to advise you to keep her in your arms. Follow your instincts, *anything* she needs to find comfort in this, you will give to her. Until your brothers resolve this quarrel, she must be able to rely on you. You can save this, Donal."

He'd never seen this youngest, happiest of his sons appear so sober. Donal nodded and nudged Nightshade into motion.

That settled, Declan could turn his full anger on the two sons who deserved it. Both had been chastened enough by Genevieve's misery to end their brawl, but Damian seethed with rage. "Why have you sent her away?" he demanded. "I should be with her!"

"You will not go near her until you have mastered your anger. Whatever Derek's sins, it was your rage at him that pushed her over the edge!" Declan turned to Derek. "How far did it go?" For the first time in his life, this most rigidly honor-bound of his sons couldn't face him. "Was there intercourse?" he demanded. Derek nodded.

Damian attacked again and Derek, never one to tamely take a blow, struck back just as savagely.

"Enough!" Declan roared. Thankfully, his word was still enough to separate them. "Whatever anger, guilt, injury either of you thinks you feel is nothing, *nothing* to what Genevieve will experience. The moment she awakens she will begin lashing herself, taking on all of the blame for this fiasco. Is that your will, Damian? Because if you cannot forgive Derek, she will never forgive herself. She would not be the first bride to break under the needs of the men of my family." Both sons were properly sobered by this. "Derek, you owe an explanation for this."

"I gave her a word. She understood I would stop the moment she wished. When I asked if she wished to continue, she said yes."

"So it is her fault, then!" Damian sneered. "Unbelievable."

"I did not mean to excuse myself at her expense, sire." It was the closest to contrite he'd ever heard Derek.

"I should hope not," Declan retorted. "I had actually warned your brother that you would find it difficult to resist punishing her if she provoked you, but I never expected to find a young woman completely inexperienced in rougher forms of play in such a condition."

Derek looked stricken. "I did not realize she had gone so deep. I was sure she would stop me."

Declan alone knew what it cost Derek to say that. It was a hideous failure, unforgivable except that Genevieve would be far more damaged if this rupture could not be repaired.

"And afterwards, when you saw how far you'd gone, you discovered that you could not punish her like that, fulfill one need, only to deny another that was equally great. That she must have evidence that she was deeply desired and cherished by you." Derek nodded. "Damian, you will find this hard to believe. I ask you to trust me. Derek's injury in this was to you, not Genevieve."

"Sire, did you see her?"

"I did. It's the kind of mistake that must first be made in order to be prevented. Neither Derek nor Genevieve understood the need for limits until they were crossed. I sympathize with your reaction, though I deplore your brawling in front of her. No man could sit quiet when his beloved was in such a state. But that state means something entirely different to Genevieve. As I said, the true injury was to you. Derek trampled your prerogative. Brother must defer to husband in matters regarding his bride. The rules are there to prevent exactly this situation." Turning to Derek, Declan said, "Knowing you as I do, I cannot imagine were your positions reversed that you would react tamely if Damian had seduced or punished your bride without your permission."

All three of them knew that Derek would have reacted far more violently than Damian had.

Declan paused to make sure they had followed him this far. "Damian, all things being equal, it is the husband's right to refuse contact, and I would sympathize should you wish to now."

Derek's eyes blazed at this.

"However," Declan added sternly, "all things are not equal. You are a Black. Your bride's needs always come first, and she has made her wishes clear. It falls to you now to accept her decision. This is my decree: you and Derek will lead the hunt for the stragglers. Talk, fight it out, do whatever is necessary. But make no mistake. You will return together, at peace, prepared to put her needs first, or do not return at all. In the meantime, I will do everything I can to make sure that she weathers this crisis. Be warned that I instructed Donal to hold nothing back, to give her anything she needs to find comfort including physical affection. The time when you could object has passed. Now go!"

Damian looked furious while Derek glowered defensively, but both bent to one knee.

"As you will, sire," Damian said bitterly.

Derek made a curt nod, and both left the clearing together.

Chapter Twenty-three

When Genevieve awoke, she was lying on her side with the bright sun on her face, a pair of masculine arms wrapped around her. For a moment it seemed like the past two days had all just been a nightmare, but she could not keep back reality for long.

The first thing she noticed was the scent was wrong. Instead of Damian's sultry oakmoss, the scent was of summer: cut grass, thyme, violets, fresh earth.

She opened her eyes to discover that she was not in her bed at all, but on the daybed in the conservatory, though she was wearing only a thin nightdress! She turned over and saw that the arms did not belong to Damian, but to Donal, who was lying shirtless next to her, wearing a pair of loose linen trousers like those that Damian favored. He was smiling. "Fever's broken! You had us worried, little girl."

She tried to edge away, but the moment she moved, she was lashed by pain—it was from Derek's spanking. The full horror fell upon her in a swoop: she was an adulteress, she'd deceived Damian with his own brother, no doubt Declan was on his way here to....

She couldn't bear to think further.

She realized Donal was speaking to her. "Genevieve, listen to me. No one is angry with you. You've done nothing wrong."

She let out a loud wail. "I betrayed Damian."

"Hush, darling. Don't say that—you didn't betray him."

Now she was just angry. "You're not listening! I... Derek...." She couldn't bear to say the words.

"No, Genevieve, *you* are not listening."

She snapped to attention—apparently it was not only his brothers who employed that iron tone.

"Within our family, we do not consider it adultery for the bride to be intimate with her husband's brothers."

Genevieve was silenced. It must be nonsense. She'd never heard anything so outlandish. Donal was trying to make her feel better, just like her parents used to. Perhaps they feared she might harm herself. "You needn't lie to me," she said finally.

"I am not lying to you, Genevieve. I swear it upon Titania's name. But if you require further proof, I am more than happy to give it to you."

He rolled her over on top of him, gripped her hair, and kissed her deeply.

"Are you ready to listen now? You know that only one of us can marry. It does not happen in every generation, but it is considered a special blessing if the bride is drawn to her husband's brothers."

It took several minutes for the use of speech to return. When it finally did, she said shakily, "That's insane."

"Isn't it? Completely and utterly insane, but honestly, Genevieve, you've spent time with my brothers. Did you really believe them sane?"

"But that couldn't be... you don't.... That's wrong," she said lamely.

"You mean morally?" Donal looked utterly struck by the notion. "Morally wrong! Well!" He pretended to ponder and then said earnestly, "I should hope so! Honestly, Jenny-girl, moral sex! Where's the point in that?"

He was too absurd.

"Are you going to start crying again?" he asked with boyish alarm. "Lords of hell, I never realized how much girls cry! I thought you might shrivel up with all that liquid pouring from your eyes. Finally I had to dunk you in the tub. Normally you're pretty enough, I own, but all that sobbing has made your face blotch something awful."

Now she punched his arm.

"That's my girl." He chucked her chin and got to his feet. There was a pitcher of water with lemon slices on the table, which had already been laid for breakfast. He poured a glass and brought it to her. She tried to sit up

259

but groaned in pain. Her entire backside still ached from Derek's beating.

"Tsk. It's worn off already. On your stomach! Now, little girl," he commanded.

Genevieve obeyed instinctively, feeling that familiar squeezing between her legs. Before she could stop him, Donal flipped up her gown, placing his knee on her back so she couldn't roll away. She protested in outrage as he started lathering her buttocks with ointment, but her protests quickly transformed into satisfied moans as the pain disappeared, leaving a pleasing tingle.

As he rubbed he said, "While I've got you in this vulnerable position, I would remind you that you made me a promise yesterday. Do you recall it?"

"Yes!" she said through grated teeth. She'd promised not to hurt herself.

"Good, because I will hold you to it, and if you even think of breaking your word, I would be happy to go to work on this lovely ass of yours." He gave her a roguish wink as he helped her up.

Genevieve thought about dumping her water glass over his head, but settled for sticking her tongue out at him, which just brought out that glorious smile of his.

"There's my girl. I take it you're hungry? I promise, no tongue, *for now.*" He gave her a lewd wink. Incorrigible! "Instead, we have coddled eggs, Roderick's special sausage pasties, and of course, fresh cherries! But I assume you're in dire need of a piss first."

She smirked—no one would ever accuse Donal of an excess of delicacy. When she stumbled trying to walk, he swung her up in his arms and carried her to the small water closet off the anteroom. "Should I help?" he asked hopefully. She slammed the door shut in response. "Spoilsport!" he called through the door.

Honestly!

When she was done, he was waiting outside, looking for all the world like a dirty-minded little boy who'd been peeping through the keyhole of his sister's door. Genevieve didn't have the energy to become offended at such nonsense and didn't object to his arm when he helped her back to the conservatory. She was truly famished and loaded her plate with two pasties and an egg, saving the cherries for dessert.

"Good girl—you need to eat. Talk about pasty—you look half-dead," Donal observed as they both dug in.

"I've spent most of the last week locked in my bedroom or in a cave," she said over a mouthful. Good manners were wasted on this brother.

He had the gall to laugh. "Be honest! You were a pale thing the day I met you." That was true enough. Too many days spent hiding in her room. "It's a good thing that I've decided you're to spend the day in the garden."

"You've decided, have you?"

"Oh yes—Declan has put me in charge of getting you better, so now it's my turn to lord it over our bride. I advise you not to disobey me, Jenny-girl, lest I take a page from my brothers and chain you to the bed or take you over my knee."

He rubbed his hands together and made a wicked-sounding cackle. He was so ridiculous, it was impossible to get annoyed with him. Even her old hated nickname didn't bother her. Indeed, for some reason she liked it when Donal called her that.

The daybed turned out to have wheels, which Genevieve thought very clever. Donal dragged it out to a spot in the garden that was warm but not right in the sun and then gave her a little push onto the bed. "Go on then, you're tottering on your feet."

He made two more trips, fetching a small table, the cherries, and the pitcher of lemon-water, and then without waiting for an invitation joined her on the daybed, his body flush against hers.

Donal's well-timed humor had eased the first wave of remorse, but sitting in the garden, Genevieve was assailed by memories of that perfect morning she and Damian had spent chatting and joking on the grass. She tried desperately to hold back the tears and then rolled to her side hoping Donal wouldn't realize.

Donal just chuckled and said, "I don't think so, little girl," and pulled her to lie against his shoulder. She cried as quietly as she could, but soon her body was shaking with sobs. After the first wave of misery tapered off, he said evenly, "Are you done?"

"For now," she sniffled. "I'm surprised you didn't run for the hills. I must look a fright."

"Hideous," he responded amiably.

Miserable as she was, she took comfort lying in his arms. Donal didn't seem eager to judge her, and he didn't pity her either, which would have been intolerable. She found the teasing way he treated her agonies infinitely more soothing than her poor mother's anxious queries of what she could do to help or her father's desperate promises that they would fix what was wrong.

"You and I are going to figure all of this out," he said cheerfully, raising the back of the daybed so it became a lounge chair. He placed the basket of cherries between them to nibble on. "Let's start with Damian. What happened that last day?"

Genevieve wasn't sure whether it was trust or desperation, but between bites of the cherries she found herself describing how she and Damian had lain out on the lawn while Damian told her all about their childhood, being raised by Declan, and Donal's stealing tarts only to get pounded by Roderick the cook. "I wanted to tell him I loved him, but I was too afraid, and then directly after we had this dreadful quarrel."

"And he tied you to the bed. I'm sure you must have done something truly wicked and disobedient—at least I hope you did." He plopped a cherry in her mouth, looking absurdly eager to hear the details.

She spat out the pit, thinking of the reason for their fight, and irritation finally began making some headway against guilt.

"Our quarrel. Well, you must understand. That visit to the garden was the first time he'd allowed me to leave the bedroom. It took me some time to notice that this house is designed as a luxurious prison, without any discernible exit. When I remarked on this, Damian saw fit to *decree* that I was forbidden to leave the house without a minder. And when I voiced an objection, he carried me upstairs and tied me to our bed." Donal looked ready to explode with laughter. "You believe I was wrong?" she asked, ready to explode herself and then grab the pitcher of water and dump it over his head.

"No, of course not. It's outrageous," he said.

He must have noticed her eying the pitcher because he picked it up, poured them each a glass of water, and then replaced it safely on his side of the lounge-chair.

"Well at least one of you is halfway sane," she said frostily, taking a sip. "Derek asked me the same thing, and when I told him, he informed me I should be *grateful* that Damian was so *lenient*. If I were his wife, I'd only be allowed to leave the house one day a year—for Titania's Feast."

Donal had been taking a sip at that moment and spat out the water, howling with laughter. "Oh, that's priceless. Did he say this before or after he pummeled you?"

Genevieve wondered to hear such things spoken of so openly, but Donal made it seem a matter of course. "Before!" she said, trying to glare at him, but finding the corners of her mouth turning up in spite of herself.

"Lord, Derek the smooth-tongued seducer," he said, feeding her another cherry. "First he force-feeds you a food you hate, then he boasts that he'll keep you locked up for life. I always wondered how our middle brother would go about wooing a woman."

She giggled then—it was too ridiculous.

"Sweetheart, I don't deny he's a complete beast, but I know Derek—he never would have continued if you'd told him to stop. Declan told me he confirmed as much. That backside of yours is a bloody mess. With any other woman, I'd have worried you were afraid, but having seen you stare down my brother, I just don't believe it."

Genevieve blushed so deeply she wondered blood didn't pour out of her ears. "I wasn't afraid." She was afraid of what she felt for Derek, but not of Derek himself.

"You wanted it then—you enjoyed it?"

"Enjoyed it!"

"Some people enjoy it. If you didn't, why on earth didn't you stop him?"

"I don't know.... I don't know why I didn't," she cried, tears threatening again.

"That's what we're trying to figure out here, Jenny-girl. Let's put it this way: are you angry with Derek? Do you never want to see him again, or are you eagerly looking forward to the next time he takes you in hand, as it were?"

"How can you even suggest that? Damian will never forgive me as it is!"

He leaned over and affectionately brushed her cheek. "Genevieve, do you trust me?"

She laughed through the sobs. "I don't know—should I?"

"Yes. I swear it on Titania's name," he said with rare seriousness. "So trust this: Damian does not forgive you." Before she could choke, he added, "He does not because he is well aware that he has no right whatsoever to be angry at you. He is angry at Derek. You see, by our rules, Damian is the husband, which means he gets to play lord and master over you and the rest of us. Derek must have Damian's permission before he can put his you-know-what, you-know-where, let alone beat your other you-know-what black and blue."

"Donal," she said impatiently, throwing a cherry at him

"Don't blame me for getting so excited," he said, throwing it back at her. "Finally, my two law-abiding brothers were the ones who got in trouble instead of me. I was hoping Declan would thrash both of them, but he contented himself with sending them away to thrash each other and kill demons instead."

"Why was he angry at Damian?"

"Because he made such a fuss, of course! Talk about tantrums. I don't blame Damian for wanting to thrash Derek, whom I've yearned to pummel for years, but he had no business doing it in front of you and making you think that you were to blame, which you weren't."

"It makes no sense. I'm the one guilty of infidelity."

"We've already established that you are a fiendish vixen guilty of murdering puppies and causing floods in the Indies, but *infidelity*? Jenny-girl, you might say that the motto of the Black family is '*what's another brother....*' So that brings us back, at long last, to the question we started with: do you want Derek to come back?" He stopped her before she could interrupt. "Assuming that Damian and Derek work everything out, and Damian is completely in accord with the *'what's another brother'* plan, how do you feel about Derek?"

"Of course I want him to come back," she said, her voice breaking. Donal searched her face as if trying to make sure she was sincere. "I'm not mad at Derek—what happened wasn't his fault."

"That's an absurd thing to say, little girl. But I am very glad to hear you're not angry with him. Genevieve," he said more cautiously, "you realize that if he does come back, this will happen again. You two are like a tinderbox. I could tell at that picnic that he was already within a hair of taking you over his knee, and he'd barely known you an hour. Then at the wedding, the moment you and he started dancing—well, let's just say, Derek's palms were itching something fierce to get at that ass of yours."

Genevieve slapped at him, her face burning with mortification.

He must have read something in her expression because he kissed her forehead and said, "You are a very special girl, and Derek is a lucky bastard. Anyone else would have shown him the door for what he did." He ran his fingers lightly through her hair. "So that only leaves your quarrel with Damian, and in that you were entirely to blame."

"I beg your pardon!"

"Beg away, Jenny-girl. This could all have been avoided if you'd been halfway clever about it. I speak as someone who spent most of his childhood being sent to his room. The great thing about people locking you up is then they think they know where you are. All you have to do is stand with your hands folded and say sweetly, 'Yes of course, Damian, whatever you say.' Then, once he thinks you are safely locked away, your accomplice sneaks you out, and voila, freedom!"

"And I suppose you are offering your services as accomplice?"

The rogue actually ran his eyes up and down her figure, coming to rest at her bosom. She was well aware that he'd selected the nightdress she was wearing. Though not as indecent as the one Damian had chosen for her, this was made of a lightweight lawn, suitable for the summer months, the thin fabric not quite transparent, but close. The dress also made it obvious that she was wearing no undergarments at all.

"Jenny-girl, if you took my cock in your mouth, you'd never need fear a locked door again."

Genevieve's eyes blazed. "You scoundrel! How dare you say that to me!"

"I never claimed to be anything else. You're the one who went all on about morality. Can you blame me for trying?" he said in a wounded tone. "Blame those blasted cherries. I was trying to torture Damian, but since then I've been able to think of nothing else but how I might get you on your knees before me!"

She took a shaky breath—she couldn't help imagining it as well, and the picture roused an intense lust. She licked her lips absently. "You'd really want to...." She was too embarrassed to continue.

"I'd really want to... sleep with you? Yes."

The words were spoken in his usual light manner, but the look he gave her was so heated, Genevieve couldn't help believing him sincere. "But you haven't...."

"Is this one of those children's games where you finish each other's sentences? I haven't... eaten squirrel brains... sailed down the Nile... tried to seduce my brother's wife? Actually, I thought I would wait for her to seduce me." Genevieve's jaw dropped. "Don't look so surprised. The truth is, I do fancy you, at least when you're not blotchy and runny-nosed from bawling, but I'm a lazy chap, and I'd prefer that you do the work."

She hit him with the cushion.

"Ouch—careful or no one will seduce anyone."

"You truly want this?"

He glanced down at his member, which was blatantly tenting the thin fabric of his pants. She laughed helplessly. Perhaps it was all as idiotically simple as Donal had said: *what's another brother?* There was a strange sort of logic to it, she supposed, and it accounted for Damian's nervousness when he first broached the topic of his brothers sharing the house with them—and what he'd said about their family trying to root out jealousy.

She met Donal's eye—he smiled mischievously and put his hands beneath his head. "Any time you're ready," he said lazily. "Climb right on. I promise I'll make it worth your while."

Beast! Badly as she wanted him, she wanted to wipe that knowing smirk off his face just as much. She thought of what he'd said—about the picnic—she licked her lips just thinking about it. She gave him a wicked smile and climbed off the daybed and knelt on the grass. "Any time you're ready," she purred.

She was ecstatic to see that she'd caught him off guard. "What are you doing?" he demanded, his voice husky.

"Don't be afraid," she said in a reassuring tone. "I promise I'll make it worth your while."

"Afraid! You little minx! You'd better not be teasing me!" he said, swinging his legs around.

"Try me and find out."

Donal stood up, yanking on the drawstring of his pants and letting them fall. "If you are, I swear I will make you pay."

"Make me pay? What are you nine?" she retorted triumphantly.

He shook his head. "You, you...."

She'd actually rendered him speechless!

However, Genevieve found her confidence wavering as he moved until his... *cock* he called it... was right in her face. She took a shuddery breath. It was still strange looking to her. His was aroused, very aroused. It stuck right up, the rounded end darker, reminding her of a plum.

It was quite large, now that she saw all of it. Really very large, flicking up and down in her face with each of his breaths.

Donal's expression was tense. He'd not been joking when he said he'd dreamt of this. When she didn't move immediately, his eyes narrowed. "You *were*! Jenny-girl, you cannot begin to conceive of how much you are going to regret teasing me."

She was not teasing! There was nothing for it. She put her hands on his hips and moved to catch it... his *cock*... with her mouth. "Gods Genevieve," Donal burst out, sounding astounded.

She was astounded herself—she loved feeling him in her mouth. His skin was silkily smooth, soft at the top but iron hard down the length. She began exploring his shape with her tongue—the sharp rim between the head and the length, the small hole at the very tip, the slight ridge of the vein that ran along the shaft, the brush of hair that just touched her face when she took him deep in her mouth. With each sweep of her tongue, Donal shuddered.

He was already aroused, but she wanted to drive him mad. She tried sucking with her whole mouth. Donal groaned loudly, gripped her head with his hands, and began pulsing into her mouth. "Ah Titania, Genevieve.... You can't.... You need to stop!" he sputtered.

She didn't want to stop—she wanted to push him all the way. She knelt up further, gripping his buttocks so she could move in closer with each of his pulses. She'd never imagined that something like this could be so exciting, but she loved how powerful she felt, loved that she could give him this kind of pleasure.

His thrusts were intensifying, his cock hardening yet more. "Genevieve.... Gods.... You need to stop now!"

She sucked harder, forcing him even deeper into her mouth.

"Damnation, you little minx!"

He let out a savage shout, and her mouth was flooded with thick, salty warmth. She was so startled, she tried to pull away, but he wouldn't let her. "No, you pushed for this. You will take every drop like a good girl."

His words sent a jolt of lust through her entire body, and she had no choice but to obey, swallowing down his release, the sensation strange but not disagreeable. When he'd finished, he pulled out of her mouth and gripped her chin, looking as if he didn't know what to make of her.

"You wicked little vixen! You think you're so clever, driving me to spend in your mouth instead of your sweet sex." He gripped her by the upper arm and pulled her to her feet. "Little did you realize, I am just getting started. On the bed, legs apart, dress up—do it now!"

"Donal!" she cried. They were outside!

"You started this game, little girl. It's my turn, and you are going to pay for your trick. Now get on that bed and spread your legs for me. So help me, Genevieve...."

He moved too quickly for her, tossing her on the bed.

In a more soothing tone, he said, "No one is here, no one can see, on my honor. But this is your last warning. Dress up, legs apart!"

As with his brothers, Genevieve found it impossible to disobey when he was like this. She reached down and pulled her dress up, letting her knees fall apart. She was nervous now—she'd never seen Donal like this.

He moved her legs farther apart and then sat at the end of the daybed, staring right at her exposed sex, making no other move to touch her, which perversely made her more and more aroused.

Abruptly his head was between her legs. Genevieve screamed. His tongue relentlessly explored, penetrated, driving her already simmering desires to a violent boil. He latched onto her bud with his lips, lightly sucking, pushing her rapidly towards a climax. She tensed in readiness, crying out, "Donal, Gods...."

But then he stopped sucking and instead used his tongue to swirl around the bud so lightly it was close to torture. "Donal, what are you doing?" she screamed.

"Revenge is sweet!" he quipped between long licks.

"No! Donal!"

"Beg!" he said, his voice rumbling into her sex, driving her even more insane.

"I'll kill you for this!"

"Not before you beg, though."

He was laughing at her! She'd be damned before she'd begged him. But Donal sensed her resistance. Suddenly his fingers were inside of her, moving in counterpoint to his tongue. She tried to pull away, but he forced her legs over his shoulders and gripped her firmly by the hips with his arms so that she couldn't move at all.

After that she was lost. "Please, Donal!" she cried shamelessly.

"Please what?"

"Please let me come!"

He flicked with his tongue right onto her swollen bud, and her whole body lurched into a hard climax. The spasms hadn't yet died down when he flipped her over onto her stomach and pulled her hips down to the edge of the daybed. She yelled in protest. The last time she'd been in this position, Derek had spanked her mercilessly. But instead Donal thrust into her—from behind! She'd no idea that was possible.

"You are the most provoking... little... vixen," he grunted as he ruthlessly pumped into her.

Then he gripped her hips more tightly and moved backwards without pulling out until her hands rested on the grass. He let go of one hip to push her head and forearms down, which was more comfortable, but made her feel even more vulnerable. And then he started to pound into her. The movement reawakened the pain in her buttocks, but insanely, the sensation was enough to push her into another orgasm. "You're not done," he growled. "One more climax for you."

"No!" she cried out. "Please!"

"Oh yes!" he said. "Thanks to your little trick, we both know I can outlast you."

Then he began lightly rubbing her rear end. She assumed it was by accident that his fingers crept closer to a spot they definitely shouldn't go near. When he did it a second time, she flinched and tried to pull away. Donal gripped her tighter than ever and said, "Oh no you don't." Suddenly a finger was circling the sensitive little hole.

"Donal!" she screamed. "What are you doing?"

"Easy, little girl. Just relax. Don't fight it."

Genevieve was as far as possible from relaxing, but his words and his implacable grip on her hips made clear he would not let her escape this. She screamed madly, unable to fathom the strange sensation. Only one thing was clear to her: she was moving inexorably towards another climax.

Donal was ruthless, swirling around that devastatingly sensitive spot until she climaxed violently a third time. As her whole body wrenched around him, she felt him driving into her until he jerked to a finish himself.

He grabbed her waist and pulled her back against him onto the grass. "I begin to see how my brothers could be driven past endurance by you," he said, squeezing her and kissing her neck. "Are you all right, sweetheart? That wasn't too rough for you, was it?"

"No," she admitted. "You're not so different from them, are you?"

"My brothers? No. Did you think I was?"

"Not really," she said, laughing nervously.

He turned her to face him and rubbed his nose against hers. "It's a lot to take, I know. For better or worse, we are all three of us the descendants of Declan, which means that when you pull tricks like that, be prepared. And I had such plans to give you control. Just goes to show!"

Genevieve rolled her eyes—his plans to give her control amounted to ordering her to climb on top of him. She ran her fingers through his hair, wondering that the three brothers could all look so similar, all share the same nature, and yet be so very different from each other.

What would happen when Damian and Derek returned? If they did?

She tried to hold the tears back. None of this was Donal's fault. He'd done everything he could to make her feel better. Donal was watching her. Thank Titania he didn't appear hurt. "It will be okay, sweetheart. I promise. But in the meantime...." He rolled on top of her and gave her a deep kiss. "I think you are ready for more lessons on the danger of taunting a descendant of Declan."

"You're not serious," Genevieve sputtered.

"Never, *ever* say that to me, Jenny-girl."

Chapter Twenty-four

Genevieve no longer fought anything, tried not to think, and just gave herself over to the closeness she felt for Donal. To her relief, they spent the night in the conservatory again, staying up late watching the stars together in between bouts of lovemaking. She couldn't bear the thought of going back to her room—Damian's room—with matters between them so unsettled.

The more time she spent with Donal, the more affection she felt for him. She'd never in her life known someone with such good spirits—or such impudent humor. It didn't seem like such qualities should accompany patience and generosity, but in Donal they did.

Even more striking was his perceptiveness. She'd noticed it from the beginning, and the more she knew him, the more uncanny his powers seemed to her. She began to suspect that his rude humor served as a camouflage for his keen discernment. She'd not forgotten that a single glimpse of her bedroom at her parents' cottage had been enough to prompt him to order her sitting room painted in her favorite color.

Likewise, the next morning when he asked if she'd like to have a portable tub brought down to the conservatory, he read something in her expression because he kissed her forehead and whispered, "Don't worry, little girl, I'll leave you to bathe in peace."

She'd hardly realized herself what was bothering her until Donal reassured her. The truth was that she'd accepted their intimacy, at least for the time being, but taking a bath with anyone except Damian would feel like a betrayal, and just the idea threw her into a panic.

Donal definitely shared his brothers' despotic tendencies, though he was not quite so obvious about it. Defiance from her didn't provoke him the way it did Damian and Derek, and he didn't seem to share their taste for binding and restraining her. Still, when they did make love, he almost always took her hard from behind, which she was positive was a taste of his—along with her giving him pleasure with her mouth while on her knees. The entire first day he only let her have a skimpy nightdress to wear, and when she asked for a proper dress, told her she was free to take it off if she didn't like it. He did bring her a proper dress the second day, but just laughed when she asked for undergarments.

But whatever contentment she found with Donal could not last. This was nothing more than a strange dream, an interlude like the cave, before her happiness fell to pieces and her life became a nightmare. Donal almost never left her alone, but in those rare moments when he wasn't making love to her, embracing her, or making her laugh, the guilt and the pain would creep back.

No matter what Donal said, she'd hurt Damian. Their family had welcomed her as a blessing, and she'd repaid them by bringing misery. Not that it could surprise her. She'd brought little but misery to her own parents for years—her parents who would have done anything to help her, but were cursed day after day to see her fall further into wretchedness.

She wasn't sure how much Donal guessed of her state, but she suspected he was aware of it, though thankfully he didn't press her to talk about it further. But she should have known he wouldn't leave matters alone. She noticed that he'd brought another chair out to their spot in the garden, but she didn't learn the reason until half an hour after breakfast.

Of course, it was Genevieve's luck that Donal was kissing her and had just reached his hand up her skirt, teasingly reminding her of her lack of drawers, when a voice said, "Good morning."

It was Declan! Genevieve prayed she might perish on the spot.

Donal was utterly unperturbed. "Oh you're here early."

She then prayed that Donal would perish—else she would murder him! He'd known Declan was coming and said nothing, and now the Black Prince had practically found them making love! Genevieve was too angry and embarrassed to do more than mumble a greeting.

"I am pleased to see you looking so much better, daughter," Declan said as he took a seat in the free chair. "You have done well, Donal."

The scoundrel laughed and gave a wicked smile. "Thank you. It has truly been a pleasure." He kissed her lightly on the mouth. "I'll leave you two to talk," the traitor added.

"Donal!" She tried to hold on to him, but he scampered out of her reach.

Declan wore the kind smile he always did with her, but today, instead of being reassuring, it only made her feel more guilty. "Sir.... Please... I am so sorry. I didn't mean to cause such trouble."

"There's no need to apologize. Surely Donal explained matters to you. The truth is that I'm the one who owes you an apology. If I had spoken to you earlier, some of your suffering might have been avoided."

This was worse than anything. "Please don't say that, please! I can't bear it." She felt his hand on her chin, raising her to meet his eye.

"Tell me what you think you did, child?" he said gently.

"I don't think, I *know* Damian was hurt by this—by *my* actions."

"Little one, Damian was not the only one who has been hurt—you were hurt by his actions, far more grievously in my opinion." Before she could protest, he said firmly, "Genevieve, the morning following your wedding, I warned Damian that if you and Derek were alone together for any amount of time, something like this would take place."

"What? That can't be." Genevieve was dumfounded.

"I speak the plain truth, daughter, and I blame myself, more than you can know, that I did not speak to you immediately. I chose to wait for several reasons: naturally, our beliefs are strange to you and opposed to what you have been taught. Moreover, though we consider it a blessing if the bride feels an attachment to her husband's brothers, such feelings must never be forced. Any intimacy must be entirely *her* choice. I felt certain that Damian would accept what is between you and Derek, and I still feel certain of it, but he needed time, which thanks to the Reavers was denied us. Though we work hard to stamp out jealousy, it was understandable that he would feel possessive, especially so early in the marriage."

"I was afraid there might be jealousy," Genevieve said. "Damian said it was a great dishonor, but I told him, you can't always control feelings like that, no matter how much you wish you could."

Declan looked surprised. "That was extremely astute. Genevieve, I will speak frankly. Derek is able to give you something that Damian can't—do you understand what I am speaking of?"

She wanted to sink into the ground—Derek had given her pain. What kind of person was she?

"Genevieve! I am well aware that most people are taught to view such desires as shameful. Within our family that is not the case. They are accepted and acknowledged. They are never viewed as subjects of right and wrong, but of need and desire. Insofar as Damian's anger led you to regard those desires as shameful, he committed a grave wrong by the principles of this family."

He spoke so fiercely Genevieve couldn't doubt him. "I don't want you to be angry at him," she said softly.

"Daughter," he said in his gentlest tone, "I promise that my anger against Damian will end the moment I am convinced you no longer blame yourself."

Genevieve almost growled—how could he say such a thing! She felt... angry at Declan. There was a wrongness to his words that made her feel bitter and hateful. He was watching her closely. Perhaps it was for the best. He would realize now that he'd brought a demon into his midst. But then he took her hand in his. "I see you will not make this easy for me. Genevieve, in truth there is one part of your conduct that concerns me very much."

Fear quickly eclipsed every other feeling. Genevieve swallowed, suddenly worried she might faint.

"Genevieve!" he said firmly. "I am not angry at all, I am concerned. Do you understand?"

"Yes, sir," she said, trying to breathe.

"I am concerned that you did not tell Derek to stop."

"It wasn't Derek's fault!" she cried defensively. "He would have stopped if I told him to!"

"Shhh, little one. I know that. Genevieve, I wish to show you something." He held out a bunch of bristles bound together with a leather-covered handle. She could feel sweat beading on her upper lip. It looked innocuous, almost like a short broom, but some part of her recognized that it wasn't innocuous at all.

"It is a scourge. It is used to punish the worst criminals—oath-breakers, traitors, rapists. As you see, the bristles bear sharpened spikes. If it is applied with even minimum force, it flays the skin."

She shuddered—it was gruesome.

"Genevieve, have you ever known anyone who deserved to be punished like that?"

"No!"

"If your friend Sally or some other village girl were to commit adultery, would you argue that she should be tied to a post and punished with this?"

"Of course not!"

"What if she were crushed by guilt and begged for the punishment? What would you say to it?"

"No! We don't stand by and do nothing when people try to take their own lives—it's no different."

"Genevieve, two nights ago when we returned, I found this inside your heartwood box."

The world suddenly turned upside down. Her vision went dark as she struggled to get air into her lungs. The sharp, caustic scent of sal volatile in her nose made her jerk her head up, but she felt as if all the strength had left her body. A cup had somehow appeared in Declan's hand—he held it to her lips and gently ordered her to drink. It was a ginger tisane. The sharp taste miraculously helped clear her head further and settled her stomach.

When she had quieted, he said calmly, "I told you the day we met that you never need fear me, Genevieve. I would never raise my hand to you. Though I always try to respect the contents of the heartwood box, I must draw a line here. Such a punishment goes far beyond what is sane and healthy. Even if you had committed adultery a thousand times, it would be in gross excess."

She wanted to curl up into a ball, to dig a hole and bury herself in the ground, anything to hide from Declan's gaze. What was wrong with her? She was a monster!

"Genevieve! It is time you learned to battle this mode of thinking. Think, child! Use your reason. If Sally begged for such a punishment, would you despise her or would you feel compassion and try to help her see that she did not deserve anything so horrible? Why should I not feel that for you as well?"

Perhaps because it was Declan, his words sank in. They were so sensible she must agree, no matter how much that voracious guilt within her wanted to scoff at them. It was far from defeated. A clamorous inner voice argued, "But that's Sally, she deserves forgiveness." But for the first time in years, that voice did not seem buttressed by all the powers of truth and goodness. The result was confusion, but in this case, confusion was infinitely preferable to certainty.

"It's hard for me," she finally admitted.

"Yes, but I hope with reflection you will be able to make some sense of this need for punishment and distinguish those ways it is safe to indulge and those that are clearly self-destructive."

"I'll try," she said but felt defeated. Just the thought that she should stop blaming herself so much raised an overpowering lash of guilt.

"That's all I ask. Genevieve, that still leaves what happened with Derek. I realize this is difficult, but I truly need to know how you feel about it. Are you angry? Do you feel my son mistreated you?"

"No!" she protested, surprised at her own vehemence. "He didn't—I told you, I know he would have stopped."

"Leaving aside everything to do with Damian, do *you* feel that things went too far?"

She blushed sharply, but she felt like she owed Declan—and Derek—the truth. "No, I don't," she confessed. "With the scourge…. It wasn't just the adultery. I know how much Damian cares about his brothers. I was sure I'd destroyed your family. What happened with Derek…. It's not the same," she finished lamely.

Declan was thoughtful. "Your response is not quite what I imagined it would be, daughter. I still believe Derek should have stopped sooner. Whatever his instincts told him, caution was warranted. It was your first time together, as well as your first time engaging in such rough play—and he most definitely did not have Damian's permission. Nonetheless, I am greatly relieved by what you've told me. I remain concerned about the feelings that prompted the scourge to appear in your box. I would like to suggest something, but I don't wish to offend you or give you the impression I am trying to sway you. I would not be disappointed or displeased at all if you reject it."

"Yes, sir.... Please, I appreciate your scruples—if there is anything you think might help me, I want to hear it."

"I think Derek can provide you a safe outlet for these feelings before they progress to something more self-destructive."

"It doesn't offend me at all, sir," she said sincerely. "I greatly appreciate how frank you've been with me. I just don't want to do anything that would hurt Damian."

"I know my sons, Genevieve. Damian will make peace with this. As I said before, within our family we firmly believe that there is nothing wrong or shameful about these needs. As long as sensible limits are observed, you and Derek should be able to explore this side of your desires. You understand why it must be with Derek?"

She almost chuckled. She did understand. There was something dark and hungry in Derek that made him relish punishing her. Damian had the same look when she was chained to the bed, but never once had she felt that he craved hurting her.

"What about Derek?" she asked.

"What about him?"

"Would it hurt him—to do that for me?"

Declan looked awestruck. "Genevieve, what I would give for you to see yourself as I see you—you have a rare spirit. Your joining this family is the best thing that has ever happened to Derek. I would not suggest it if I

289

thought it would hurt him—if only to protect you from further guilt. In fact, if it were kept within limits, it would satisfy a strong need in him."

"Why—why does he want to hurt me? Is he angry that I'm here?"

To her amazement, Declan looked almost abashed. "That is a complex question, one that I've never answered completely to my satisfaction. The best I can come up with is that there is a deep though dark kind of pleasure that comes from exercising complete dominion over another, challenging them to work through the pain to find the pleasure that hides behind it. I can say emphatically that such acts are not incompatible with deep affection and love. Some unfortunate people are driven to give pain from hatred of the object, but surely you can tell that Derek cares deeply for you. I suspect what happened between you was partly driven by his fear of how strong his feelings are, but the desire to punish and give pain has always been a part of Derek's nature."

Genevieve knew her face was burning as Declan's words reawakened those dark desires she'd first felt in the cave. "This... feeling inside, I used to think it was a demon. It was so ugly, and it made my parents so unhappy. But then with Derek—it was like he knew it was there, but it wasn't ugly to him. He kept calling me angel—I could feel that I'd given him something... I could give him pleasure."

"If you hadn't felt guilt towards Damian, then the experience would have fulfilled something for you?"

Tears started streaming down her face. "It probably sounds foolish to you—I know he and I are so different, but the day I met him, I thought, Derek is like me. He can't control his moods. He knows what it's like to make the people he cares for unhappy."

"Not foolish at all. Does he make you unhappy, Genevieve? Would you be happier if Derek were not in your life?"

"No!" She wanted to say that she loved him—she loved all of them, but she couldn't stand being disloyal to Damian.

"So perhaps the same is true of you," he said softly. "Despite your troubles, your parents are deeply grateful that you are in their life." She gave him a shaky nod. "I think you will find that all of my sons consider the troubles of the past few days a trivial price to pay for the blessing of having you in their life. So the question for you is: can you accept a life where you are intimate with all three of them?"

She forced herself to suppress her embarrassment. That would be a poor return for the respect and sympathy Declan had shown her. "I care for them—I love them," she answered. "I just don't want to hurt Damian—or Derek or Donal."

Genevieve could not mistake the joy that lit up the Fae Prince's otherworldly features. "I swear upon all that's sacred that I would not counsel you to any course that would hurt you or my sons. And make no mistake: you are Damian's wife. His brothers must defer to him and obey the rules he sets in the household. I do not expect you will try to undermine those rules, given how much you've suffered seeing the brothers in conflict."

"No!"

"I would remind you that you too must set limits. It is my sons' nature to try to dominate, but that does not mean you are obliged always to give way. In all marriages there are quarrels and misjudgments, and this is no different. Working through them requires patience and negotiation, but they are crucial if this arrangement is to work."

She smiled to herself, remembering her discussions with Damian. For the first time, she felt something like confidence, rather than a blind hope, that they would be able to talk things out and reconcile.

"It is probably a good thing that you will have another day or so. Derek and Damian are proving stubborn as only two Black males can be. I advise you and Donal to treat this as a holiday and enjoy yourselves as much as possible before you must face those two more... demanding natures."

"Thank you, *Declan*, for everything," she said kissing his cheek.

"Finally, she begins to learn."

Chapter Twenty-five

The field was littered with the bodies of demons and Reavers. They'd managed to cut off the retreating stragglers as they tried to regroup. Damian had lost track of how many he'd killed—for the first time in his life, he'd fought more brutally than Derek. He'd actually grabbed one poor sodding Reaver and crushed his neck with his bare hands until he practically ripped his head off. It was that or rip Derek's head off. Derek had watched him warily but hadn't said a word.

At the end of the battle, Damian ordered their men to gather a huge pile of wood while the two of them silently dragged the bodies to the pyre. As the sun went down, they watched the flame consume them to ash.

Damian was frantic to get home, but he could not even contemplate forgiving Derek while his brother refused to apologize. And since Derek had never in his life apologized for anything, he was trapped. Damian felt like he'd made a hundred thousand allowances for him their entire life, but this time Derek had gone too far. Every time he thought about Genevieve's backside, the way she'd huddled miserably when she exited the cave, he wanted to roar with rage. And then there was the fact that

Derek would have *killed* him if their situations had been reversed—and still, he'd not said a word to him!

In the meantime, Genevieve was home, possibly suffering. Declan had worried she might harm herself! Damian needed to get back to her and reassure her. He'd never dreamt their sire could be guilty of injustice, but how else could he regard Declan's decree? He'd set an impossible condition for their return and then given Genevieve, his wife, over to *Donal*.

"Have you nothing to say to me?" he burst out, too incensed for once to abide by his resolution not to speak before Derek did.

Derek looked at him stonily. "You know what happened—what more should I say?"

"You sodding ass! How about, I apologize for belting your wife and then screwing her."

"I am not sorry for that—you ask me to lie," Derek returned, actually looking offended that Damian would think he would.

Damian couldn't murder him. If he did, he could simply confide Genevieve to Donal's life-long care. He knew his youngest brother's powers of seduction and his taste. He wondered how long it would be before she was on her knees before him, while he sat here with Derek watching demon corpses burn!

He needed to get through to Derek. "For once, Derek! For once! Can't you at least say that you were wrong! Is that too much for you! How could you hurt her like that?"

"You know the answer to this. She already blames herself. Must she endure your blame as well?" The savagery of Derek's anger caught Damian up short. It was more than anger; it was almost disgust. Damian wanted to roar that he blamed Derek, not Genevieve—never Genevieve—but it suddenly occurred to him that for her it might well amount to the same thing.

For the first time he began to wonder what had really happened between the two of them in that cave. He realized he knew that this was not a simple case of a man taking advantage of an inexperienced girl.

He collapsed against a tree, covering his face with his hands. How on earth had his life fallen apart so? Genevieve had looked so vulnerable, so wretched. What if she tried to injure herself? He hated himself for feeling even a moment's jealousy of Donal. Pray Titania Donal did everything in his power to comfort her even if she fell in love with him.

"We quarreled," he said before he could stop himself. "Just before you arrived."

"You feel guilty about that quarrel!" Derek said indignantly. "You were completely in the right! She's your wife—she may leave the house when it pleases you to allow it. If she were mine, that would be once a year!"

Damian laughed at that. What else could he do? Was there another man in existence equal to his brother for sheer gall? "I'm sure that pleased her."

"It should have! She was fortunate you only tied her to the bed!"

"Is that why you punished her?" he grated.

Derek appeared surprised. "Of course not. She's not my wife."

"Well, I'm glad we have that clear!" Damian snapped out. "Since you went ahead and slept with her, I'd wondered if you'd forgotten that fact."

Derek had ever refused to acknowledge sarcasm and only glowered in response. Damian was forced to pull back from his anger, unwilling to walk away now that they were finally talking. "I'm afraid I don't quite understand the distinction you're making, Derek," he said with patently insincere patience.

"You're her husband—you'll discipline her as you see fit. I would never undermine your authority with her." Derek sounded annoyed, as if he were being asked to explain that the sun rises in the east.

Damian wanted to yell, "You just fucked her instead," but he forced himself to suppress his rage. Derek was incapable of even minor prevarication. He meant what he said. He would never deliberately undermine what he saw as Damian's authority as husband.

Damian realized he must try to speak to Derek in an idiom he would understand. "I'm glad to hear that, Derek. And now as husband, I would like to know why you saw fit to discipline my wife." Damian didn't bother erasing the irony from his tone.

"Of course," Derek said with no irony whatsoever. For the first time that Damian could recall, Derek looked uncertain. "From the moment we met, she has not stopped pushing me. She must have sensed how I would react to her defiance. I gave her many warnings, but she only pushed harder. I do not mean to suggest that she consciously sought to provoke me. I know she couldn't help it. But I knew that she wouldn't stop until I gave her what she sought from me. In the end her need was too great—I couldn't resist it."

Genevieve's needs. Damian thought of the heartwood box. When he brought out the crop, she'd almost fainted. She needed something he couldn't give her. The thought was agonizing. Was that why Derek was so angry? "You think she would have been better off with you?"

"What the devil are you thinking?" Derek barked.

"I don't know!" Damian almost wailed, wondering how the conversation had ended up going in such a perverse direction. "I gave her no choice. At the Bridal

Picnic, I pushed until I was sure her box had changed and then rushed the marriage before she could back out. She understood nothing of what it meant to marry me! She said as much when we quarreled—she accused me outright of deceiving her."

Derek spat in disgust. "Listen to yourself! A few angry words spoken during an argument, and you question yourself! She is the bride of a Black! You are her husband—her *master*. You did what you must to secure her to you. Had I been in your place, the moment I knew her box had changed, I would have dragged her from the picnic and tied her to my horse!"

His brother was completely sincere. Damian chuckled humorlessly. What would it have done to the poor Mirans if they'd had Derek for a son-in-law? "If you'd married her, you would not have shared."

"No," Derek said without a hint of apology. "I would honor our traditions in any way I can, but I could never share what is mine."

"And yet you expect me to?"

Derek shrugged. "It's best for our family that she married you and not me." There was his brother's thinking in a nutshell. From Derek's own perspective, his logic was irrefutable.

"So the rules are nothing to you—my rights nothing?"

"I didn't say that, but the bride's needs come before any rule."

"And so you must beat her black and blue and then sleep with her?"

"What would you have me say, Damian? She craves punishment—I wish now I'd understood the extent her craving went beyond a desire for pain. I fear she suffers from some sort of morbid guilt. But I don't think I would have acted differently even if I had known, and once I'd begun, I couldn't turn away from her without far more grievous cruelty. My only regret is that she believed herself guilty of infidelity. If there had been time, I would have tried to explain our ways, though I doubt I could have done it in a way she could understand. I think Donal can explain it better—or if not, Declan."

Damian could not have believed there was anything Derek could say that would lessen his guilt in this, or that he could even contemplate forgiving his brother without a contrite apology—which was as likely as a demon turning healer.

But hearing him, Damian found he understood Derek's perspective and could even accept it, though it irritated him to no end that he must be the one to back down from his anger. Derek's one regret was that Genevieve blamed herself. He felt none towards the brother he had injured. Somehow things had twisted

300

around so much that if Damian pointed this fact out, the complaint would sound like childish carping. One would think Derek was a master of casuistry, when in actuality he was the polar opposite.

Arguably he even owed Derek a debt. Derek could have thrown it in his face that Damian had allowed anger at his brother to come before Genevieve's needs. Must he credit *Derek* with delicacy now? Were pigs flying as well? He recalled what Derek said about how he would have "courted" Genevieve at the Bridal Picnic and decided that there would be no shortage of bacon for the foreseeable future.

So there it was. He could accept his brother's actions in what had been a very fraught situation, but that did not mean that Derek could simply discard centuries of family rules. "I am husband," he said firmly. "You and Donal will abide by our traditions, which means that you do not touch my wife or discipline her without my permission. Don't ask me to overlook such a transgression again."

"I won't," Derek said. There was no challenge, no resentment in his tone at all.

They sat staring at the dying flames as the stars appeared in the sky. Suddenly, he heard Derek's voice from the darkness. "I... regret... I am sorry if my actions caused estrangement between you. I believe now that I was guilty of jealousy—or perhaps covetousness. I did not seek to usurp your place or divide you—I swear it on my honor, Damian. But I was caught off guard by how much I desired her. At the picnic, I tried to provoke her. I thought she would refuse to allow me to share the house. I know it was wrong—my duty is to protect her. Then she agreed anyway.... It was only when she spoke to me afterwards that I realized I'd been guilty of cowardice. I'd never before felt disgust in my own actions, but I'd never even imagined a nature like Genevieve's."

Talk about pigs flying: Damian could not have been more astounded if Derek had sprouted wings and lifted off the ground. He felt he owed his brother to answer in kind. "Genevieve sensed there was jealousy between us— or at least the potential for it. Would that I had taken warning and examined myself more closely."

"Why on earth would you? I always took for granted that if either of you found a bride, she would feel nothing but aversion for me. The very idea that *you* could be jealous of me was too improbable to believe without proof."

In anyone else the words would be ironic or accusatory, but Derek was making a simple statement of fact. There was no self-pity in his manner at all. Until now, Damian had never dreamt that Derek might realize how difficult he was and wish he could be different.

Damian felt something shift within himself, almost like a door opening. His brother's words had made something clear to him: Derek was in love with Genevieve. Was it possible that Genevieve loved Derek, his impossible brother? He knew his wife—she must. She would never have let things go so far if she didn't.

Though he'd never breathed a word of it to anyone, for the last twenty years, Damian had yearned to somehow create a home where his brothers could be safe and happy. He adored Declan, who'd been the best of fathers to them, but of the three, only Damian remembered their mother and could measure what the Reavers had stolen from them.

But as they'd grown older, he'd begun to fear for his dream. Damian had no idea how much of Derek's off-putting behavior was due to the tragedy and how much was simply his natural temperament. Not that it mattered really, but Damian had grown increasingly worried that when the time came, his bride would refuse to allow Derek to share the house with them. And every surly word or unsocial action of Derek's just reinforced that she would be entirely justified.

And then he'd met Genevieve, his miracle of a wife, who hadn't hesitated to welcome Derek—who *loved* Derek. But instead of doing everything he could to nurture his dream, within days of his marriage he'd come close to destroying it. Their house was supposed to be a safe haven for her, but he'd threatened to make it her prison. Even worse, instead of celebrating Genevieve's love for Derek, he'd exploded in a jealous rage.

And yet Derek was right that it was best for all of them that Genevieve had married Damian. Derek would have seen no reason to set limits on the submission he demanded from his wife so long as she was experiencing pleasure. That kind of pleasure could be highly intoxicating, but Damian honestly didn't think it was enough of a life for Genevieve or any woman. And Derek could not have shared her no matter what she wanted. If Donal had married Genevieve, he would have shared her with his brothers, but the situation would have been dangerously volatile. Derek could not have tolerated Donal's contempt for all rules, and the two of them would have constantly been at each other's throats with Genevieve caught in the middle.

They needed Damian if the four of them were to actually form a family. He could only pray that Genevieve and the fates would give him another chance to get it right.

Chapter Twenty-six

To Genevieve's relief, her days of staying locked away in the garden—or the bedroom or cave—appeared to be over. As soon as Declan left, Donal returned holding out her boots and a key. "Before you go on the rampage, I have a little gift by way of apology."

"What gift?" she said suspiciously.

"This is the key that opens the dining room door." He smiled ruefully. "It's yours on one condition. You can't go out on your own, Genevieve." When she frowned, he said gently, "I'm not sure if Damian explained matters, but the truth is that the Reavers would give anything to kill you. They believe if they do, the Black line will end. With us gone, they could seize control of the demon gate, open it permanently. This house is warded with Fae magic, but anywhere else…. Damian defeated this latest push of theirs, but they're like an infestation of bedbugs. No matter how many times you keep eradicating them, they just keep coming back. They'll be waiting for a chance to find you unprotected. Please promise me you won't."

"This is not an excuse, is it?" When she saw his expression, she quickly backtracked. "I'm sorry, I shouldn't have said that."

"Don't Genevieve—don't apologize, Gods," he said, looking abashed. "I suspected Damian hadn't told you. I'm sure he had notions of not wanting you to worry, mixed with guilt because marrying him endangers you in a way you wouldn't be otherwise."

"Don't ever say that!" she protested.

He kissed her cheek. "I just wanted you to know that it wasn't a matter of keeping you locked up." She gave a skeptical humph, and he said, "Well not entirely, at least."

"I understand. You needn't have worried about the promise. Derek already got it out of me—by different means." It amazed her that she could even laugh about it. It felt good, though. She kissed him lightly on the mouth. "But I promise you as well. Thank you, Donal, for explaining matters to me. Neither of your brothers chose to."

"I can't say I'm surprised. I doubt he'll be too happy about this key either, but as he's absent at the moment...." He gave her a mischievous wink and said, "Come on, George and Thomas can't wait to meet you." He showed her how to unlock the hidden door in the dining room, and for the first time Genevieve actually entered the kitchen without being carried over a man's shoulder.

George and Thomas turned out to be brothers in their fifties. The two men couldn't say enough about the honor of being entrusted with caring for the bride's house, causing Genevieve to turn crimson. The brothers acted as if they were meeting Queen Titania instead of a village girl whose family had never employed more than a neighbor's boy or girl to help out. There was also the problem of her and Donal's activities in the garden and the conservatory. If anyone even guessed, let alone witnessed some of them, Genevieve prayed she might expire.

Unfortunately, Donal seemed to have been born constitutionally immune to embarrassment. He gave her a roguish wink and handed Thomas a key. "You two can get in there now. We'll be out for a few hours. Make sure to change the linens on the daybed in the conservatory. Why don't you have a bath ready there for five?"

Genevieve said nothing as Donal led her out the back door to the stable yard. Once they were out of sight, she punched his arm. "Why don't you just say outright that we're sharing a bed! What if one of them came in?" They'd been making love at all hours, right out in the open.

"Enough, you little harridan! In the first place, their family has been serving the Blacks for generations—trust me when I say that *nothing* surprises them about us. In the second place, didn't you see me give them the key?"

"You mean they don't have it?"

"You can blame Damian—or better, thank him. He's the one who set the rules. Because of what happened with our parents, he's been rabid about security in this house."

"What happened with your parents?"

"I was a baby. I don't remember anything and they never talk about it. All I know is that two Reavers somehow got themselves invited to the house and proceeded to murder our parents. They had a knife out to slit Derek's throat when Declan burst in and pulverized them into Fairy dust." She must have gone pale because he said, "I'm sorry, Genevieve. What a thing to tell you!"

Genevieve quieted him with a light kiss on the lips. "You were right to."

"I love you—you know that, don't you, little girl?"

"I do. I love you too. Finish your story."

"There isn't much story after that. The three of us were moved to the fortress, and Declan gave up most of his duties at Titania's court and moved back from Faerie to raise us himself."

"He must have been wonderful."

"He was," Donal said feelingly. "I never knew anything else, so I can't say I was affected by what happened. It was only when the preparations for the Bridal Week started that I began to wonder about Damian. He and Declan had lots of talks behind closed doors. The upshot was a decree that no one would be allowed in this house except for the family and a handful of servants he trusted absolutely. The door from the kitchen was to be locked at all times, and the servants would only enter your part of the house when one of us opened it for them. It struck me as rather extreme, to be honest. I realized then that he'd never fully gotten over it."

"Derek either, I suspect." Donal shrugged, obviously uncomfortable with the idea.

It was impossible not to be influenced by Donal's account. Genevieve decided she could forgive Damian a fair degree of high-handedness, but she was grateful that Donal did not see the same need for caution. She did not want her life held hostage to a tragedy that occurred before she was born. She also recognized that both Damian and Derek were motivated to restrict her freedom by something other than mere concern for her safety. Luckily, their younger brother did not seem enraptured by the idea of locking her up.

Never one for melancholy topics, Donal gave her a kiss that left her dizzy and then pulled her along to the stables. "Come, I have a surprise for you." He led her to a stall where an ethereally beautiful grey mare stood placidly. "She's yours," he said proudly.

"What?"

"Declan had her brought—from Faerie. So my brothers won't squawk about the dangers. She's gentle as a lamb but could outrun a demon if she needed to, and no Fae horse would ever throw a rider. Her name is Mist."

They led the horse out to the paddock. Genevieve's family had not had the means to keep a horse, and she'd never learned to ride, but with Donal's encouragement, she climbed up on Mist bareback. She proceeded to giggle like a halfwit as the horse sedately walked about.

Unfortunately, her rear end was still healing. The moment she began to shift uncomfortably, her eagle-eyed brother ordered her to get off. She ignored Donal, encouraging Mist to a trot, which she quickly regretted because it caused her to bounce up and down, which *hurt!* For the first time she felt serious annoyance at Derek for leaving her in this state.

In the meantime, Donal had caught up to her. "Off! Now!" he ordered.

Genevieve dearly wanted to defy him, but she was pretty sure her little adventure had just reopened some of the welts her beastly brother had given her. She gingerly dismounted. Donal was the picture of masculine disapproval, which just made her laugh. "What's got into you?" she asked innocently.

"I am beginning to understand how your backside ended up in that shape if you behaved like this with

Derek. I never thought I'd say this, but he can't come home soon enough."

"No!" she snarled.

"Oh yes. I have a feeling you are going to be spending a lot of time in the study—and good thing!"

"You are such a hypocrite!"

"In other words a male, sweetheart. Come on, I have more surprises for you."

They left the stables, and Donal led her through a short forested path, hardly a quarter of a mile long, that led to the back entrance of the fortress. She almost laughed at the sight of an ordinary poultry yard, kitchen garden, and paddock with several draft horses munching quietly. The formidable Black castle seemed far less intimidating from this perspective. They entered the house through an unassuming door that led directly to the kitchens where she was presented to the infamous Roderick.

Roderick turned out to be barely taller than she was, though so stout he must have been thrice her weight. She'd been expecting an ogre who would terrify her with his wooden spoon. Instead he lit up into an almost childlike smile. Within seconds she was seated at the kitchen table, being offered plates of tarts, homemade cheeses, and a sausage pie fresh from the oven. At her invitation, Roderick joined her and proceeded to interrogate her on all of her favorite foods, any special dishes she wished him to make and, to her great relief, any foods she disliked.

When she bemoaned her poor cooking skills, he put his hands to his cheeks and exclaimed, "Well then you must learn! Any time, my dear, come! I'll teach you to make any dish you wish. Beginning with the sweet-cheese rolls you told me of. I'll send someone today to your mother to request the recipe."

"My mother would be honored, sir," she said, utterly charmed.

"Well, I cannot have Damian's bride pining for the foods of home." He whispered confidentially into her ear, "And you will not be offended when I say that you must eat more—you need more meat on your bones. What if you were to take sick, Titania please it never happen? You'd waste away."

Genevieve laughed and promised she would eat more. After she and Donal left, she realized that he'd barely spoken the whole time they were there—truly a marvel. "You goose," she said. "How could you make him out to be such an ogre? He could not have been sweeter!" Donal looked at her as if she were possessed. "What?"

"You're dangerous. You appear so shy and kittenish, but I begin to suspect that beneath that sweet appearance, you're actually a witch, or perhaps a demoness."

"How dare you!"

"HOW DARE I!" he roared. "You just called Roderick, RODERICK, SWEET! The bane of my childhood, the author of my sufferings, the terror of the tart-taker! You think your backside is bad? I don't think a day went by when he didn't crimson my rear end with that spoon of his."

"You were stealing food!"

"Titania, give me patience! Roderick sweet! I could not have believed it. I suppose you think Derek is sweet as well. Did you call him peach-i-kins? Honey-pie? Sugarplum? Perhaps that's why he felt the need to tan your hide."

Genevieve took a swipe at him. "I did no such thing, you louse! And I never called Derek sweet—he who made me eat a tongue sandwich! Roderick is sending to town so he can learn the recipe for my mother's sweet-cheese rolls!"

Luckily Donal's noisy rage over Genevieve's friendliness to Roderick did not prevent them from visiting the fortress the next day for another surprise. After saying hello to Roderick, Donal ushered her into a dark and rather shabbily decorated sitting room, which provided ample evidence that no woman had lived in the fortress for decades, if ever.

Genevieve forgot all about it, though, when Sally was announced a minute later! She was delighted to see that Peter Crane had accompanied her friend. One glance confirmed the obvious: that Sally's box had changed to blue. They were to be married in a fortnight.

Genevieve was well aware that Sally's assertiveness was not precisely to the taste of the men of her family, and she worried that Donal might prefer not to leave them alone. She was consequently relieved when he immediately invited Peter to tour the fortress. The suggestion pleased everyone. As an artist, Peter was eager for the chance to explore such a dramatic building, while she and Sally were just as eager to be rid of the men so they could freely discuss Sally's news.

Roderick sent in tea along with a platter of small sandwiches and a delicious butter cake soaked in ginger syrup. Genevieve was highly gratified to have the chance to repay Sally's kindness and listened contentedly to all the details of Sally's courtship and wedding plans.

Though Sally was understandably full of her own concerns, Genevieve should have realized that her sharp-eyed friend had not suddenly become oblivious. "I can tell something's going on with you, Jenny, but don't worry. I won't press you for the details. Whatever it is can't be too bad. You're looking well enough—and you're finally getting some color."

Genevieve realized something at that moment: she truly wished to remain friends with Sally, but for their friendship to work, she would have to make a few things clear. She returned Sally's penetrating glance with one of her own. "You're right. There have been some difficulties, but I believe they are in train to being resolved. I would appreciate your not pressing me for details, Sally."

She left off saying "now or in the future," but trusted that Sally would understand her implication.

"Well enough, Genevieve. If you need a woman's ear, you know where to come," Sally said briskly.

"Thank you for understanding."

Genevieve knew that in the long run there would be little hope of completely deceiving someone as observant as Sally. If they were to stay friends, Sally must accept that there were parts of Genevieve's life that were not open to discussion.

She finally understood why Damian had been so determined to keep her from speaking to anyone about his family before their marriage. It was a measure of the distance she'd come in the last twenty-four hours that she didn't believe there was anything wrong or shameful in her intimacy with Donal and Derek, but that did not mean she wished others to know about it. There was simply no way for someone outside their little family to understand their unusual arrangement. She felt an unexpected elation when she realized that she instinctively thought of them as a family.

The men returned soon afterwards, both in excellent spirits. Peter was a good-humored, easy-going man, a perfect match for Donal. As they were leaving, Donal surprised her again by inviting Peter to return to sketch— and of course to bring Sally.

Genevieve exchanged a glance with Donal at this, which she was positive he interpreted correctly. She was determined that he act as host for these visits instead of Damian or Titania forbid, Derek. She strongly suspected that Damian and Sally would merely tolerate each other at best. Damian would not be able to resist the temptation to prove his dominance over her in front of Sally, and Sally would definitely disapprove of his tendency to domineer. Derek and Sally spending time together did not bear thinking of.

Genevieve took Donal's hand as they walked back to their house at the end of the visit. "Thank you," she said, kissing him on the cheek.

"I'm sure you can come up with a better way to thank me," the scoundrel answered.

She tried to rip her hand away, but instead he pushed her up against a tree and took her mouth deeply. He immediately began lifting her skirts to fondle her sex, easily accomplished since she wasn't wearing drawers.

When she tried to shove him away, he murmured, "Please, I'll be quick. No one will catch us."

"No—when we get home, not here," she said decisively, recalling Declan's advice about setting limits.

This was the main path between their house and the fortress. She didn't care if George and Thomas were beyond surprise. She would not get caught with Donal pumping into her against a tree! Donal grumbled something about Sally being a bad influence, but he did respect her tone, and they continued their walk. "So you and Peter got along?" she asked to break the slight tension.

"He's a good chap and doesn't seem to mind that pint-sized dictator you call a friend."

"I thought you liked her."

"I'm teasing," he said. "I like Sally very well—she's loyal, smart, honest. I admit she's a good friend for you."

"I'm worried Damian won't agree," she confided.

"Let me talk to him," Donal said firmly. "I doubt Damian will make trouble but if he does, Declan will back me."

She felt certain then that Donal would make sure that she and her friend had the chance to see each other. After a minute, he added, "Peter mentioned something to me: that you used to play the pianoforte. You were reputed extremely good, but then you just stopped one day."

317

Genevieve froze and stared at Donal in alarm. He gave her an almost mocking look, for all the world like an obnoxious brother teasing his sister for being scared of a mouse. She prayed she sounded tolerably indifferent as she said, "Yes. I used to play and then I stopped."

"I'd love to hear you some time," he commented, and then they continued walking. They were almost home when Donal cried, "But you know what I want right now? Cherries! Race you!" Donal, insufferable wretch, took off towards the orchard at a speed she couldn't hope to match, calling back at her, "Slowpoke!"

When she finally caught up to him, he pelted her with a cherry. "You rotten scoundrel," she cried and grabbed some cherries off the ground and started throwing them back.

Donal shot more cherries at her, mocking, "You sure do throw like a girl!"

"You... you... I'll get you, Donal Black!" she cried, resolving to come up with some better taunts as soon as possible. A full on cherry fight ensued, which left Genevieve's face and dress spattered with red juice—and Donal practically pristine.

"Enough, truce!" he called. Genevieve sent a few more his way before finally holding up her hands in capitulation.

She eyed the cherry trees for fruit fit for eating instead of ballistics, but the lower branches had been picked clean. Donal noticed of course and got a devious expression on his face. "I can see that my lovely Genevieve is craving cherries. How about I climb up and get you some, and in return you can suck me off after dinner?"

"You beast!" she yelled furiously.

"It's not my fault girls can't climb trees."

"I can too!" she insisted. At least she used to be able to.

"I'll believe it when I see it!" Donal leapt for a branch and swung himself up like a monkey and then rose to his feet, effortlessly balancing on the branch without holding on. He reached for some of the fruit. "Oh, so delicious! These trees come from Titania's own orchard. Did you know that? Heavenly. Poor Jenny, stuck on the ground like a girl."

"We'll see about that!" she snarled between her teeth. She untied her boots and pulled off her stockings. She found a tree that looked promising and after a few tries managed to pull herself into the crook. Of course, the moment she was stable, Donal pelted her with a cherry.

"You'll be sorry!" she shouted and struggled to climb high enough to reach the fruit. She climbed out on a branch that looked sturdy and lying on her stomach managed to reach some cherries hanging from one of the upper branches. She ate a few, closing her eyes with pleasure—until another cherry hit her! Donal had climbed higher in his tree and began shooting cherries at her.

Unfortunately, when she tried to return fire, she lost her grip and tipped over the branch. She scrambled to keep her hold but wasn't strong enough and went tumbling down. "Blast!" she cried, but when she looked up, she almost fainted.

Damian and Derek were standing right in front of her, their arms folded, looking anything but pleased. Genevieve bit her lip: how was it that the two of them standing together was more terrifying than the two of them trying to kill each other?

Donal, that traitor, scurried down the tree, easy as a squirrel. "Look who's back!" he said brightly, wearing his tart-stealing expression.

She tried to get up, but found to her mortification that she'd twisted her ankle and couldn't stand without holding onto the tree. Derek's already dark expression became thunderous, while Damian's smile was pure menace.

"Brother?" Derek asked.

"You take Donal. I'll deal with my wife—this time," Damian said. A moment later she was being hauled over Damian's shoulder while Derek tackled Donal.

"Damian! Put me down! Don't you dare!" she shrieked.

"Genevieve, I am not home one minute, and already you are in deep trouble. I strongly recommend you be quiet."

"What about Donal! Make Derek stop!"

"Donal has it coming. You'd best worry for yourself, darling."

She caught a glimpse of Derek flipping Donal onto the ground, before they arrived at the kitchen door. Damian said a quick hello to George and Thomas, who looked understandably stunned to see the master of the house home again—carrying his wife over his shoulder like a blasted sack.

"Damian, put me down!" she pleaded.

"Be silent, Genevieve," he said, unlocking the door to the dining room and moving quickly through the anteroom, up the stairs, and down the hallway to their room. He finally put her down in the bathing chamber and immediately turned the water on to fill the tub. "Forgive my state, darling. I'm in dire need of a bath." Taking note of her juice-stained face and twig-strewn hair, he added, "And you as well."

Now that they were alone together, Genevieve gulped and tried to speak, but her voice was little more than a whisper. Before she could stop them, tears started rolling down her face. "Damian...."

"Shhh, no tears," he said and pulled her into his arms.

"I'm so sorry, Damian... Gods."

"No, Darling, *I'm* sorry—you don't know how much. Genevieve, you cannot imagine what the past five days have been like."

She gripped him as hard as she could, worried that she might shake apart. "Don't say sorry, please.... I can't bear it... please Damian. I wanted to tell you I loved you, but I was too big a coward, and then... I was so afraid I'd lost you, that you hated me..." To her mortification, she began heaving, she was crying so hard.

"Never, darling. Impossible. You are so dear to me." His voice cracked as he whispered in her ear, "I love you, Genevieve—I cannot even express how much."

The tub was almost full. "We'll talk about everything. Now I just want to hold my little wife in my arms," he said.

He quickly undressed both of them, helped her into the tub, and then climbed in after her. Genevieve had never felt anything equal to the comfort of lying in his arms again. She splashed her face, trying to rinse the tears and get a hold of herself. Damian had come back— he and Derek had reconciled—he loved her. Whatever their troubles, they were together again.

Chapter Twenty-seven

Damian clutched Genevieve to him for a few minutes, trying to bring his emotions under control so that he didn't behave like a madman. When he felt calm enough, he began soaping her back and arms, taking note that Genevieve was sporting a new tan line and even had a little sunburn on her nose. His clever brother had kept her outside, and she was clearly better for it.

Within minutes, Genevieve was practically purring from his strokes, looking like a contented little kitten. He was already sporting a vicious erection from seeing her on the ground looking adorably guilty. He tried to get his lust under control. He wanted to seduce Genevieve slowly, gently, give her the control. He was horrified that she'd witnessed his brawl with Derek, by far the most brutal fight he'd ever had with one of his brothers. She'd need time to feel safe with him.

He forced himself to hold back from massaging her breasts though he was yearning to take them in his mouth. Instead, he used the pitcher to dampen her hair. "I missed this," he murmured.

"Me too—I wouldn't let..." Genevieve cut off abruptly. Suddenly she looked miserable and guilty. It took him a moment before he guessed that she'd been about to say something about one of his brothers—Donal probably.

He knew this moment was crucial if he was to repair some of the damage he'd done and start all four of them on the right footing. "Tell me," he said, keeping his tone light.

Of course, Genevieve tried to turn her face away, but he caught her chin and made her face him. "Please Damian," she begged.

"Were you going to speak of Donal?" He smiled warmly and whispered, "Trust me, Genevieve. Please—I'd never lie to you. I know you've been intimate with Donal. You can tell me anything at all about my brothers." When she still didn't respond, he decided on a different tactic. "Genevieve, I am your husband. I must know anything that happens with my brothers. Is that clear?"

"But..." she tried to protest.

"No. No excuses will be accepted. While I am ecstatic that you have developed feelings for them, I am master of this house. As far as this family goes, my word is law. There are no secrets between us. If I ask you a question, I expect you to answer it."

"I don't want to hurt you."

"I understand that, darling, but that's for me to decide, not you. Now please finish what you were saying."

"I didn't want to take a bath with Donal," she said nervously.

Damian just caught himself before he sharply demanded what she meant by that. This entire disaster started with his getting angry at Derek. He must never forget for even a second that Genevieve would blame herself if he fought with his brothers.

He plastered a light smile on his face. "You don't have to bathe with him. Why? Did he try to persuade you?"

"No, of course not. I think he guessed that I wouldn't want to—with anyone but you. I don't know why, but I just couldn't bear the thought of it." Genevieve was watching him carefully, trying to gauge his reaction.

He chuckled. "I am very happy to hear that. I never want you to feel pressured to do something that makes you unhappy, Genevieve." He saw something in her eye. "I know that's not what happened with Derek. I promise we will talk about it, but would you mind if we save him for later? I've just spent the last three days with Derek, and honestly I could use a little break." It was the right thing to say: she bubbled over with knowing laughter. "I'd much rather hear about Donal—especially since it looks like you two had a grand time getting into trouble."

"I don't think I've ever met anyone as good-tempered as Donal," she admitted.

"I owe him eternally. He did an excellent job cheering you up."

"It's funny, he's so humorous and carefree, but I find he's very observant and considerate. Like with the paint in the sitting room. I have not been back to the bedroom once since we came back. We stayed the whole time in the garden or the conservatory. He guessed that I wouldn't want to, just like with the bath. He purposely hides it, I think, but he can be very perceptive...."

She trailed off, afraid she'd said too much, but he could sense what she was trying to communicate. "It is fitting that my brother is a master of stealth. And I thank Titania that he has used his gift to sneak into your heart." He kissed her gently. "Though if I'm to be fair, I suppose I must feel equally thankful that Derek battered his way in!"

He winked at her, which elicited one of her captivating blushes. He then gave her his most autocratic smile. "I believe I will issue my first decree as master of this house and all its occupants: my lovely wife will bathe only with me."

Genevieve's eyes glazed as they always did. He rubbed her buttocks knowingly, enjoying her shudder. "In fact," he added, "I can think of quite a few other decrees I wish to make now that we are all home together. I see that I'm going to enjoy this."

He stood abruptly and helped her out of the tub. Gods, it had been too long. Genevieve practically threw herself at him, rubbing against him like a little cat. He gripped the back of her head and tilted it so he could kiss her properly, loving the way she melted when he took possession of her mouth.

Suddenly he couldn't bear to wait another moment. Without bothering to towel them off, he carried her to the bed, tossed her on, and climbed on top of her. He continued to take deep kisses, while she squirmed wantonly beneath him, opening her legs without his having to tell her to.

"I want you," she moaned. He reached down and brushed his fingers through the folds of her sex—she was soaked.

It was almost as if the scent of her desire triggered some instinct in him. All of Damian's virtuous intentions crumbled to dust, as if a lifetime of playing the responsible older brother, the reliable commanding officer, the reassuring lover and husband finally became too much. He was gripped by a primitive need to assert his dominance. His brothers might share in loving her, but she was *his*.

Genevieve saw something in his expression because her eyes widened with alarm, which only fueled his need. He shoved a cushion under her hips and pinned her wrists above her head. "I am going to take you now," he growled. "Deep and hard." Her eyes glazed with desire, though she was still wary, which pleased him. She should be wary.

He thrust in hard, growling with satisfaction at the rightness of it. He shifted her wrists to his right hand and used his left to pull her leg over his hip so he could go even deeper. He began driving into her, shocked at the violence of his need. He was pounding her so hard, their heads edged dangerously close to the wooden headboard. "Grip the headboard—brace yourself!" he ordered, releasing her wrists.

He wrapped his hand around her hair and forced her head back so he could kiss her vulnerable neck. He realized he had left a mark, which caused something to snap. Suddenly his mouth was everywhere on her throat, her breasts, her chest, as he left at least a dozen love bites on her fragile skin.

Genevieve would be furious, which didn't bother him a bit. More importantly, he knew the moment they saw the marks, his brothers would know what they meant— that Damian was her master, and they touched her only at his sufferance.

Neither of them would dare mark her like that—only him.

He took her mouth again, feeling that she was building to her climax. He tightened his grip on her hair. "Keep your eyes on me," he ordered. "This orgasm is mine!"

Genevieve's whole body shuddered, but her desire was amply mixed with apprehension. Fear made her fight the climax, but his wife could never resist being dominated.

"You are mine, Genevieve," he snarled. "Say it! My brothers can touch you, but you answer to me!"

"Damian!" she begged.

"Say it," he growled harshly.

"I'm yours," she cried.

"You obey *me*—say it now, or I won't let you come."

He knew it was only the frenzy of lust that made her gasp, "I obey you."

"Good girl—come now!" He shifted in a way he knew she wouldn't be able to resist and roared with satisfaction to feel her convulsing helplessly as she cried out his name. His pumping became frantic then as he slammed into her, bringing himself to his own climax.

As he relaxed and the fury of possessiveness receded, he realized that he'd just behaved like a crazed animal. He clutched her to him. "Gods, Genevieve, I didn't mean.... Can you forgive me?"

Genevieve reached for his face and pulled him close for a gentle kiss. She looked perfectly happy. He didn't think he'd ever seen anything as beautiful. "No," she said smiling. "There's nothing to forgive."

Chapter Twenty-eight

Genevieve was completely sincere when she promised there was nothing to forgive. She understood why Damian had attacked her, and she couldn't complain about the result when he brought her to such raptures.

However, she was less pleased when she noticed the result of those passionate kisses. "What is this?" she exclaimed.

"Love bites. I already apologized, love. I'm afraid in the heat of the moment...." He shrugged apologetically, but his expression was pure masculine triumph.

"How long will these last?" she demanded, incensed by his smugness.

"I'm not sure—perhaps a day or so."

"Or so?"

"It might be a week," he admitted.

"A week! I can't go out like this!"

He rolled over on top of her, thumbing her breasts and pushing his leg between hers. "We can always stay here. I was hoping we could eat in tonight, just the two of us," he murmured between little kisses along the edge of her ear. Her completely disloyal body began humming with desire as her infernal husband well knew.

When it was time for dinner, Genevieve found she had even more reason to wish she'd not forgiven Damian so easily. When she tried to stand, her ankle gave out. It turned out she'd strained it falling out of that blasted tree. Damian practically pounced on her. All signs of the apologetic lover vanished like smoke in a high wind, and his despotic side returned in force.

"Why on earth were you in a tree?" he demanded as he examined the swelling.

"I wanted the cherries, and there were no more on the lower branches."

"And so you must climb high enough to break your neck?"

"It wasn't that high!" she protested. "And Donal dared me." Genevieve instantly realized that was the wrong thing to say.

"He dared you! I hope Derek beats him to a pulp!"

Unfortunately, that wasn't the end of it. He helped her over to the little table and then noticed that she was also having trouble sitting. He pulled her to stand and lifted her skirt up. "What happened here? You've had three days to heal!"

"It's not what you think," she squeaked.

"Genevieve, you have no idea what I think. What did I say about answering my questions?"

"It wasn't Donal—at least—you see, Declan got me this beautiful horse—named Mist—and Donal told me to climb on, just for a few minutes...."

"You climbed on—you mean bareback—without a saddle or bridle?"

"Well it is a Fae horse," she argued. "Even without a saddle...."

"I don't need to hear about the merits of Fae horses, Genevieve," he said sternly. "Don't even try to pretend to me. This happened in more than a few minutes. Now I will have the truth right now. Did Donal tell you to get off or not?"

"Fine. Declan told us we should enjoy ourselves as much as possible before the two more *tyrannical* brothers returned. But it seems that Donal can be as despotic as either of you when the mood strikes him."

Damian shook his head, his expression dangerous.

"Damian!" she cried.

"No—this is too much. You cannot possibly imagine I would ignore this."

"I forgave you for pounding into me and then behaving like a hound marking his territory!"

"And that was very sweet of you, but I am not you. Fortunately, I know the perfect punishment."

"What?"

"That I will save as a little surprise for later," he said, pulling her in for a thorough kiss that left her lightheaded. "Frankly, you should be glad I am not sending you to Derek."

"You wouldn't!"

"Wouldn't I? I see now that he is exactly what you need."

"That's just what Donal said," she grumbled, wondering if perhaps she might come to regret this new spirit of cooperation between the brothers.

"I'm not surprised. Now can you sit in that chair, or shall we play our favorite game by the divan, because I have no objection whatsoever to feeding you while you are on your knees."

"And now you sound like Derek," she huffed.

He laughed, his voice rich and relaxed, as he served her up a generous helping of her new favorite dish, Roderick's creamed chicken, this time served with delicate herbed crepes and some lovely green beans with butter and a hint of tarragon.

He poured them each a glass of chilled white wine and then said, "So speaking of Derek, I really do need to know everything, darling, and please, no apologies. Just tell me what happened."

So she did, becoming more and more comfortable as it became clear that Damian did not seem hurt or disturbed by anything she was saying. "I truly don't know how long it had been when Donal found us," she said at the end of it. "I can't explain it, but my thoughts were very disordered. I think Derek was apprehensive about my state—at least that's what I recall."

"Thank you," he said feelingly. "I cannot tell you how much I appreciate your openness with me, Genevieve. I will do everything in my power to be as open with you."

"I want you to be, Damian. I hate worrying about what you're feeling."

"Come, let's sit by the hearth. I find I need to hold my beautiful wife," he murmured.

He led her to one of the armchairs and pulled her in to sit on his lap. He just clutched her for a few minutes, as if he wanted to reassure himself she was still there, still his.

Finally, he said, "I don't think it's news to you that I was not comfortable with the state you were in the other day. I am well aware that my behavior was completely inexcusable." He stopped her when she tried to interrupt. "Please hear me out, darling—I need to say this. It took me several days to make some sense of it, but it is clear that in addition to feeling horribly guilty about our quarrel, I suffered a bout of lunatic possessiveness and jealousy towards Derek. I could not have handled it worse and you suffered terribly for that, and I am truly, truly sorry for it."

"I know," she murmured. "Please, don't apologize. Please."

He looked at her a bit too knowingly and then kissed her nose. "I won't say any more on that. However, we still have the issue of your state. Understand I am not speaking of the need for punishment itself, or the fact that Derek is the one who can satisfy it for you. I am speaking only of your state afterwards, and the truth is that I am not comfortable with it. So far, you have needed three days of healing, during which even a few minutes on a horse set you back another few days. I would give anything to take you riding, but I can't until you are fully healed, and even more seriously, I cannot possibly spank you myself now...."

Genevieve slapped his arm.

"I'm jesting. I do not mean to make some proclamation for all time, but I am hoping there is a way to meet this need without leaving you in that state. I want you to tell me how you feel about what I'm saying."

"Declan spoke to me. He did not like it that I did not stop Derek sooner. I don't think I could have—I don't understand why I didn't. I don't mean to defy you, or make problems with Derek...."

"Shhh, love. I'll tell you what I am thinking, Genevieve. I am not going to interfere between you and Derek. If you provoke him, whatever the motive, you must be prepared to accept the consequences of his temper—no different than Donal when he used to provoke Derek. I will use the riding as a rule of thumb. Unless he clears it with me first, he will not administer any punishment that leaves you unable to ride a horse the following day. Does that seem fair to you?"

"Yes." She felt an odd sense of relief. She desperately wanted to avoid being the cause of conflict between Damian and Derek, and she felt Damian's objections were reasonable and well within his rights as her husband. The problem was that she didn't trust herself to say no to Derek. She agreed with Declan that she must set limits, but there was a kind of madness between her and Derek, and she could see matters going too far without someone to stop them.

"Excellent." He kissed her and then shifted her off his lap onto the chair. As he walked towards the dressing room, he said, "That leaves only the matter of your punishment for behaving so irresponsibly."

"Damian! No!"

He returned holding the green leather cuffs. "I'm sorry, darling, but it would send exactly the wrong message for me to ignore your risking your neck by tumbling out of trees or riding a horse when you haven't even healed up yet. Hold out your wrists, please."

"Fine!" she grumbled.

He got a glint in his eye that made her want to hide under the bed. "Here is my decree: from now on, you will submit like a good girl to sleeping bound to the bed and you will not make any fuss."

"From now on!" she said breathlessly.

"When you sleep in this bed, you sleep bound. It will serve as a daily reminder of how I will react if I find you risking yourself like that."

Chapter Twenty-nine

Genevieve and Damian spent most of the next day in their bedroom. Damian argued that they were owed the rest of their honeymoon, and Genevieve was just as eager as he could be for time together.

Fortunately her ankle was better, so Damian had no excuse to keep her locked up. He was as despotic as always, but he grudgingly agreed to visit Mist at the stables and even suggested that they eat a picnic lunch in the garden.

Genevieve was more willing to spend most of the time in their bedroom when she made an unexpected discovery: she did not feel comfortable being intimate with Damian in the garden. Somehow, that space had become Donal's, just as the bath was Damian's.

Surprisingly, she did not feel any awkwardness when Donal joined them for the picnic. Outside of their bedroom, Damian did not engage in the endless fondling that he did at other times. She realized it was his way of respecting the garden as her domain.

Donal also didn't try to touch her, even when Damian left them alone for a few minutes. It was only after the picnic was over that she grasped how relieved she was. Donal was showing his usual perceptiveness. It was tacitly understood that these days were Damian's, and Donal would not put her in the position of having to choose between them or somehow be intimate with both of them at the same time, which was frankly unimaginable to her.

She wished she could feel the same relief about Derek's absence. But she was growing more and more uneasy about him though she tried her best not to let Damian see. She'd not seen Derek once since she fell out of the tree, and she got the decided impression he was avoiding her.

She knew Damian must resume a more regular schedule with the garrison in two days. Though she'd agreed to this unusual arrangement—happily agreed— she'd no idea how it would work in practice. At least as far as intimacy went, she knew what to expect with Donal and Damian, but Derek was a different matter.

When it came to the point, she'd spent very little time with Derek, and the few hours they had been alone together had been among the most tumultuous and emotionally wrenching of her life. How on earth was she to share a bed with a man she'd yet to have a civil conversation with?

The next day was Damian's last before he must leave for four days. He suggested that they take advantage of the beautiful weather to have another picnic, which Genevieve happily agreed to.

He'd not mentioned whether Derek would attend, but Genevieve did check his little room on their corridor and then the dining room and study, hoping that they could at least speak for a few minutes. Of course she saw no sign of him.

However her worry for Derek was quickly eclipsed by a more immediate concern. As she crossed the conservatory to get to the garden, she saw something that almost made her faint: a pianoforte now occupied the corner.

She silently cursed her meddling brother—and Peter Crane, who had undoubtedly informed Donal of everything he knew or suspected of her crisis four years ago. Her only question was how much Donal had told Damian. She hoped he'd said nothing and decided he'd probably said as little as possible.

It took her a minute to regain her composure enough to go closer. She could tell at a glance that the instrument was first-rate and must have cost an absolute fortune—it was much finer than the one her parents had scrimped to purchase all those years ago, which she'd so wantonly destroyed.

She didn't know whether to laugh or cry when she saw the body was constructed of cherry. Who other than Donal would do this?

Her eyes began streaming—apparently it would be crying not laughing. They should dub her *Genevieve the perpetual watering pot,* she thought crossly.

"Play the piece your father played at the wedding." Donal was standing in the entrance—of course. As if she could hope to hide something from him. She gnawed her lip, wondering if she could actually bring herself to touch it.

"You...." She swallowed, trying to find her voice. "You really don't understand, Donal."

"I do, better than you might imagine," he said softly. "Derek is my brother."

She closed her eyes tightly. She would not start sobbing.

"One song," he added. "And then I promise, say the word, and I'll have it removed by tomorrow."

She forced herself to brush her hands along the elegant curve of its rim. Was there any more perfect shape in the world than the curve of a pianoforte? It was so sensuous. How could she have forgotten how beautiful it was?

Enough.

Donal was right. One song. She sat down and immediately began to play.

For the first minute, she played without thinking, allowing her fingers to flit lightly over the keys by rote.

But Genevieve could never play anything by rote for long. Music had always seemed like a living thing to her, constantly evolving and adapting, becoming something different with each musician, each instrument, each performance.

Inevitably, it was as if the song found its way into the muscles of her hands. Once there, it could no longer remain fixed. New dimensions began unfolding, new possibilities. And as she'd found since that fateful, cursed day, no matter how she fought it, those dimensions were dark—dissonant, strange, difficult.

She couldn't bear to appear cowardly before Donal, so she allowed the piece to develop fully, to go where it would. When it finally came to the end, she forced herself to look at him. His expression was the last thing she might have expected.

He looked... angry. *Furious.* Donal, who never got angry.

"I take back my promise," he said, his voice literally quaking with emotion. "I won't get rid of it. If you give up playing again, I'll throttle you."

He walked out into the garden, leaving Genevieve utterly stunned.

Chapter Thirty

Damian had only been back two days and he already wanted to kill Derek.

In almost every way, the past two days with Genevieve had been glorious. She was growing more confident with him, and their lovemaking was everything that was passionate and tender. But now their honeymoon was coming to an end. He had to leave the next morning, and he knew Genevieve was anxious though she tried to hide it from him. It was no puzzle that Derek was the cause: Derek who'd not shown his face once since their arrival home.

He was all the more annoyed because he'd deliberately tried to come up with a way to ease Genevieve into her new life with the three of them. His wife adored picnics. What could be simpler than for the four of them to recreate that first extraordinary picnic they'd shared the day before the wedding?

He'd invited Donal, who of course instantly agreed, and told him to pass the invitation on to Derek, never imagining that Derek would not appear. Donal smoothed over the awkwardness of Derek's absence, but Damian could tell Genevieve was bothered by it.

Damian was relieved but not surprised that he and Donal instinctively settled into a mode that respected Genevieve's needs. It helped immensely that Genevieve's expressions were so easy to read. The moment they entered the garden he could sense her anxiety, and he quickly guessed the reason. She'd been intimate with Donal here, and now she considered it his domain. It was exactly the same as with the bath.

He could tell that Donal was also careful to keep matters completely nonsexual. He must have sensed the same thing: Genevieve considered this Damian's time, and she would not welcome advances from Derek or Donal.

Damian knew then that these boundaries would be very important to Genevieve, and though they might eventually be able to take a few liberties, the basic spirit of them must be respected.

Unwilling to give up on his brilliant plan, Damian ordered a second picnic basket from Thomas the next day. He found Donal just before noon. "Where is he?" Damian demanded.

Of course, Donal merely shrugged for an answer. Damian rolled his eyes at his younger brother's unconquerable aversion to anything that smacked of squealing. Damian was angry enough, he actually forced himself to enter the main house, which he always avoided at all costs, and wasted half an hour searching through every room, but there was no sign of Derek.

As he carried the picnic basket into the garden, Damian reminded himself that murder was not an option. It was for him to solve this problem, and he must control his temper to do it.

His ruminations were diverted when he got closer to where Genevieve and Donal were sitting. Donal had taken her hand and was saying something. Even from a distance Damian could tell that Donal was deeply disturbed. He'd never seen his brother like this before.

Genevieve was far easier to read: she was shaking her head the way she always did when she was denying the need for an apology. Damian knew without being told that it must be about the new pianoforte. Donal had been far too cryptic about its purchase. Clearly there was a story behind the instrument—a momentous one. But Donal hadn't told him, and Damian suspected he might never know the full truth.

Damian permitted himself thirty seconds to indulge his envy. It was clear to him that Donal had become exceptionally close to Genevieve during their days together, and worse, that his brother understood aspects of her character better than Damian did. It wasn't just the business with the pianoforte. The conversation yesterday had been full of lighthearted remarks about Roderick, cooking lessons, and Sally, which Damian couldn't entirely follow. These were activities that she would pursue with Donal, not him.

But Damian had learned some hard lessons over the past week, and he forced himself to master these ugly feelings. It helped when he made a discovery that surprised him: Donal was deeply in love with Genevieve.

Just as with Derek, that realization reordered the world for Damian. Donal was not the same man he'd been a week ago. There was a new intensity to him. For all his and Genevieve's antics, Donal was deeply protective of her, only in a different way. Just that morning, Donal had almost bitten his head off after Damian made a snide remark about Genevieve's visit with Sally. The message could not be clearer: the friendship was important to Genevieve and Damian must support it.

Damian found it was enough now to remind himself of the vow he'd made at Titania's Altar to always make Genevieve's happiness and well-being his priority. Which meant that he must battle his anger at Derek and solve this problem.

It only took Damian another fifteen seconds to realize that he would have to make a very painful sacrifice. He laughed ruefully that this was the price of leadership. The first rule of a successful command was to know what and when to delegate.

His decision made, he joined the other two and did everything he could to lighten Genevieve's mood. However, he took a moment when she'd gone to pick some of her beloved mint to say to Donal, "Find him, now. I'll see both of you in the study in ten minutes."

Donal could follow orders when he had to and left immediately. Damian went to find Genevieve. "Darling, would it be all right if we all met in your sitting-room in, say, half an hour?"

"Of course," she answered, clearly surprised that he would ask her.

"It is your domain, darling," he said simply. "I will not use it without your permission."

His brothers were waiting in the study when he arrived, as Damian knew they would be. He got immediately to the point. "I have asked Genevieve to meet with us in her sitting room in twenty minutes so we can go over the rules of this household. However, I wished to speak with you first without her present. A few things have become clear over the past few days."

He explained his observations about her need for boundaries, asking Donal to add his thoughts.

"I believe these boundaries may become more flexible as she grows more comfortable, but until she is less worried about showing a preference or injuring one of us, I expect them to be respected. Especially the bath," he

348

added with a wry smirk. "I want to hear your opinions, but *I* will decide when and how they are pushed. I hope it goes without saying that she should not be feeling a moment's anxiety about us. Even if she screams out someone else's name during her climax, I expect you both to have her giggling over the mistake within half a minute. Do I need to say more?"

"No," Donal said, chuckling. Derek shook his head.

"Good. Derek, I have decided that you will be in charge while I am absent."

Since Derek was resolved to remain a pestilential blight on humanity, he showed no reaction whatsoever to this.

Damian was forced to forge ahead. "I have discussed what happened between you with Genevieve already. She was very open with me about the fact that she does not feel confident setting limits, so it falls to me." He then succinctly informed Derek of the limits he'd established. "Do you have any problem with that?"

"You set the rules," Derek said curtly.

In anyone else, that response would be sarcasm. He knew it wasn't with Derek, but Damian still clenched his fists, forcing down his temper yet again.

Ah the joys of command.

"I have not spoken to Genevieve again about her leaving the house on her own. For now, you will both need to keep an eye on her."

Both brothers spoke at once. "She promised not to leave," Derek said harshly, while Donal said, "That won't be necessary."

"I explained the situation with the Reavers," Donal added. "She understands the danger. I also gave her the key that opens the dining room door."

"You did what?" Derek snapped. "You had no business...." He cut himself off.

For once, Damian completely agreed with Derek about their youngest brother's compulsive need to break every bloody rule ever set down by god or man. But he was not willing to risk a replay of his quarrel with Genevieve to undo Donal's gross overstepping of his authority.

He stifled his anger and said mildly, "Well then, I won't worry about that. That's all I have to say for now. Meet in the sitting room in five minutes."

Derek walked off without saying anything.

Donal touched his arm. "It will be okay. She can handle him."

Damian took a deep breath and decided to trust Donal. For as long as Damian could remember, one of the basic facts of his existence had been that Derek was impossible—why would he expect *this* to be easy?

When he arrived in the sitting room, he immediately noticed Genevieve's disappointed expression and saw that Derek had chosen the farthest possible spot from her.

He counted to twenty.

That done, he smiled warmly and said, "Thank you all for coming. I've called this meeting so that we can have everything clear between us. We have seen how destructive conflict can be, and the importance of avoiding it. I will be brief because in fact I have very few rules. I'll say first that I have discussed all of them with Declan. I invite you in turn to discuss them with me if you have any problem, but unless I say otherwise, I expect them to be obeyed."

He paused to allow all of them to nod agreement. Poor Genevieve looked like a frightened doe about to be run to ground by wolves. He prayed he'd made the right decision, but there was nothing he could do but continue.

"Excellent," he said brightly. "First rule: within this house, our relations are out in the open. No one will say or do anything that cannot be repeated to the others. We will not attempt to keep secrets from each other, nor will we expect others to refrain from telling us things to spare our feelings.

"Second rule: if one of you is unhappy for any reason, I expect to be told immediately. If you find it difficult to speak to me, you will speak to Declan. Problems or resentments will not be allowed to fester. I remind my brothers that Genevieve will almost certainly be the one to suffer if they do. I hope that is all I need to say to ensure this rule is obeyed."

"It is," Donal said quietly. Derek nodded.

"Good. Third rule: it should go without saying that Genevieve is not a bone to be fought over. I have decided that it will be easiest for her if she need cope with only one male's attentions at a time. To that end, we will divide the week. I will take three nights, and my brothers will each take two, with the caveat that Genevieve is always free to say she wishes a night off, whether for her bleeding days *or any other reason*. For the males especially, I expect everyone to be flexible. I will not tolerate quarrels or complaints about the scheduling—and I include myself in that."

He paused for a moment and then continued. "Fourth rule: physical affection. If it is not your day or night, then you may demonstrate affection, but nothing beyond what you would show a beloved friend. I should be clear that this rule applies to the males only. Declan was adamant that Genevieve must feel at liberty to show affection to any one of us *as she wishes*, without being made to feel she is showing an unfair preference. When she is spending time with one brother, no matter their activity, it is for *her* to decide if she wishes to invite another of us to join them *or not*; whatever her decision, she is *never* to be made to feel like she is injuring either party."

His brothers both nodded.

Turning to her, Damian said, "Genevieve, it is crucial that you speak up if you feel overwhelmed by our demands and set limits if need be. I will remind you that this room is your domain. If you wish for privacy, you need only shut the door, and none of us will bother you unless there is a compelling need."

She laughed nervously and said, "What if I don't wish for privacy?"

Damian could feel her pain, but he managed to control his features and answer warmly, "You need only speak. I promise you are in no danger of male neglect— quite the opposite. But just to be clear: it is for you to decide how you wish to spend your day and with whom, but unless you say otherwise, we will divide the days as we do the nights."

She gnawed her lip, which of course made him yearn to take her mouth, but he stayed his course.

"When I am absent, Derek will be in charge, and I expect you and Donal to respect his authority. Genevieve, I have only two rules for you. First, I expect you always to be truthful with me, and second, I expect you to take care of yourself and act in a safe way. These rules are not subject to debate, and if they are violated you will present yourself to Derek in the study for punishment. Is that clear?"

Derek knew how to school his features when he wished, but Damian easily detected his surprise. For once Genevieve was more difficult to read. She was surprised and also aroused by the idea, but most of all he still saw uncertainty.

This matter with Derek *must* be resolved.

More gently he added, "I wish to make it clear before everyone that I do not expect blanket obedience on other topics. You are *not* accountable to me for how you choose to spend your time. Arguments, debates, even defiance are all to be expected, and no one should punish you for that. Discipline that occurs during bedroom play is also not my concern—I have made clear the limits I expect you and Derek to observe, and Derek has promised that he will abide by them. I speak only of examples such as what happened with the riding. If one of us tells you to stop an activity because it is dangerous, I need to know that you will obey, darling."

She frowned and said, "What about climbing a tree? Donal didn't think it dangerous. I don't want to be treated like some fragile flower."

Damian chuckled. "I understand, darling, truly. Can we leave it like this—you promise to abide by the spirit of this rule, and I promise I will ask Donal to referee when we honestly disagree about how risky an activity is?"

"Yes, I think that's fair," she answered.

"Excellent. Does anyone wish to say anything at the moment?" When no one spoke, he took Genevieve's hand. "Darling, I *am positive* I speak for all three of us when I say that our first priority at all times is your happiness and comfort." He shot Derek an unmistakable look. "I hate that you worry about us, and I would command you not to if I thought it could possibly work. I can only hope that when you understand how much joy you have brought to this house, to all of us, you will realize how ridiculous these fears are."

He forced himself to abide by his own rule and kissed the top of her head.

Now came the test.

He said lightly, "Tragically, I must depart this evening to visit my abominable troops, so we will begin our new schedule today. Derek, you will take the first two weeknights, and Donal the second."

"What?" Genevieve cried, looking terrified.

Damian swallowed down his instinctive response and pressed forward with his plan. "I am afraid so, darling. I will return Friday, and I promise I will be counting every minute."

Derek was obviously close to rage. Damian gave his brother a look that contained the full weight of his authority in this house. "Derek, I presume you will wish to use the main bedroom."

For once, Derek's temperament worked to Damian's advantage. Derek forced himself to acknowledge the silent command with a grim nod. It was the best he would get.

So Damian loosed his final bolt.

He smiled dangerously at Genevieve, and then said to Derek, "I will not ask it of Donal, but Derek, I would be grateful if you would see to it that Genevieve sleeps chained to the bed. I think it would be good for her, and I will find the thought comforting on those nights I must spend alone, away from all of you."

It was up to the two of them now.

Chapter Thirty-one

Damian's announcement did away with any remaining anxiousness about the new pianoforte and Donal's unexpected explosion. Genevieve hardly noticed as both Donal and Damian kissed her cheek and vanished, leaving her alone with Derek.

Suddenly her enormous sitting room felt far too stuffy and confining. "Can we walk in the garden?" she said breathlessly. Derek scowled but followed her outside. They walked for a few minutes in silence, Genevieve hating that she felt so awkward with him. Finally, she asked lamely, "How have you been?"

"Well enough," he said curtly.

Genevieve was divided between the impulse to burst into tears and smack his face. How on earth was she to share a bed with him?

Derek, as if reading her thoughts, said, "If you ask to skip your nights with me, I won't make trouble."

"And what happens if I don't ask?" she snapped out, the desire to smack him triumphing for the moment. He gave her one of his glares. How could she get through to him? "I need to be able to live with you," she tried. "I can't be constantly afraid."

He actually looked horrified at this.

She gave him an exasperated sigh. "Afraid of hurting you, afraid that you're unhappy."

At first Derek looked as if she were speaking some incomprehensible gobbledygook; then his expression hardened into outright anger. "Why on earth would you think something so lunatic? Weren't you just listening to Damian? I should spank you just for saying that." He was not joking.

"You'll do nothing of the kind until we've resolved this!" she astonished herself by crying out. She forced down her temper and said quietly, "Derek, do you *want* this... this... with me?"

"Yes." One short word, but with Derek it contained so much.

There was nothing for it. Declan had told her she must set limits, and the time had come to set one with Derek. "Then I want something from you—I have not asked this of your brothers, but I ask it of you."

"What?"

"I want four hours in which you do not tyrannize over me, in which I choose what we do, and you cooperate with me. If you wish something from me, you can phrase it as a request or a suggestion instead of as a command."

Again his expression suggested she'd spoken in some ancient lost tongue instead of perfectly clear English.

"I've had no time with you, Derek. I am not asking you to go to the dressmaker's or bake pies or visit Sally, only that you spend some time with me."

Derek made a noncommittal shrug. She forced herself not to be hurt and said with excessive cheer, "Do you like lavender? It's one of my favorite flowers—did you know that? I'd like to have a bouquet for our bedroom. You are planning to stay there, are you not?" She almost added, "Now that Damian specifically asked you to keep me chained to the bed." She strongly suspected Derek would be far stricter about enforcing that "rule" than Damian— as Damian well knew. She started walking towards the back wall, calling over her shoulder, "Why don't you help me?"

"Help you?"

"Yes Derek, help me. I'd like to pick some flowers, and I'd like you to help me."

Honestly, the man acted as if she'd asked him to eat garden slugs!

She couldn't help taking a small bit of revenge by handing him the stems to hold as she gathered them. She blathered at him as they walked, telling him about Roderick's offer to teach her to cook, Sally and Peter Crane's visit, sleeping out in the conservatory. She got only grunts until she mentioned Mist.

"A Fae horse? Donal!" Derek growled angrily.

"It was *Declan's* gift!"

"And he had no business giving it to you!"

"What's your problem with it? I'm told the horse is extremely safe," she shot back.

"They should have waited for Damian to return. It should have been his decision whether you're to have a horse, just like giving you that key should be Damian's decision."

"You say that because you know he'd prefer I never leave the house."

"Yes, he would prefer it. And as his wife, you should abide by his wishes. I suppose you mean to ride her?"

"Yes, Derek, I mean to learn how."

"You don't already know?" His face was darkening with each second.

"Whatever you are going to say, don't! No tyrannizing, Derek, you promised."

"I didn't promise."

"Is this really so much to ask, Derek?" she exploded, catching him by surprise. "One bloody afternoon?"

She tried to walk off, but he grabbed her arm and refused to let her go. More despotism from him! Genevieve had reached her breaking point.

"I'll tell you something else I never told your brothers!" she screamed. "You all thought I looked so ill at the picnic? Four years ago, I went mad. I thought a demon had possessed me. I tore apart a pianoforte with a hammer until my fingernails were shredded. An instrument my parents had saved for years to buy for me! I spent the last four years of my life shut up in my room—too afraid and miserable to leave the house. I did that to myself, do you understand? I won't let you and Damian put me back there to satisfy your... lust, obsession, fear—whatever it is those Reavers did to you!"

She tried again to wrench her arm away, and when he didn't let go, she barked, "Parole!"

Derek instantly released her, and Genevieve stormed over to the fountain and splashed her face repeatedly, trying to keep from sobbing over him like some pitiful, lovelorn female.

She was startled when Derek said from about three inches behind her, "Four hours?"

She turned and faced him. "Four hours, Derek."

He had a calculating look in his eye. "When this is over, I want four hours too."

"What?"

"I want four hours where you obey me without any defiance."

"Derek, I have never been with you...."

"I won't ask anything my brothers wouldn't," he said intently.

Genevieve considered that highly unlikely. "One hour," she countered.

He nodded grudgingly.

"No gags. Never again unless I consent. Declan said I must set limits and this is one." He hesitated. "Derek, you took away my ability to speak the moment I tried to resist you."

"We were under attack—you were struggling."

"Yes, and if you'd said, 'Reavers are after you, Genevieve,' I would have stopped. At the very least, you could have tried that before binding and gagging me and tying me to the horse. We both know neither of your brothers would have had to!"

Another grudging nod.

"Then I agree," she said, praying she didn't regret this.

There was a pause while she pondered what on earth she should do next, when Derek said thoughtfully, "I'll teach you to ride the horse, but you need to be stronger."

It took Genevieve a moment to make sense of what he'd just said. "Stronger?"

"If you wish to ride, you must be stronger," he repeated. "You can barely lift a glass of water, and you plan to manage a sixteen-hundred pound Fae thoroughbred."

"Aren't you afraid if I'm stronger I'll be able to fight the three of you off when you try to domineer?" she said tartly.

Derek gave her an insultingly blank look. "There is no risk of that," he said flatly.

"Perhaps you should teach me to use weapons then," she muttered. To her amazement, Derek turned on her. "That was a joke," she started to say.

But his expression made clear it was no joke to him. He reflected for a minute before saying, "Crossbow and throwing knives. We'll start today." She thought she might just have caught a glint of humor when he added, "Good suggestion."

He grabbed her by her upper arm (Titania forbid he hold her hand!), and dragged her back towards the house. As they reached the door of the conservatory, he looked at the hand that held the lavender as if wondering what on earth it was.

"If you drop them, Derek, *you* can go pick a new bouquet."

"What do you want done with... these?" he grated. From his tone, he might have been saying, "What do you want done with this maggot-ridden animal carcass?"

"They are flowers, Derek. They require a vase with water," she answered as if speaking to a toddler.

He just nodded. When they got to the anteroom he said, "Wait here!"

This was Derek Black *not* tyrannizing.

He went into the dining room, presumably through the door to the kitchen, and came back two minutes later with her bouquet in an extremely fine crystal vase—much too fine for an unruly bunch of herbs.

Truly there was something astonishing in the sight of Derek carrying a vase of flowers. But he grabbed her upper arm again and led both of them upstairs.

"Do something with this," he said, handing her the vase.

While he went into his little room, she took the flowers to the bedroom and left them on the small dining table, trying not to think about what it would mean to share this room with Derek.

She was thirsty and poured herself a glass of lemon water from the pitcher that Damian had ordered always be left on the coffee table. For the first time in her life, she wished she drank brandy. She met Derek again in the corridor. "We'll start with the crossbow today. You can carry it when you go on rides," he said.

Genevieve *had* wanted time with Derek. She supposed it was easier to spend it learning about weaponry than picking flowers. On their way out of the kitchen (she walking on her own feet, not being carried over a man's shoulder), she asked George for a lump of sugar for Mist—to Derek's blatant but *silent* disapproval. They paid Mist a short visit and then went out to the empty paddock.

And so once again she got to learn the art of shooting projectiles, evidently an important activity for the Black brothers. Of course, instead of spitting cherry pits, she was shooting a crossbow—and for three hours instead of twenty minutes.

Derek was usually so taciturn, but it turned out he had plenty to say about crossbows, which were clearly a favorite topic.

Truly a great deal to say!

By the end of the first hour, he'd lectured her at length about quarrels and other bolts; the primary differences between yew and ash bows; the competing merits of hemp, linen, and mulberry for strings; culminating with a very extensive analysis of the special features of the Fae crossbow, something called a "recurve"—apparently a very powerful innovation!

Genevieve struggled to take in all of this. Derek didn't *tyrannize* precisely, though teaching clearly put him in a position of ordering her about. In fairness, he was a good instructor, patient with her mistakes without unreasonable expectations as to her skills, even if he did not readily distinguish between information that was truly necessary to shoot the damn thing and information that was only of interest to the curious (curious in this case referring to him, not her).

But it was far from terrible, and she acknowledged that learning to fire this weapon might come in handy—if only to make Derek and Damian more comfortable about her riding to the village on Mist.

The best moment came after about her hundredth shot when she finally grazed the target they were using.

Derek Black actually made a small smile.

Genevieve was so excited she clapped and kissed him on the mouth. They both froze. She kissed his brothers so often and easily, but this kind of intimacy had never been possible with Derek.

She nibbled her lip, watching for his reaction. "Kiss me," she murmured.

With surprising gentleness, Derek took her face in his hands and brushed his lips against hers. His expression was usually so harsh, those times he relaxed she noticed how full and sensuous his mouth was.

She parted her lips slightly, inviting him to go deeper, but he held back. So *she* went deeper, slipping her tongue into his mouth to find his, excited to discover his taste again.

She felt his jolt of surprise, but then he stopped the kiss and shoved her away almost roughly. Genevieve bit her lip miserably, wondering if she'd somehow repelled him.

"We still have seven minutes," Derek grated.

"What?"

"Seven minutes until the four hours is up."

Genevieve laughed. "You've really been keeping track?"

His stark expression should have warned her. Though he'd largely abided by her rule about tyrannizing, it had truly been a challenge for him.

And her time was rapidly running out.

"Has it been so horrible?" she demanded. "Not domineering over me for a single afternoon."

"It is not easy," he admitted.

"Then perhaps it is a skill that can be learned—like shooting a crossbow?" she said with a bright smile.

"Perhaps," he responded dourly.

As they began the walk back to the house, however, Genevieve noticed something. Derek's expression was changing before her eyes. The awkward, earnest crossbow instructor was fading away. In his place was the man she'd only seen in the cave.

This Derek was a graceful predator—one who was preparing to pounce.

Chapter Thirty-two

Genevieve couldn't help edging away. Was she truly ready to share a bed with this man? "Derek?"

"Your time is up. It's my turn—one hour, complete obedience." Genevieve couldn't help hesitating. "One hour," he repeated. And then he said, "I need this."

Derek never lied. He did need this. And she admitted to herself that she'd never given it to him before. She'd fought and defied him at every point since she'd met him, far more than she'd fought his brothers. But complete obedience? Could she really in honesty give this to him?

"I'll try," she gasped.

"Go back to the bedroom. Take everything off but your shift and stand at the end of the bed until I come for you."

Genevieve shuddered, astounded at how violently her desires fired when he spoke to her like this. Thank the Gods she passed no one else on the way back to their room. She couldn't have met anyone's eye.

Once in her room, she undressed mechanically. If she allowed herself to think about what was happening, she'd probably try to flee like a terrified rabbit—she couldn't bear to imagine what Derek would do if he had to hunt her down.

She went and stood at the end of the bed, wondering that her hands were shaking so much. Her breathing was quick and shallow, and she feared she was getting dizzy.

Why was this so much harder with Derek?

The door opened, and she clutched her sides, trying to control her nervousness. Derek moved so silently, she almost squawked when he suddenly wrapped his arms around her and nuzzled her neck. He'd removed his shirt and was wearing the loose linen trousers his brothers favored. "Easy angel," he whispered.

"I'm sorry," she pleaded like an idiot.

"We'll take this slow today," he said, "but I will spank you if you disobey me. Unless I ask you a question, you do not have permission to speak. If it's too much or if you're frightened, say the word 'parole' and everything will stop." She nodded at him, spellbound by his voice and the intensity of her desire. "Kneel in front of me."

Her face turned bright red, but she obeyed, closing her eyes.

She felt his hand on her chin. "Always keep your eyes on me unless I tell you otherwise, angel." She looked up at him. His harsh expression had mellowed into something sensual and seductive, and his voice had taken on a velvety quality. "Hold out your wrists." When she obeyed, he buckled the green cuffs on. "Stand up and face the bed again.... Good, now raise your arms." She trembled as

Derek slipped her shift over her head, leaving her completely naked. "Good girl. Now I am going to inspect you. Clasp your hands behind your neck and hold them there."

She felt a surge of alarm, but she obeyed him. She couldn't suppress a shudder when she felt Derek's hands on her breasts. His touch was so... knowing.

He slowly trailed a finger around the outer rim of each breast and then cupped them with his palms as if to weigh them. Afterwards, he began kneading them. She desperately wanted to slap his hand away, but she felt restrained by his command. His touch was almost too soft at first, but it steadily became firmer until he squeezed hard enough to cause her to cry out.

He nuzzled her neck, murmuring, "Keep still, Genevieve. I am testing how you respond to my touch."

He moved to her nipples. He lightly traced the rose tip of each breast with a finger and then began exploring. His touch was exquisitely pleasurable, and the erotic effect was magnified tenfold by being forced to stand passively while he freely touched her body. As always with Derek, she felt completely out of control, as if he had somehow taken over her body, and it now answered to him and not her.

"Do not move!" he ordered sharply, and all of a sudden he squeezed and twisted first her right and then her left nipple. Her body wrenched into a short, sharp climax as strong spasms of sensation shot from her breasts to her sex and through the rest of her body. Genevieve screamed and flinched, but somehow she kept her position. She shuddered when she realized that pain in such a sensitive spot had actually driven her to orgasm—and that Derek had known it would.

Derek gently caressed her breasts, soothing them, and then stepped back. "That was good. Now I want you to spread your legs as far apart as you can and bend over, placing your hands on the end of the bed."

"What?"

She felt a sharp slap on her buttocks. "You do not have permission to speak. No hesitations, Genevieve. When I give you a command, I expect immediate obedience without any questions." His tone was calm, but granite hard.

He nudged her legs and she complied, widening them so far apart it was difficult to balance. She bent over and clutched the bedspread to steady herself. A few tears dribbled down when she realized how utterly exposed she was. Derek gripped her hips to make sure she was stable and then brushed his hands over her buttocks and thighs, up her back and around to her stomach. She let out a scream as she felt him pull open the cheeks of her buttocks and use his thumb to gently knead the little hole that Donal had played with.

"Stay still, Genevieve," he warned in the same calm tone. She couldn't help letting out a groan at the sensation, invasive though it was. Derek murmured, "You're very sensitive here."

Thank Titania he stopped, and his fingers moved to her folds. To her shock, he knelt behind her and blatantly pulled them apart and blew on them, his face inches away. She flinched and tried to pull away and felt another stinging slap on her rear end. "You will stay like this until I tell you to move."

She froze, reminding herself that she'd given her promise. He placed a single gentle kiss on her sex before standing again. To her surprise, he placed his left hand on her lower stomach with his fingers spread widely. Then he began exploring her sex with his right hand. He ran his fingers through her folds, swirling, rubbing, pressing at different points. After he'd touched everywhere, he began to massage her bud, moving it a dozen different ways, each more arousing than the last. Finally, he thrust his fingers inside of her. Again he touched everywhere, exploring every last bit of that most intimate part of her body.

She was so desperate by now, his movements felt like torture though she was sure it wasn't his main purpose.

Unlike Donal, Derek didn't tease. He was doing exactly what he'd said—testing her responses. And she just knew he was keeping track of every tremor of hers no matter how small. It was deeply unnerving. From the first time they'd met, she'd felt cornered by Derek, as if he were a hunter and she his prey. She felt it again now. He was stalking her, methodically uncovering every weakness of her body, which he would then ruthlessly exploit to dominate her.

By this point, her sex was soaked, and the self-control needed to submit passively to this "inspection" was making her crazed. Finally, he pulled out. "That was very good. Stand up again." When she obeyed, he said from behind her, "Every night we are together, you will perform these same acts—undress, stand by the end of the bed and wait for me, kneel so I can put on your cuffs, and then stand for inspection. Do you understand?"

She was staggered by the audacity of his demand and by her body's shameless response. She nodded before she could stop herself. "I expect a verbal answer to my questions, Genevieve."

"Yes, I understand," she said weakly.

"Good. Turn around and face me."

She obeyed but instinctively raised her arms to cover her breasts. Derek yanked them down. "Never cover your breasts in front of me, Genevieve! Do it again and I will give you a real spanking."

Genevieve groaned just imagining it. She lowered her arms, clenching her teeth with the effort to keep them in place. She could practically feel that demon of hers waking from its five-day slumber and raising its head to sniff the wind curiously. She'd learned in the cave that the demonic part of herself reveled in punishment no matter how severe, and if she wasn't careful, it would rise up and seize control.

But badly as she craved that, she needed something else from Derek as well. That state of intoxication came at a high price. When she was under his control, she felt utterly out of her mind. Those feelings shut out everything else, leaving no room for simple affection. She'd been trying all day to find some middle ground with him, some way of spending time with him without letting him drive her into a frenzy.

She met Derek's eye—he knew she was thinking about his punishing her, and he was strongly aroused by it. "Not today, please Derek," she pleaded. His gaze hardened at her speaking without permission. He was moving to spank her. Before the demon took over and matters spiraled out of her control, she whimpered, "Parole."

Derek dropped his hands, his face suddenly hard and cold. "I'll leave," he rasped.

"NO!" she practically sobbed. The very idea that she'd hurt him threatened to make her start bawling like a hysterical child. "I want you so badly I'm going to go mad. Please, I just need...." She cringed at how desperate she sounded.

"I know you want me to punish you," he said angrily.

"I need to touch you," she shouted back, wondering to hear herself repeat the words she'd said to Damian in this very room. Somehow it gave her courage. Damian had always insisted she speak up about what she desired. This matter with Derek went beyond desire: she needed something from him, and it was worth fighting for. "I submitted to you, and we both know I will again, Derek, but I can't always live like that—in that state of intoxication. I need affection from you. I need to be able to *be* with you. I need you to hold me!"

To her astonishment, some recognition passed over his features. He nodded slowly and said, "You need it."

He scooped her up and carried her to the bed, clasping her tightly to him. She clung to him then, trying to squelch the tears of relief. She'd not realized how desperately she needed to feel close to this man she loved so very much, but who made things so difficult.

She reached to touch his face, again wondering at how extraordinary but right it felt. She threaded her fingers through his hair, pulling it away from his face to fully show his eyes. For once there was no anger or aggression in them, none of that intense need to master her. She saw desire, but it was quiet, almost gentle.

She moved closer so she could kiss him. To her surprise he didn't plunder her mouth as Damian usually did, but brushed his lips coaxingly, invitingly over hers. She'd always thought his full lips sensuous, soft, like an odd *dolce* passage in an otherwise *brusco* composition.

She parted her lips enough to invite him in. When his tongue touched hers, she felt a strong jolt, as much emotional as physical. Genevieve knew herself well enough to know that the demon he'd unleashed from her in that cave hadn't been exorcised. Shockingly, she no longer wanted it to be. But if they were to live together, she needed this tenderness, this connection to him.

She ran her hands over his arms and shoulders, digging her fingers into the carved muscles, finally able to revel in that tremendous strength of his. She broke the kiss, so she could rub her lips over his chest, licking his nipples, nuzzling her cheek and ear against him like a kitten.

She moved closer, bringing her body fully against his. He clasped her shoulders, but made no move to push things further. Though he was being so gentle with her, she could tell he was painfully aroused. He was letting her set their pace, she realized with shock. *Derek!*

"You go on top, love," he murmured. "You control it."

"Are you sure?" He nodded. "Why?" she couldn't help asking.

He looked thoughtful. "I'm a Black. I swore to put your needs first. You need this." He stopped her before she could protest. "We need this."

"Thank you." It seemed a little foolish to her, but she felt a rush of gratitude towards him. Neither of his brothers had done this for her. She had no quarrel with them, but she needed it with Derek, and for all his stubbornness he knew it. She pulled at him to move towards the middle of the bed and lie back so she could climb on top of him, loving the feel of her breasts against his chest.

Suddenly, she was desperate for him to be inside of her. She reached down and untied the string to his pants and pulled them down. She froze at the sight of his straining cock.

This was no shadowed cave, but her bedroom with the late afternoon sun streaming in. She swallowed and gripped it, but he clasped her hand and shook his head. "Don't, angel."

"What?"

"Genevieve, I'm about to die. If you do that...."

She nodded and then straddled him. She gnawed her lip, wondering then what she was supposed to do. "I've never done this before," she confessed.

Derek smiled almost in wonder. "You've really never been on top?"

"No."

That seemed to excite him. "Well then, I see we will have a riding lesson today," he said with an almost *roguish* smile. "Come, angel, slide up a little... that's right." He reached down to position himself. "Help me," he said. She moved until his cock was right at the opening of her sex.

"What do I do now?" she asked, giggling.

"You ride," he said. He gripped her hips and pushed her down his length. Genevieve let out a loud scream— she'd never taken anyone so deeply before.

"Are you all right, angel?"

"Yes," she gasped. "That just feels.... It's so deep."

She wanted him to thrust into her, which was when she realized what he'd meant. She must move—she must ride him. He lay still while she pushed herself up and down his length, wondering that it could feel so different like this.

He'd closed his eyes tightly. She recognized that look. He was trying to keep control. She leaned down and rubbed her forehead against his, slowing her movements. "Derek, open your eyes," she whispered.

Miraculously, he obeyed.

"I love you," she said. "I just wanted you to know that."

His face contorted with pain, and he squeezed his eyes shut. It was like watching herself in a mirror. She knew exactly what he was feeling at that moment.

"Derek, open your eyes," she said gently.

He did.

"I love you."

This time his features relaxed. "You're impossible," he said.

"You would know," she murmured. He actually chuckled at that.

"Derek," she said a third time.

"What Genevieve?" he said smiling.

She leaned down and whispered in his ear, "You don't have to say it because I know."

He nodded and even looked relieved. Before he could say anything she braced her arms and ramped up her movements again. Unfortunately, the more she pushed and wiggled, the more frustrated she became, though she was becoming impossibly aroused. No matter how she shifted herself around, she couldn't hit the spot she needed to bring herself to a climax.

When her arms collapsed under her, she was forced to acknowledge that she really did need to get stronger. She propped herself up and tried again, riding up and down, growing close to frantic, but release kept eluding her.

Derek was watching her struggle, his eyes bright. For the first time since she'd met him, he reminded her of Donal.

Genevieve narrowed her eyes. "You'd better not be laughing at me."

"Never," he said. He pulled her down against him and whispered in her ear, "Let me, angel. Let me bring you."

"I can do this," she growled.

"Genevieve, let me." She'd never heard his voice so gentle.

"Oh fine," she huffed.

To her astonishment, he gripped her arms and pulled them behind her back. There was a click, and her wrists were attached together.

"Derek!" she protested, unable to do anything but collapse on top of him.

He gripped one of her thighs and pulled it up and hooked her knee under his arm, and then shifted her slightly to the side, changing the angle he entered her. He wrapped her hair around his wrist and forced her head back, giving him better access to her breasts. He took her left breast in his mouth, and then he began to move in small, subtle pulses that just brushed the spot she needed.

Genevieve had never felt anything like it. Damn him and his inspection! He really did understand her responses. And of course, it was impossible not to struggle against the bonds. Being restrained raised the stakes of her sensations, forcing her to new heights of urgency.

"Please Derek!" she cried.

But his expression had darkened. Like Damian, seeing her struggle helplessly strongly fueled Derek's desire—and his need to master her. He shifted again, thrusting harder. Genevieve screamed out, unprepared for how suddenly her body shot to ecstasy. With her arms bound behind her, she couldn't brace herself or fight the climax. She felt like a bottle being tossed in the waves as pleasure wracked her body.

Meanwhile, she could feel Derek tensing. He was getting close, but their position restricted his movements almost as much as the bonds did hers. He could only make small thrusts, which were badly testing his control. His face had twisted with frustration as he had to fight for his own release. Genevieve wanted to do something— touch him, help him—but she was helpless.

Finally, she could feel that telltale sharpening in his thrusts. He let out a groan that grew louder as his climax took a torturously long time to arrive.

When it came it was explosive: he roared out, clutching her almost desperately.

When the tremors finally died off, he rested his forehead against hers, his eyes tightly closed as both of them lay panting, recovering. Genevieve was sure they were both feeling the same sense of shock at how intense that had been.

As if echoing her thoughts, he said, "I've never felt anything like that—you make me insane."

"That's funny, because you have the opposite effect on me," she murmured.

She felt his chest rumbling. He was actually laughing at a joke!

He took her face in his hands and kissed her tenderly. "I love you, angel," he said smiling. He shifted her off of him and stood to pull his pants on. He made no move to unlock her hands, but instead walked towards the bathing chamber.

"Derek!" she squeaked. He returned with a damp cloth. "Derek, you have to unlock me!"

His smile was every bit as dangerous as Damian's. "Is that so?"

He flipped her onto her stomach. With her hands tied behind her back, it was next to impossible to move. She tried to kick her legs.

"Lie still, now!" he warned in his iron tone. When she struggled even more frantically, he crashed his hand down on her rear end.

Gods did it hurt when he did that.

"What did I just say, Genevieve?" He pushed her legs apart so he could rub the cloth along her sex, being every bit as thorough as he'd been during his inspection.

"Derek!" she screamed.

"I still have forty-seven minutes," he said coolly.

"What?"

"You promised me an hour of complete obedience— my inspection only lasted thirteen minutes.

He flipped her onto her back. With her hands trapped beneath her, she was if anything more helpless. Genevieve groaned, wondering that she could become aroused so soon after one of the most wrenching climaxes of her life.

Derek rubbed one of her breasts thoughtfully. She'd never seen him like this before, and she had a feeling no one ever had. In the cave, he'd been driven by desperation, but now he seemed to be enjoying himself. It was a side of himself that he'd kept locked away. It was both terrifying and exhilarating to see it released.

He leaned down and roughly tongued her left breast, sucking hard, until she screamed out, feeling herself spiraling out of control. He examined his handiwork and then took the other in his mouth and repeated his treatment.

"Derek!" she shrieked.

"Much better," he observed, squeezing them both almost to the point of pain.

He reached between her legs and began fondling her sex almost casually as he said, "It's almost time for dinner. I seem to remember warning you would eat tied to your chair if you gave me trouble over your meals. But I'll settle for you on your knees, hands bound behind your back."

"Gods Derek...." She was close to coming.

"My only question is whether I should blindfold you. I haven't forgotten how aroused you were by my description."

"Derek please..." she pleaded.

"I love it when you beg, angel," he murmured as she screamed out another climax.

Chapter Thirty-three

Four weeks later

The weather that evening was stormy, but summer was so well established, they could sit out in the conservatory, enjoying the patter of the rain on the glass without any fear of damp or chill.

Genevieve was seated at the pianoforte, trying to recreate a variation she'd improvised earlier that day. Though these improvisations usually unfolded effortlessly at the time, they were far more difficult to recapture later. But Donal had particularly liked this one, saying it perfectly captured the mood of a summer rainstorm, so she was determined to get it down on paper this time.

It took her forty-five minutes, but she was pretty sure she'd succeeded. She got up to fetch her composition book so she could record it when she noticed that Donal was reclining on the lounge chair. Since dinner ended, he'd changed into his linen pants and removed his shirt. Thankfully, he appeared relaxed after what had undoubtedly been a trying day.

She'd been so desperate to get in a visit to town before Damian got back from a five-day absence, she'd managed to wheedle Donal into riding down with her, despite the threatening skies. The visit to Sally and Peter's had been as enjoyable as always, the visit to her parents' less so. Mama had been unusually fretful, first about the rain, then about how tan Genevieve was getting. Genevieve's temper had begun rising, her tan turning to angry scarlet, until Donal stepped in, diverting her mother's focus to Roderick and their ongoing exchange of recipes.

Predictably, during the ride back, the skies had opened up drenching them. Equally predictable, Derek had been livid when they got home, beginning an argument that had lasted through half of dinner, until Genevieve had finally burst out that if Derek didn't stop, she would ask *him* to accompany her to Sally's instead of Donal, after which there was finally peace.

She efficiently jotted down the notes in her book, only needing to replay two passages. She always wondered how Donal could bear listening to her bang around when she was working out a piece, but he claimed it was fascinating. As soon as she was finished, however, she began improvising on one of his favorite tunes. She'd been growing worried about Donal and was always trying to come up with ways to show him how much she appreciated him.

As it happened, none of the problems they had worried about had come to pass: there had been no conflicts between the brothers. Damian's fears that she would be overwhelmed by male demands proved completely unfounded. She'd even learned to canter on Mist. She adored her life with all three of them.

But Genevieve knew she had Donal to thank for much of her comfort. Today had been the perfect example of the problem: his easygoing nature meant that he was the one who most often gave up what he wanted for the sake of others—most often her.

Though Damian had boasted that she was free to spend her days as she wished, in fact he ruthlessly monopolized her time the days he was home. Derek was not quite as bad, but there were only certain activities one could do with Derek. Those included riding lessons, practicing her crossbow, trying (and generally failing) to hit something (anything!) with a throwing knife, or "hunting." (Genevieve refused to participate in killing animals, so "hunting" was another word for tramping through the woods, teasing Derek whenever he complained about all the game they were letting escape.)

She didn't mind any of this, but it did mean she was especially desperate on Donal's days to pay visits in town or go to the fortress for a cooking lesson or any of the other activities that she could only do with Donal. Donal, of course, knew this and steadfastly refused her offers to do something he'd prefer, though she suspected he'd much rather lounge about the garden making love—or at least sit quietly at home instead of riding around in the pouring rain.

Over the past few weeks, she'd had occasion to think back to her wedding day and the vows the four of them had made. She'd no regrets, no blame to cast that she and Damian and Derek had not all immediately lived up to them. Vows like those must be earned, something that turned out to be a wrenching process, requiring painful mistakes.

At the time of her marriage, she'd barely understood herself—neither the impulses that had caused so much misery for the past few years, nor the need to take responsibility for her own well-being, beginning with trying to forgive herself.

Both Damian and Derek had been sincere when they promised to uphold their family's values, but those values were like lessons they'd memorized. They loved each other so much, but nothing had ever threatened their loyalty before, so they weren't fully prepared to cope when jealousy finally hit.

But Donal had not needed these painful lessons. He was the only one of the four who'd understood at the time what he was promising, who'd never once failed to live up to those vows. She owed him an immeasurable debt for helping her during her darkest hour, and for giving her back her music. He was happy, she knew, but it sat ill with her that he might suffer for being less selfish than the rest of them.

She'd finally spoken about it to Damian, who'd teased her that the only complaint she'd made was for the sake of his brother and not herself. When she persisted, he'd kissed her and promised he'd think on it, but then he'd had to leave for five days for some troop exercise. He'd finally returned this evening just as they were finishing dinner. She wished to remind him again, but she hadn't had the chance.

She played another of Donal's favorite pieces, smiling when Derek wandered in, also shirtless and wearing identical linen trousers. She'd come to relish their habits, especially these little reminders that for all their differences the Blacks were still brothers.

Derek and Donal began their nightly card game, which both played as if the fate of humanity and Faerie hinged on the outcome. Damian came in half an hour later, dressed like his brothers, except that he wore a shirt as usual. He had taken a quick bath and had a plate in the kitchen and now settled down at the other end of the table to tackle the mountain of paperwork that always followed his visits to the garrison.

It was an ordinary evening.

"Play the new piece," Donal said, not taking his eyes from his cards. Genevieve was happy to oblige, quickly becoming absorbed with revising and making further marks in her book. When she finally looked up almost an hour later, she realized all three brothers were staring at her.

"What?" she asked. Damian was giving her his treacherously bland smile. "What are you up to?" she demanded.

"Darling, it's time to say goodnight."

"Is it?" she said suspiciously.

Damian prowled towards her. "Yes, and I think you should say goodnight to Donal, love."

Genevieve stood up herself and began moving back, though there was nowhere to go except out into the storm. "What... what do you mean?"

"I wish you to say goodnight to Donal—in whatever way you think he would best like. Do you know what that is, darling?"

"The way that Donal likes?" she squeaked, disbelieving. Damian raised his eyebrows at her. "Now? In here?"

She looked at Donal, who appeared surprised but decidedly willing.

"Yes darling," Damian answered. "In fact, I think you should make a habit of saying goodnight to him on his off nights. I'm sure my brother would greatly appreciate such a gesture." When Genevieve still hesitated, Damian said, "Derek, would you help Genevieve, please."

Derek was instantly on his feet, moving with that panther-like grace of his. He took her by the elbow and guided her over to Donal, who was also standing now.

"Kneel down, darling," Damian ordered.

When she didn't instantly obey, Derek put both hands on her shoulders and forced her down and then took hold of her hair and wrapped it around his hand tightly.

"Darling, are you going to obey me or must I send you to the study with Derek?" Damian asked.

Genevieve felt dizzy, overwhelmed by the combination of Damian's sultry voice in her head, Derek's intense presence directly behind her, and Donal's wicked smile before her. Donal was already aroused, his cock straining against the fabric of his pants. She untied the drawstring, freeing him. She reached forward to grip him, but Damian said, "Hands down—use only your mouth."

As happened so often when Damian gave her a command, she obeyed without thinking, leaning forward to catch Donal's cock in her mouth. She could feel his shudder of pleasure as her tongue ran down his shaft, but then she remembered that they weren't alone. She shut her eyes tightly.

"Eyes open! Whenever you take one of us in your mouth, you will keep your eyes on his face the entire time," came Damian's command. "Donal make sure she obeys."

Damian's iron tone had its usual effect, and Genevieve moaned, her mouth filled with Donal's cock. Donal gripped her chin and held it as her mouth worked over him. Though she'd enjoyed taking him like this before, she'd never imagined doing it could get her this aroused.

Damian of course noticed. "I think our girl likes saying goodnight. Derek, check and see if Genevieve is enjoying herself."

Derek knelt down behind her. "Her legs are pressed together," he growled.

"I think it's time Genevieve had a lesson in how to kneel properly," Damian said. "Genevieve, pull off of Donal for a moment." She was almost mindless now, so Donal guided her head back. "Derek, take her dress off."

That roused her: she clutched her dress to stop him, but Derek pushed her forward into Donal's grip and gave her buttocks three stinging slaps.

"Arms up, Genevieve," Derek ordered. She didn't dare disobey again. He whisked the dress off, leaving her in only her stockings and garters. "Don't you dare cover your breasts!" he barked, giving her another slap on her rear end. "You are on your knees to please Donal, and he wants to see them!"

"Derek, instruct her on how to kneel properly," Damian said calmly.

"Knees apart, Genevieve!" Derek ordered. "Farther apart... farther!" Finally, he just reached down and spread her knees as far apart as they would go.

"Excellent. You may continue saying goodnight to Donal now, darling," Damian said in his lordly tone. Donal stroked her cheek, and she reached for him with her hands, earning herself a sharp command from Damian. "Mouth only! Put your hands behind your back and lace your fingers. Do not forget again."

Genevieve instantly obeyed and leaned forward and caught Donal in her mouth again. Each command, each correction sent another jolt of lust through her until she wondered that she could stay upright.

"Derek, check and see if Genevieve is enjoying saying goodnight."

Derek pulled her tightly against him with his left arm, the bare skin of his chest hot against her back. He ran the fingers of his right hand through her folds. She must be soaking by now.

"Aye, she's good and roused," Derek said, holding his hand before his face and then up for Donal's inspection. To her shock, Donal took Derek's fingers in his mouth.

"I can vouch that our girl's enjoying saying goodnight," Donal said.

"Excellent. Feel free to reward her if you wish, Derek," Damian said lazily.

Derek massaged her right breast with one hand, while brushing his fingers lightly over her sex with the other, but he steadfastly refused to touch her bud. It was such torture Genevieve tried to yell his name, though her mouth was filled.

"You can yell all you want to, but you will keep your mouth on him," Derek whispered so only she could hear. "I want to see you try your hardest to please Donal—as if your life depended on it." Derek's voice had taken on that rich, velvety timbre that he saved for their most intimate moments. It was pure seduction. "I love seeing you like this, angel. Such a dutiful little bride, saying goodnight to your husband's brother just like an obedient wife should. Take him deeper. Relax your mouth so you don't choke. I know you can work him with that beautiful mouth of yours."

She obeyed, allowing Donal to thrust all the way to the back of her throat.

"Good girl," Derek murmured. He pinched her nipple between two of his fingers, scissoring them until the sensation was just shy of pain—only Derek ever touched her that way. She groaned loudly again.

Donal began running his hands through her hair, confusing her with all the competing sensations. Suddenly Damian was very close, just over her shoulder.

"I want her to come with him," Damian said. "Donal are you good?"

"I can wait for our girl," Donal answered, slowing the pace of his thrusts into her mouth.

"Genevieve, you will keep your arms behind your back, or all three of us will take turns thoroughly spanking you, which I would regret since I had been looking forward to our ride tomorrow."

Her body lurched with a mixture of fear and desire at his threat. She tightened the grip on her fingers until her knuckles ached, lest that demon of hers surface, as it occasionally did, and prompt her to some insane act that earned her a punishment.

"Derek, work her breasts. I'll bring her to the point."

She tried to look at Damian to see what he was doing, which earned her a brutal slap on her buttocks from Derek, sharp enough to make her eyes water. "Keep your eyes on Donal," Derek growled. "You are on your knees to please him, not yourself."

"Poor little girl," Donal soothed. "She pleases me very much. Keep your eyes on me, sweetheart."

Thankfully, Donal's warm eyes and reassuring tone were enough to hold her. She didn't turn when Damian knelt right at her side and reached down between her legs and began exploring.

She groaned loudly, both from the surge of pleasure and the struggle not to look. "Stay with me, little girl," Donal said, sensing how hard it was for her. "You know there's nothing I love more than watching you take my cock in your mouth."

Somehow Derek and Damian happened upon the same rhythm, Derek massaging her breasts, Damian her bud. Donal sensed it and began to match them, pumping into her mouth. She screamed then, building dangerously close. Damian pulled back just enough. "Donal?"

"Soon. Damnation that feels good," he hissed. Donal's cock hardened palpably, and his movements became more urgent. Damian began again, manipulating her bud until her whole body was tensing as her climax approached.

"I'm going to bring her now," Damian said, making a little swirl with his fingers that caused her whole body to seize and left her trying to scream as Donal pumped into her mouth.

"Ah, Gods, Genevieve," Donal yelled just afterwards. He thrust four or five more times, and then came the spray of warm fluid into her mouth, which never failed to surprise her. He immediately put his hand on the back of

iting

five

had

d by

and

' he

got
ce
ve

he

d

a

t

l

.t I want. Swallow it, every drop,"

released her, Genevieve collapsed
, utterly mindless. Derek put his
ng her neck, whispering in her ear,
gel. I'm proud of you."
.e for our girl," Damian said.
Genevieve in his arms, kissing her
: handing her to Damian. Damian
al could kiss her goodnight as well.
art," he said, ruffling her hair.
darling," Damian said.
e murmured.
ny turn," Damian said in a tone that
It told her that no matter how aroused
on being absolutely ruthless with her.
see you tomorrow, but don't fear.
ne down before bed to say goodnight to
' and all of your off-nights. Derek, you
e doesn't forget."

Epilogue

Six months later

Damian and Donal were seated at the table wa
for the other two so they could begin lunch. After
minutes, Damian decided to check where Genevieve
gotten to when his home's usual peace was shattere
ear-piercing screams.

"Oh brother," Donal groaned. "Here it comes."

Damian downed the full glass of wine before him
then decided to pour another. "Would you like one?"
asked.

"Yes, please!" Donal said in a mournful tone.

They both fortified themselves as the screams
closer. Finally Derek appeared in the doorway, his fa
dark with fury—with an equally enraged Genevie
heaved over his shoulder, frantically pounding his back.

"Genevieve and I have some business to discuss. S
will not be able to ride for several days," he announced.

"Don't you dare, you bastard," Genevieve screame
and then let out a string of expletives that would make
demon mercenary blush.

"I warned you what would happen if you used tha
language!" Derek roared at her.

There were several more expletives followed by, "I'
kill you Derek! I swear it!"

"Very well," Damian replied in a studiously reasonable tone. "I needed to attend to some matters with the garrison anyway. Perhaps Donal will come with me."

"That might be best," Derek said and exited. Next they heard the door to the study slam shut, which muffled most of the shrieks.

"Do I have you to thank for my wife's new vocabulary?" Damian said, pouring himself one final half-glass of wine.

Donal had the grace to look abashed. "Peter finds it amusing to annoy his wife by teaching our girl to swear like a quartermaster. I'd never have guessed a painter would know so many obscenities. He's really quite impressive."

Damian prayed for patience. He was convinced he deserved to be canonized for tolerating Genevieve's continued friendship with the diminutive blond virago, whose lovely face, in his opinion, did not atone for her shrewish disposition.

However, he did concede that Peter's pastel portrait of Genevieve standing in a flower-filled meadow, which currently graced the wall of the dining room, perfectly captured his wife's fresh, unforced sensuality. He'd since commissioned a full-length oil portrait that would look perfect in their bedroom.

"Should I speak to Thomas and George?" Donal asked, getting to his feet.

Damian rose as well. "Fine. How long do you need to pack?"

"Actually, I'm packed already. I had a feeling an explosion was imminent."

"You might have mentioned it to me. I just got back!" He'd been looking forward to three nights—and days—between his wife's thighs.

Donal just shrugged. "I'll try to remember next time I sense the demon about to awake."

Damian could only laugh ruefully. There had been surprisingly few adjustments to the initial plan, which had worked almost miraculously well, thanks most of all to his highly tolerant and adaptable wife. Certain habits had emerged: for example on his nights, Donal preferred to sleep in the conservatory with Genevieve. Derek, on the other hand, always stayed with Genevieve in their bedroom, of course rigorously enforcing the rule about chaining her to the bed.

On his brothers' nights, Damian visited his troops, falling into a pattern of working four grueling days and then having three heavenly days with Genevieve, the largest part of which were spent in their bedroom.

Derek and Donal, in contrast, preferred to alternate their nights rather than have two in a row. The days

Damian was away, Genevieve usually spent with Donal practicing her music, visiting her parents or friends in town, or learning to cook with Roderick.

The only surprise was that Genevieve never once did anything to get herself sent to the study. In the early weeks Damian had worried about it, entertaining and discarding several theories as to why: she was afraid of how severe Derek would be; she was afraid of injuring Damian's feelings; Donal was lying to cover for her.

The reason was predictably more complicated. Genevieve spent far too much time worrying about the three of them, relentlessly scrutinizing herself for any sign of preference or hint of unfairness. Her anxiety made her unconsciously avoid doing things that might upset one of them.

He also realized that temperamentally, it was difficult for her to disobey when one of them issued a serious command. Still he wasn't happy with the situation and resolved to intervene. Though he truly didn't want her to do anything that put herself at risk, he couldn't stand the idea that his wife was monitoring her behavior to that degree.

It turned out that his worry was unnecessary, though he would never have predicted the reason. Two months after they set up their household, Damian had been stunned to see Derek drag a shrieking Genevieve into the study and lock the door.

An hour later, Derek found Damian and Donal in the dining room and announced he needed four more days. Damian had to acknowledge that Derek had actually been civil when he requested that his brothers stay at the fortress and order the servants away. Derek also promised he would make up their lost days after "it was over."

Damian was proud of how he'd reacted. He'd not punched his brother or tried to knife him. Instead he'd calmly asked, "What is happening with my wife?"

"She needs this," Derek answered curtly and then added, "I don't think she'll be able to ride for the next week." With that he'd left the room.

There had been a long moment of silence while Damian debated various ways to murder Derek, when Donal said, "Leave it. If he says she needs it, then she probably does. You've not been here, but something has been brewing with her over the last week."

Damian was about to say something, when Donal added, "You don't want to know. Let me take the two days afterwards. The worst will be over by then. And then you and she can spend a whole week together. Derek and I will cover you at the gate. You'll have the house to yourselves."

"Are you sure?" he asked Donal. Donal was still the one who always seemed to make the compromises to accommodate his less flexible brothers.

"Of course," Donal said without hesitation. "Stop worrying, Damian. I dealt with it the last time. I know how to help her."

So they had left.

Damian had, however, sought out Declan, who advised him that he must allow matters to play out.

"Derek said she wouldn't be able to ride for a week," he protested.

"Your rule is a sound one," Declan responded. "However, you must accept that there are times when that limit is too stringent. Did you allow Derek access to her heartwood box?"

"Yes, I did what you recommended," Damian said. "I left the box unlocked; he knows where it is."

"I know it is not easy, Damian, but you made the right choice."

"I don't think she'll stop him."

"I realize that. Do you think if she wished him to, she would keep silent?"

"I just wish I understood this," he confessed.

"You know, Genevieve once asked me why Derek craved punishing her. She was concerned it might injure him to fulfill her need." Damian shook his head. Who other than his wife would even think such a thing? "Do you ever wish you were different, Damian?"

Damian smiled at Declan, who'd watched generations of his descendants cope with these dark, unruly passions, always guiding them with love and patience. "I used to, but not since I met her."

Declan's eyes grew hazy. "I used to curse Titania for banishing me—and to find *love* of all things. And then a little thief fell into my arms, cursed me out, and tried to break my nose."

Damian was astonished. Declan never spoke of the woman who had won his heart so long ago. "I always imagined your wife was like our mother."

Declan barked out a laugh and then said ruefully, "I've seen few women who could match your mother for gentleness; not my wife, certainly." He chuckled at some memory. "Desire is a great mystery, Damian. You can trust Derek."

Damian examined his heart and found that he did trust Derek, so he had adapted. When another explosion occurred six weeks later and then a third eight weeks after that, he accepted that this would be a regular occurrence in his life.

He learned during those interludes to throw himself into his work, keep as busy as possible, not dwell on what was happening, and ultimately accept the mystery that was Genevieve, his gentle, sweet, tenderhearted wife, who every so often flew into violent rages that could only be sated by equally violent responses by his brother who had nothing sweet or gentle about him.

Invariably at some point during those days, Damian would find time to visit Titania's Altar to thank the queen of light for the gift of the heartwood and for blessing not only him, but his brothers, with the woman who had made the happiness of each of them.

The End

About the Author

At different times, Lilia Ford has worked as a cashier, paralegal (sometimes called the fourth circle of hell), doctoral student, and English professor. Now she divides her time between herding cats (otherwise known as being a mom to two lunatic boys), and writing. She and her family live in New York City.

Lilia loves to hear from readers. Visit her web site at LiliaFordRomance.com or find her on Facebook.

3276275R00218

Printed in Great Britain
by Amazon.co.uk, Ltd.,
Marston Gate.